His Crazy Obsession

His Crazy Obsession

Book One of His Crazy Obsession Series

Ana Denise

Prologue

Kyla

The slap that connected with my left cheekbone almost gave me whiplash. Lightly caressing my cheek, my eyes settled upon the monster before me. The monster that I once was deeply in love with years ago. The monster that caused the searing pain that was spreading across my face. Brad's forest green eyes were wide, filled with rage and hatred. The anger and hatred directed right at me were redundant and uncalled for.

"Why do you have to flirt with him?" Brad asked in a stern voice.

"I was not flirting with him," I tried to reassure him.

"Yes, you were. You do it every time he comes over here to hang out with me," Brad growled in a loud, bone-chilling voice.

As Brad continued grilling me, tears filled my eyes as I looked around the house I once called home. Now this place felt like absolute hell. Looking over at our daughter Bria's closed bedroom door, I hoped and prayed that Brad's yelling did not wake her up, as it had done many times before. After all, it was a few minutes after midnight.

"I just asked him if he wanted something to drink." I attempted to reason with him, to no avail. It was as if I was trying to reason with him every night, but it was no use.

"I don't give a damn what you did. You are always acting like a slut."

One would think each degrading word that came out of Brad's mouth would hurt my feelings and further tear my soul down. The truth was, it didn't even bother me anymore. I had dealt with the physical, mental, and emotional abuse for the past five years, and I was almost numb to it. The only abuse that I have yet gotten used to was physical. It left scars I had no choice but to look at every single day I looked in the mirror.

"I am not a slut." That statement was more of an affirmation to me. Brad's opinion was insignificant, as his mind was already made up.

"What?" Brad asked me, stepping closer as if he needed to hear me better.

"Nothing," I mumbled, looking down at the ground in shame.

Staring into the eyes that I adored once before and now hated with deep passion just reminded me of the horrible situation I could not see any way out of.

"No. You want to be brave tonight and talk back to me? Say it so I can hear you loud and clear."

Looking up, my eyes locked with Brad's. I stated in a very calm voice, "I am not a slut."

Brad's rage wavered somewhat as he chuckled and rubbed the brown, overgrown stubble on his chin. "If I say you are a slut, Kyla, you are a slut."

"I said I am not a slut," I yelled, surprising myself.

This was the first time I had stood up to Brad in the past five years. As the words left my mouth, a sense of pride came over my body. The feeling left my body when my feet were swept from under me by the force of a powerful fist connecting with my jaw. My body hit the floor with a loud thud, causing my neck to snap back with force. My head struck the floor hard and caused immediate, searing pain to radiate through my head and neck. As I lay on the cold, tiled floor crying my eyes out, Brad pummeled me to a pulp on the floor. The pain from the strikes was unbearable as I heard a loud, piercing scream that echoed throughout the house. Attempting to look out of the only eye that was not trying to swell shut, I saw Bria running out of her bedroom door. She clutched her stuffed teddy bear she slept with in her bed. She ran into the living room screaming, tears streaming out of her eyes and down her cheeks. The look of sheer terror was displayed all over her sweet face. That view alone would not stop the brutal beating I endured.

"Mommy," she shrieked as she ran towards us.

"Bria, get back in your room now," Brad yelled as he stopped hitting me long enough to point his index finger toward her bedroom.

A scared Bria continued to scream, but knew better than to disobey her parents. So, doing as she was told, she ran back into her room.

As Brad continued to hit me, even after seeing our daughter cry, I knew I had to get my daughter out of this horrible living situation. I knew what would happen if I did not take it upon myself to get us out of this situation fast. I knew that if I continued to stay, it would only be a matter of time before the forensic crew would come to this house to scrap my lifeless body off the floor and place me in a body bag. A silent vow was made that night as my body took that ferocious beating. I would not allow it to happen again. Bria could not lose me. I was going to make sure of that with every fiber in my body.

Chapter One

Kyla

Four months later
I picked up the cup of burnt, lukewarm coffee I had been sipping on for the past three hours. Unconditionally, I despised coffee, but at the moment, it was my best friend. My body was almost exhausted, but there were a few more miles to drive on the interstate until I was due to get off my exit.

As my fingers drummed on the steering wheel, my eyes flickered to the backseat. My eyes landed on Bria, sleeping restfully in her car seat. She clutched her favorite stuffed rabbit in her chubby, tiny four-year-old hand. Her cup of milk was sitting upright in her lap.

The day after the horrible beating I endured for speaking back to Brad, I plotted a plan to get us away from the abuse and to safety. With grace, I ignored the two million apologies thrown my way from that following morning until two weeks after it occurred. Having spent the past five years believing in those lies just to be betrayed yet again, I had learned my lesson more than enough times.

I just hoped the four months of intense planning that I had done would pay off in our favor. Bria and I had disappeared two days ago without a single trace. Knowing that Brad had a tracking device on my phone, I left it on the nightstand right next to the bed we once shared. The goal was to ensure he could not reach out or track us.

"In two miles, please get off on the next exit," the maps app told me on the phone I purchased two days ago.

The device was not as fancy as the phone Brad had bought me, but it didn't matter. Brad always wanted me to have a top-of-the-line phone. The phone I had bought for myself was one of the cheapest phones I could find that I could afford.

Once the exit came up, my heart pounded out of my chest. It was a mixture of nerves and excitement. Nerves because I was no longer traveling north, away from Florida, far away from the home I once lived in for far too long. Excitement since I was traveling to Branchville, South Carolina. Branchville, South Carolina, was a small town that did not have a large population. I had never heard of the town before I searched for small, remote towns. After my extensive research, I could locate the perfect destination for a small family that did not want to be found.

Continuing to drive for another few miles, I noticed a gigantic pylon sign from afar with the words Meg's Coffee Shop. Right next to the word 'shop' was a steamy mug of coffee, with half a bagel leaning against the mug. Meg's Coffee Shop was the local cafe I had been in contact with over the past two months. I had been in contact concerning a full-time waitress position. It was in a small shopping plaza, along with four other businesses.

Pulling the unfamiliar car into the crowded parking lot, I slipped into the first unoccupied parking space I could find. Killing the ignition on the car, I reached up and touched the silver dream catcher I had placed on my rearview mirror.

Secretly, regret was sneaking up on me for the switch of vehicles I had done. I went from driving a brand-new blue BMW sedan to a used silver Honda sedan. I had no other choice for fear that Brad had a tracking device installed in my car. I had to get rid of it four hours into my journey north to avoid being tracked. After I abandoned the car in a mall parking lot, I met up with the woman that sold me the Honda. It had over 100,000 miles, but it was cheap and the best option I could find.

Pulling the sun visor down, I opened the mirror up. I took off my huge, black designer sunglasses that covered my serene brown eyes and more than half of my face. Brad had purchased them four years ago as a 'sorry I gave you your first black eye for talking back to me' present. As I stared at my face, my heart ached. Even though I had a naturally dark skin tone, the black eye Brad had given me four days ago would be visible to any person within a thirty-foot radius of me.

Brad had become angry with me that night. I did not have dinner ready for our once-a-month dinner night before his mother and father arrived at our home. Later that evening, after dinner was over, I suffered those consequences the second the tires of their Mercedes sedan left our driveway. The swelling of my eye had gone down plenty, but the pain and nasty bruise were still apparent. Unzipping my purse, I pulled out the emergency bag of makeup I always kept on me. Occasionally, I would apply a stroke of mascara or eye shadow for a striking look. I never wore pounds of makeup on my face until Brad gave me my first bruise. My beauty never needed to be covered up, but the bruises that appeared once the damage was done needed to be hidden from the entire world. A sense of relief settled around me as I applied the makeup to my left eye. Once this bruise was healed up and gone, I would never have to pack makeup on my face again.

I adjusted the black bangs with a partial shield over my eyes that I installed at the start of my trip. The best thing I could do was hide my identity by concealing part of my face with clip-in bangs.

Closing the sun visor, I turned around to focus on Bria. Our different heritages came together in full force and created a beautiful interracial baby girl. She had big brown eyes and light brown curly hair. Bria was the only beautiful thing that came out of my five-year relationship with Brad.

"Bria, wake up, baby girl," I whispered in a low tone. I reached into the backseat and rubbed her cute, chubby cheeks.

Bria stirred in her car seat briefly as I caressed her face. Whenever I talked to Bria, it was best to speak calmly and quietly. Bria was used to Brad yelling, and I did not want to further traumatize her.

Bria blinked her delightful, light brown eyes a few times before she looked out of the side windows. "Where are we, mommy?" she asked in an adorable, sleepy voice.

"We are finally in our new town."

"Yay," Bria cheered.

I had been having positive conversations with Bria about our move for the past two days since we left. I had not mentioned it to her before, as I was afraid Bria would slip up and tell Brad about our plans.

"Mommy just needs to go in here and talk to some people before we see our new home."

"Okay," she responded, being the sweet daughter I adored from the first time I held her in my arms.

"Are you ready to see our new home?"

"Yeah." She was full of excitement.

"Well, let's go in here for a few minutes, and then we will go to our new home."

I scanned the parking lot, looking for any signs that Brad might've already located us. When I saw no such signs, I stepped out of the car and fixed my clothes. The weather in South Carolina was less humid than Florida's weather. It was a pleasant change of scenery. There was a chill in the air since we were coming to the end of winter. Opening the back driver-side door, I reached in to unfasten Bria's car seat before I kissed her forehead. Once I had Bria safely in my arms, we walked up to the coffee shop.

As I was about to open the door, an older gentleman opened it from the inside. He walked out of the shop, carrying a cup of coffee. He held the door open, so I could walk in with Bria.

"Thank you," I called out as the gentleman nodded at my response.

The smell of freshly ground coffee beans danced in my nose as soon as we entered the shop. I looked around the coffee shop. Almost all the booths and tables were occupied by happy, chattering customers. Walking up to the long counter, I sat Bria on a counter stool and sat next to her. As I waited to be addressed, I imagined myself scurrying around the coffee shop, eagerly filling up cups of coffee and handing out various delicious pastries.

"Good morning. Welcome to Meg's Coffee Shop. My name is Sabrina. What may I get you two?" the strawberry blonde-haired woman asked me as she took out a small pad of paper and a red pen.

"We would like two chocolate donut holes, a medium black coffee, and the manager, please."

Sabrina smiled, revealing a mouth full of colorful braces. She wrote the order down on her pad of paper. "I will have your items up soon. Let me go grab the manager for you."

She disappeared into a swinging door leading to the coffee shop's back.

Reaching into my pocket, I pulled out my phone. Unlocking the phone, I handed it to Bria. "Here, you can play some games on my phone. We will go buy you a tablet later tonight once we get settled in."

Bria took my phone with glee in her little eyes.

A few moments later, a heavy-set brown-haired woman with a formal bun walked out of the back with Sabrina. Sabrina smiled at me as she walked by, heading to collect our food items.

"Good morning. I am Kelsey, manager of this establishment."

"Good morning, Kelsey."

"What may I help you with?"

"We have been in communication these past two months concerning a job."

She snapped her fingers and nodded. "Are you Tiffany?"

"Yes, ma'am."

Tiffany was the fake name I had come up with, so it would be even more difficult for Brad to locate us. I had planned everything out in these past few months, down to the small details.

"I am happy for your start on a new life," Kelsey said.

Over the course of the months, I explained how Bria and I were starting a new life in another state. She had a soft spot in her heart for us since I had told her I was a single mom.

"I am just so appreciative of you giving me this job," I replied.

Sabrina sat Bria's donut holes in front of her and my coffee in front of me. I smiled a thank you. She smiled back as she walked away.

"No problem, sweetheart. I felt the need in my heart to help you out."

"It is amazing to know there are still nice, caring people in this world."

Kelsey smiled. "I know. I'll just need you to shadow someone during your first few days. Once you feel comfortable, you should be okay working on your own."

"Thank you."

Kelsey smiled as she directed her full attention to Bria. "Who is this pretty girl?" she asked as Bria took a bite out of her donut hole.

"This is Bri," I said, shortening her name. I wrapped my hand around the cup and quickly sipped the hot coffee.

The coffee was of much better quality than the day-old gas station coffee I had been living off for two days.

"Hi, Bri. You are so pretty."

Bria looked up from the phone, and she gave a toothy smile. "Thank you," was her response.

Kelsey redirected her attention to me. "Do you think you can start on Monday?"

"That sounds great to me."

"That will give you a few days to get settled in."

"Perfect," I responded as I took another sip of the coffee.

"Did you find her a daycare yet?"

"Yes. It's about a mile up the road."

"That is a great daycare." She placed her hand on her hip. "All my children went there. I'm glad you could get her enrolled there."

"They are going to allow her to go to preschool for free. I qualified for a scholarship."

"That is so wonderful. Your start on a new life is so exciting."

"I am excited too. I'm going to head out now. There is a lot I must do in these next few days to get settled in."

"Good luck unpacking," she said.

"Will I see you Monday morning?" I asked, as Bria finished her last donut hole.

"Yes, you will. Be here 6 A.M. sharp."

Once we said our goodbyes, I placed a ten-dollar bill on the countertop and picked Bria up. Once I approached the door, I quickly surveyed the parking lot before we headed out of the coffee shop.

I strapped Bria into her car seat, her safety most important. "Time to go see our new home," I exclaimed.

"Yay," Bria cheered as she clapped her tiny hands together.

As I left the coffee shop that morning, I had a genuine smile. This was the start of our new life. The perfectly imperfect life I had yearned for many years.

Chapter Two

Kyla

I parked in front of the two-bedroom, one-bathroom home. Over the past two months, I had been eyeing the house on the internet. It was in a quiet neighborhood, which screamed a green flag to me. The house was on a corner that bordered another street. I had arranged for the homeowner to meet me here at eleven that morning, and I was ten minutes early.

"Mommy, is this our new home?" Bria asked as she looked out of the front windshield at the house.

"Maybe." I stared at the house sitting in front of me.

The outside looked exactly how the internet portrayed it to be. The house was a small bungalow-style painted light gray with white trimmings. The landscaping of the home was immaculate and maintained, green and vibrant. Excitement coursed through me as I stepped out of the car. Going into the backseat, I grabbed Bria out of her car seat. As soon as Bria and I walked hand in hand up the three steps leading to the front porch, a newer model Nissan truck parked right next to my car in the driveway. Moments later, a man in his late forties that had a slow, receding hairline, stepped out of the truck and approached us.

"Good morning, Tiffany," the man greeted me.

"Good morning, Mr. Abraham," I replied, showing the respect I had learned in my years of being raised in a foster home. Most children in the foster system grew up to be very disrespectful, but while I was in the system, I held on to all the manners that were taught to me.

"Are you ready to see this beauty?" he asked me, swaying his right hand towards the house.

"Of course. Give us the tour."

Mr. Abraham walked up to the house. Using the set of keys he carried, he unlocked the door. Before pushing the door open, he turned around and smiled at Bria.

"Who is this little angel?"

"This is Bri."

"Nice to meet you, Bri."

Bria smiled as she held my hand tight. She stood close to my side.

Mr. Abraham opened the door. Right away, I fell in love with the house and its spacious layout. From the front door, I walked right into the small living and dining room area. To the left, two doors led to the bedrooms. One room was Bria's, and the other room was mine. Off to the right was the bathroom. Towards the back of the house was a door leading to the backyard.

"I'll give you a few minutes alone to tour the house on your own and make your decision. If you have any questions, I'm right here" Mr. Abraham stated before he walked out the front door.

As soon as the front door closed, I envisioned the furnishings I wanted to purchase and decorate. The furnishings would be on the color line beige. I could never choose the color of the furnishings when I lived with Brad. Every decision made in our relationship was based on what Brad desired. Dark brown furnishings were what I had to deal with. Dark brown furnishings were what I was going to avoid.

I walked over to view the two bedrooms. The master bedroom was a bit bigger than the other bedroom by a few feet in width. It had a nice walk-in closet that I would use to its fullest potential. Walking into the bathroom, I observed the elegant, marbled shower bath. After a long day of serving my customers, I envisioned taking a steamy hot shower. Walking to the back door, I unlocked the deadbolt lock and opened it. Stepping into the backyard, I noticed it was maintained just like the front yard. The backyard was surrounded by a privacy fence that would keep wandering eyes away. I imagined us running around the backyard playing tag. Bria playing in the sprinklers during the summer while I read a book and sipped on fresh, homemade lemonade. Bria being a child without having to be exposed to her mother being abused 24/7.

"Bria, do you like it?" She stood next to me in the yard. A toothy smile grinned up at me.

"I like it a lot," Bria said as she clapped her hands with excitement.

"I like it also, sweetie."

This house was small compared to the one Brad had provided for us, but I thought a small, intimate place would be what Bria and I needed to bond on a deeper level.

Hand in hand, we walked from the backyard through the house to the front yard. Mr. Abraham stood on the edge of the property, looking across the street at another home. I closed the front door behind us. The sound of the door closing caused Mr. Abraham to turn around and give us his full attention.

"Do you like it?" He walked back up to the front porch.

"I love it," I admitted.

Mr. Abraham went over the house's details,

explaining that the rent included the maintenance of the landscape.

"You will be responsible for all utilities. When would you like to move in?" he asked.

"How about right now?"

Mr. Abraham's eyeballs bugged as he smiled. He nodded as he said, "I will need first, last, and security."

Digging into my purse, I found my wallet. Stuffed inside was a wad of big bills. I had saved every dollar earned from my part-time job at the bookstore for the last four months. Pulling out the exact cash, I handed it over to him. As he fingered through the bills, counting them out, Mr. Abraham would look at me every so often.

"I'm going to need you to sign some paperwork, and I'll be on my way."

Relief rushed through me as I stood at the kitchen counter, looking over my first lease.

I scanned over the small print.

"Is this a six-month or a twelve-month lease?" I asked him.

"That's negotiable. Whatever works best for my tenant works best for me."

After contemplating the pros and cons, I decided it was best to settle with a six-month lease. I had become independent, and it felt good. It felt good not having to depend on Brad to help me out. I was taking care of my daughter by myself at twenty-two.

"Thank you so much, Mr. Abraham." I walked him to the front door.

"No, thank you. I will be back in one month to collect next month's rent." Mr. Abraham was about to leave when he stopped in his tracks, turned around, and laughed.

"What is funny?" I asked. I could use a good laugh.

"I forgot to give you a key to the house."

I giggled at the mistake. I was so excited to sign my lease, I had forgotten the one thing I needed most, to lock us up safely.

"I hope you have a great day settling in. Congratulations."

Once Mr. Abraham handed me the key to the house, I locked the door. Grabbing my phone, I turned on a song that Bria and I both liked and had heard on the radio a few times. We danced together in our new living room. Giggling and dancing around with Bria warmed my insides as I saw Bria's smile. The life that I would provide for her would be amazing.

***

Brad

Taking a gulp of whiskey from my flask, I sat slouched in my dark brown, lazy-boy chair. It was torturous being in my empty, quiet home all by myself. Bria was no longer in the house, giving it life with her various cartoons playing in the background while her laughter echoed throughout the house. Kyla was no longer in the house, buzzing around and making it feel like the perfect home with her presence alone. My family hadn't been in the house for two days, and I didn't know what to do.

At first, I was mournful. I thought something horrific had occurred when my family had not arrived home the first night. Maybe my family had been kidnapped, or worse, my family had been killed while I had stepped out. But then I looked throughout the house. I noticed some of Bria's stuffed animals were missing, and most of her clothes had disappeared.

Most of Kyla's clothes were gone from our shared closet except for a few pairs of jeans and t-shirts. Kyla's BMW was gone, along with her car keys. Kyla's phone was the only thing left behind that was close to being valuable. Kyla never left the house without her phone, but it sat on the nightstand beside our king-sized bed. That was the biggest telltale sign that something was not right, and I was going to get to the bottom of it.

The whiskey burned my throat and chest as I continued to guzzle it down. I wanted to drink until I imagined my family still in this house with me like they had been these past five years. But as I continued to drink, everything around me slowed down but my mind. My mind raced as I put two and two together. Kyla and Bria were not kidnapped. Kyla had grown tired of the shit I had put her through for the last five years, and she finally developed the courage to leave me.

Rage coursed through my veins. I could not believe it took me two days to figure it out. They could be anywhere in the United States by now.

They could be in another country for all I knew, and I had no clue where to even search for them. I would search for the two of them until I could locate them, even if it killed me.

I had told Kyla many times over the years that she could never leave me. She belonged to me for life, for eternity. Unfortunately, she didn't take my words seriously because I would only give her two options once I found her. She was coming home with me to deal with some very serious consequences, or she would say goodbye to our daughter forever. If I couldn't have her, then nobody would.

A smirk touched my lips as I rubbed the stubble on my chin. I needed to formulate a solid plan for getting my family back. It would be like taking candy from a baby. I was ready to make that baby scream and cry for mercy.

Chapter Three

Kyla

After spending hours dancing with Bria, I purchased a few furnishings online. They would be delivered to our home late Monday afternoon after work. I would buy furnishings little by little as I earned money to ensure we'd always had a nice stash of cash, just in case of an emergency. Bria and I went shopping at the local retail store. We purchased groceries, everyday necessities we would need around the house, a few books that captured my attention, and the tablet I had promised her.

Shopping with Bria had always been such a joy over the years. This shopping trip was nothing different. As we walked around the store, Bria loved to play games such as 'I spy' and 'would you rather?'.

Due to us being in a new house, Bria only felt comfortable sleeping with me in my bedroom. We ended up cuddling all night on the air mattress we purchased earlier at the store. Sleeping on an air mattress was nothing like sleeping on an expensive king-sized bed. Having my baby tucked safely in the comfort of my arms made me sleep soundly for the first night in years.

Waking Bria up at five in the morning was difficult. She had never gotten up that early for school, a day in her life. Once I got her up in the morning, she was grumpy. If we were lucky, that grumpy nature would dissipate quickly.

I sat her in a bean bag chair with her tablet to distract her with cartoons as I bustled around the kitchen preparing breakfast. As I scrambled eggs on the stove in a frying pan, I cut up some strawberries and a banana.

"Breakfast is ready, sweetie," I sang as I placed Bria's plate of eggs, bananas, and strawberries in front of her on the carpet.

I fixed myself the remaining food and sat beside her on the floor.

As we ate our breakfast, we talked about her attending her new school for the first time today.

"Are you excited about going to school?" I asked before I took a bite of my eggs.

She took a sip of her milk from her cup. "Yes."

"What are you most excited about?"

"Making new friends."

Bria was a sweet, outgoing child, and I knew she would have no problem getting along with her new classmates.

Once we were finished eating, I got us both ready to start our official first workday and school day.

With caution, I opened the front door. I looked around the front yard. The cool, refreshing air hit my face as my eyes tried to adjust to the darkness of the morning. My nerves were on edge. I didn't see any sudden movements or shadows that I should be wary of. With speed, I locked the house before I walked to my car, holding Bria's hand tight. Once I fastened Bria into her car seat, I slid into the driver's seat and pushed the button to lock the car.

Inhaling and exhaling, I closed my eyes. My nerves had me on edge.

"Mommy, are you okay?" Bria asked from the back seat.

"Yes, sweetie," I replied before I started the car up.

The electronics in the vehicle brightened up the car, and I looked in the rearview mirror at Bria. She was the warrior in my life. She was the reason I kept on going every single day.

Traveling a few miles down the road from home, I pulled my car into the small daycare Bria would be attending. It was a convenient location, since the coffee shop was only a mile down the road.

I helped Bria out of her car seat. Together, we walked into the daycare hand in hand. Once Bria was signed in, I handed her a lunchbox that contained a ham sandwich, a bag of pretzels, sliced cucumbers, and a bottle of water.

"I love you, Mommy."

I bent down to give her a kiss on her forehead. "I love you too, sweetie. I will see you later."

I watched as the woman at the front desk grabbed Bria's hand. She led her down a hall. Before Bria was out of my sight, she turned around and waved at me. Waving back, I blew a kiss at her as I walked out of the daycare with confidence. Most parents had to peel their tear-streaked child's hands off their bodies as they tried to leave their children in daycare, but Bria was different. She had no problem being around kids all day. She would make plenty of friends.

I drove the mile to the coffee shop and pulled into the parking lot. My eyes scanned the area for a brief second before I straightened up the black dress pants and the beige collared shirt I wore as I stepped out of my car. The dress code for the coffee shop was neutral colors. I walked into the coffee shop ten minutes before six, clutching tightly to my purse.

Sabrina wiped down the countertop Bria, and I had sat at a few days ago.

"Good morning." Her tone oozed with

happiness.

"Good morning," I replied.

"Your name is Tiffany, right?"

"Yes, it is."

"Welcome back. You will shadow me all day today to get a feel for how things operate around here."

Sabrina had finished wiping down the countertop, the scent of lemon wafting into my nose.

"Sounds great. Where can I put my purse?"

She pointed towards the swinging door she entered to find Kelsey the first time I came in.

"We have a mini locker room back there. Come follow me."

I followed close behind Sabrina as she led me to a hall with three doors. She walked to the first door on the right. There were approximately ten lockers in the room. She pulled out a piece of paper from her pocket and held it out for me to take.

"This is your locker and your locker combination."

"Thank you."

I took the piece of paper and stared down at the three numbers written in red ink.

"Do you need any help to open it?"

I shook my head. "No, I think I have it from here."

Sabrina smiled. "Goody. Get situated and come out when you are ready. I will let Kelsey know you are here."

Sabrina walked out of the locker room while I fumbled with my lock. I messed around with the lock a few times before opening it. Once opened, I stuffed my purse inside and locked it up. Kelsey walked in as I was about to walk out of the door.

"Good morning Tiffany. I see you arrived a little earlier than expected. That is great to see."

I smiled, appreciating the praise. "There was no way I would mess up this great opportunity you gave me. Thank you again."

Kelsey shook her head. "You don't have to keep thanking me."

"It's hard not to," I admitted.

"I could tell with how persistent you were that you were serious about this job." As Kelsey and I talked, we headed out to the front of the coffee shop.

"My focus is taking care of my family. Being persistent is a necessity."

"Where did you move here from?"

"Miami, Florida."

"I could not imagine moving from that big city to this small town. I'm planning a vacation there in a few months."

"You will have the time of your life."

At that moment, I noticed an older white-haired couple had walked in and was seated in a booth. Sabrina walked out from behind the counter as she looked at me and asked, "Ready to get to learning?"

Throughout my entire shift, Sabrina showed me the ropes of the job. I observed how she handled every customer she came across. At first, I was overwhelmed with all the business that we had received. However, the tips at the end of the day, plus the money per hour that was promised, made it all worth the while. There was no doubt in my mind that I would make enough money to provide for my small family.

By two o'clock, the coffee shop doors were locked, signifying the end of the work day was near. We did the end-of-day cleaning. Fifteen minutes later, my shift ended, and I headed to the locker room. I was greeted with warm smiles from my coworkers. I opened my locker to grab my items as Sabrina entered the locker room.

"So, how do you think your first day went?" Sabrina asked me as she worked on her locker, which was three to my left.

"I think it went better than I expected. This is my first time being a waitress."

"Wow, that is awesome." Sabrina looked over at me and smiled. "I can't tell. You are getting the hang of it fast."

"Thank you. I'm sure I would not be doing this well without your great training."

Sabrina grabbed her bag out of the locker and closed it shut. "I am pretty good at what I do, but you must take full credit."

Sabrina and I headed out of the locker room as we continued to talk.

"So, where did you move here from?"

"Florida. I thought a change of scenery would be great for my family."

"I have always wanted to vacation there growing up. Do you recommend any vacation spots?"

"Panama City is stunning." That was the only location Brad had taken us to over the years that we all enjoyed. On that specific vacation, we had gotten along fine. No arguments occurred. No bouts of jealousy had surfaced. If it were up to me, we would not have ever left.

"Thank you for the suggestion. Your daughter is so adorable."

"Thank you," I responded, feeling prideful in the daughter I had.

"When you two came in, I just wanted to pinch her cheeks."

Sabrina and I laughed. "She is my everything."

"It is very clear," she pointed out as we approached the coffee shop doors.

My heart thumped out of my chest as Sabrina pushed the door open. With caution, I walked out the door. The smell of exhaust was thick and pungent in the air. I did a quick yet careful scan of the entire parking lot. I sighed in relief when I did not see Brad's black BMW SUV among the twelve cars still inhabiting the parking lot.

"Are you okay?" Sabrina raised her right eyebrow as she placed her attention on me.

"I'm fine," I responded, forcing a smile. "Do you have any children?" I asked.

The best thing to do was to steer the conversation in a different direction.

Sabrina nodded. "I have a five-year-old. Her name is Emily." She pulled her phone from her purse and showed me the lock screen. On the lock screen was an adorable little girl smiling wide with brown pigtails on each side of her head.

"She is so precious," I cooed.

Sabrina smiled as she tucked a piece of hair behind her ear. "Maybe we can do a play date one day soon?" Sabrina suggested.

"That would be great."

Getting together with another mom and daughter for a play date sounded awesome. I knew Bria would enjoy it. We had never arranged one before, and it would be a fantastic experience. I was excited to get together with someone I might share common interests with. There had been several years since I had a friend to spend time with and confide in.

"Will I see you tomorrow?" she asked me as we approached the employee parking lot.

I scanned the parking lot once again before I responded to Sabrina's question. "Bright and early."

"Awesome. I hope you have an amazing day."

"Same to you, bye."

I got into my car as Sabrina walked over to her white Toyota sedan. She waved at me as I started my car. I waved back before I looked over my shoulder to back out of the parking space. The sun peeked through the trees, temporarily blinding me before I drove out of the parking lot.

Drumming my fingers on the steering wheel, I drove to Bria's daycare. My heart ached when I passed a family of four riding their bicycles on the sidewalk. I yearned to provide Bria with a life where family activities resulted in happiness and laughter instead of sadness and tears. I pulled my car into the parking lot and walked inside. The office had a faint stench of burnt popcorn that caused my nose to wrinkle in distaste.

Within minutes of checking in at the front desk and having a small conversation with the front desk attendant, I heard an excited, "Mommy."

My heart burst with joy as Bria ran towards me with her arms extended. I squatted down as she ran into my arms and squeezed me with all her might. Picking her up, I spun her around in a circle.

"How was your day, sweetie?"

I waved goodbye to the attendant as we headed out the door.

"It was good. I made new friends, and my teacher is nice..."

Bria continued to talk as I led her to the car.

I was in love with being Bria's mother. I wouldn't trade it for the world.

Chapter Four

Brad

I stared at the address displayed on my phone's screen. I stared so hard that my eyes blurred, making the words on the screen indistinct.

My heart skipped a beat. I felt a buzz of excitement tingle down my spine. I hadn't felt this way in a while. I had been living in a drunken haze for the past few days. The haze was so intense that I had forgotten about the device I had placed in Kyla's car when I first purchased it.

I grabbed my keys off the dark brown end table next to the front door. Locking up my house,

I was grateful it was early. The sun wasn't beaming hot at this time of the morning. I ran to my SUV and got in. The vehicle roared to life as I pressed the start button and the brake at the same time. Backing out of my driveway, I headed towards the highway. I had a four-hour and twenty-seven-minute trip I had to make. I planned to make that trip a hell of a lot shorter.

With aggression, I tackled the congested morning traffic as I maneuvered between all the vehicles that littered the highway. As I zoomed by the other cars on a morning drive, my mind wandered in many directions.

When did Kyla finally realize she was tired of dealing with the shit I put her through? Was it the day I punched her in the stomach for overcooking my steak? Was it the day I called her every horrible name I could think of when I caught her flirting with the man at the grocery store? Was it the day I kicked her in the shin for not using the right detergent on my clothes? Was it the day I mentally abused her for hours on end for not making me feel wanted? Or was it the day I gave her a black eye for allowing Bria to make a mess of my house before my friend came over to hang out with me?

Even though I had put her through hell on Earth, that was not enough for her to just up and leave me. Let alone take my daughter without a trace. Our relationship was far from perfect, but I was under the assumption that the good outweighed the bad. I was wrong.

I just hoped when I saw her in nine minutes, she would be apologetic for allowing me to go through hell for the past few days. If she was not sorry, there would be hell to pay.

Confusion hit me hard as I pulled into the parking lot of a tow yard. Somehow, I made the trip shorter by forty-five minutes. Why was Kyla at a tow yard? Did her car break down, and she couldn't afford to take it to the dealership and have it fixed? I turned the vehicle off as I quickly scanned the parking lot. From here, I couldn't see too much.

Opening the driver's door, I stepped out. Today was a sunny and bright day, making the air sticky hot, and humid. There was not even the slightest breeze flowing through the air.

Running my fingers through my short brown hair, I walked over to the chain-linked, gated fence that outlined the back of the property. From here, I could see cars ranging from different makes and models. Her car was nowhere in sight.

"Hello, Sir, welcome to Mike's Tow Yard. My name is Edward. What can I help you with today?"

Turning towards the voice, a man dressed in a T-shirt and jeans approached me.

"I'm searching for a car that was towed here a few days ago."

Edward raised his left eyebrow as he made eye contact with me.

"Did you receive a call about the car?" he asked me.

Rage boiled in my veins. It irritated me that Edward questioned me on how I found out the car was here. Pulling my phone from my front right pocket, I placed it inches from his face. "No. The tracking device I installed on the car states it is at this location. Should I mention I paid for the car in cash?" I growled.

Edward's eyes widened to look at the screen of my phone.

Edward studied the information on the phone. "Let me see if my boss can speak with you," Edward stated as he pulled his eyes away from my phone and walked towards the building.

Once Edward walked into the building, I decided to follow. Walking to the entrance, I pulled the door open, and a blast of cold air greeted me. Six eyes landed on me. Edward looked as if he was a deer caught in headlines. He pointed at me and said, "This man would like to speak with you."

"Hello, my name is Mike. I am the owner of this establishment." Mike, a white-haired man dressed in business casual attire, walked over to me. He reached his hand out to shake mine.

I gripped his hand a bit firmer than I had intended. I shook it with intent. "It's nice to meet you, Mike."

"What can I help you with?"

"Can you tell me when my girlfriend's car was towed here?"

"I'm not sure which car you are referencing. We can go look." He extended his hand toward the backyard, where all the towed vehicles were sitting.

I led the way, walking out of the back door. Dust kicked up under my feet as I walked further into the yard as I did a quick scan. Before long, my eyes zeroed in on the dark blue BMW sedan I knew all too well. Defeat washed over me as I made a beeline right over to it. Cupping my hands over my eyes, I peeked into the back seat. Bria's purple car seat was missing. I looked into the front seat. The car was stripped of Kyla's favorite silver dream catcher, which always hung in her rearview mirror. I remembered the day we purchased it like it was yesterday.

The clouds hugged the sun, making the temperature drop by five degrees. The five degrees made little difference, as the humidity was still muggy. Kyla was seven months pregnant, and we were taking a peaceful stroll through the local flea market that came to town once a month. She wore a light-colored blue maternity dress that stretched perfectly over her baby bump. She rubbed her stomach when she stopped in her tracks, something catching her attention. She waddled over to a booth manned by a petite, breathtaking woman with long, luscious black hair. Hanging from the booth was an immense variety of dream catchers ranging from different colors and styles.

Kyla reached up and fingered a silver dream catcher. I walked up to the booth and stood beside her. Gleam glistened in her eyes as she stated, "I love this."

The woman approached Kyla from the opposite side of the booth.

"This dream catcher is 100% authentic."

"Did you make it yourself?" Kyla asked her.

She nodded. "My tribe back home specializes in this craft," she responded.

"That is so wonderful." Kyla gasped as she admired the dream catcher.

"You won't find another like this one," she responded.

"We will take it," I said before Kyla could even continue the conversation.

The look in Kyla's eyes had my credit card out of my wallet before she even approached the booth.

"This is the car." I snapped out of my memory.

Mike's gaze danced over the vehicle as he responded, "How are you so sure this is it?"

Pulling my spare key out of my back pocket, I pushed the unlock button. All the locks on the door lifted at once. "I am sure you need more proof." I walked to the back of the car, opened the trunk, and pulled out the small tracking device. I had placed it in the trunk the day I brought Kyla to the BMW dealership to purchase it. The car was purchased brand spanking new off the showroom floor five years prior. "This is how I knew where to locate it."

"We towed it here a few days ago." He stuffed his hands into the front pockets of his dress pants.

"What's wrong with the car? Has it broken down?" I asked him.

Mike shrugged. "I don't think anything is wrong with it. We got a call from an owner at a local mall. The car hadn't moved in a few days, so they called for us to pick it up."

Rage coursed through me as my mouth watered for my whiskey. Even though I made sure Kyla had everything she could have ever desired, it was still not enough. She abandoned a car in perfect shape at a mall. What was Kyla up to? Where was her mind? Was she losing it?

"We can go inside. Look up the paperwork. If the car is in your name, I can release it to you."

"I can't take it away from here today."

"Come inside. Let's look at the information that we have on file."

I followed Mike back into the building, giving Edward a side-eye stare before I sat at Mike's desk. After twenty minutes of verifying the car was in my name and receiving an overload of information, I learned the car was towed here four days ago from a mall five miles away. The pieces of the puzzle were gradually coming together, little by little.

Mike walked me out of the front door and handed me a business card. "I will see you soon."

I nodded as I headed for my SUV. There was one destination in mind. The mall. The traffic there was no better than in Miami. After cursing under my breath every five seconds, I arrived at the mall. I located several cameras that were placed on the buildings. I hit the jackpot. The cameras would tell me everything that I needed to know. After speaking with a security guard, I was informed of where to find the main office. Following the directions provided, I knocked twice on the closed door.

A tall, scrawny, balding man wearing a suit opened the door. "Hello, how may I help you?"

"I'm Brad, and I need your help."

"Well, come on in, Brad. My name is Zackary." He motioned me to walk into the small, cramped office, where I sat on a metal folding chair. "How may I help you?"

"My girlfriend's car was towed from here four days ago."

"I am sorry to hear that. If a car is in the parking lot for a few days without being moved, we have no other choice but to have it towed. It's company policy."

"Listen." I exhaled as I folded my arms across my chest. I had no interest in the policies of the mall. I would not pretend to care. Time was ticking, and Kyla and Bria were nowhere to be found. "No disrespect to you, but I don't care about company policy."

Zachary raised his bushy eyebrows. "How may I help you?" He placed his hands on his desk.

"I need to have a look at your cameras. I must

see how my girlfriend and my daughter left from here."

"I'm not able to show you that footage."

I locked eyes with Zachary, my body feeling hot. "Why is that?"

"Video footage can only be viewed by police with a valid warrant."

The response I received was far from what I hoped would come out of his mouth. I stood, the chair legs screeching on the tile. My fists balled up at my sides as my face changed into a scowl. "No. You are going to show me that video footage now. My girlfriend and daughter might be in danger."

Zachary's eyes zeroed in on my balled-up fist at my sides. He defensively raised his hands as he stood. He backed up a few feet away from me. The cowardice seeped out of his pores.

"Listen, I do not want any problems. Please leave, or I will call the police."

Smirking, I rubbed the overgrown stubble that was on my chin. I pointed my index finger right at him. "I expected a coward-ass response like that when I saw the man I was dealing with," I said with venom.

I pushed the chair over in the office before I walked out of the mall. As soon as I was situated inside my car, I dug into my glove compartment and pulled out my emergency flask. Gulp after gulp, the alcohol burned my throat as it traveled to my stomach.

I took a deep breath as I closed my eyes.

Kyla suspected I had placed a tracker on her phone and her vehicle, which I had done with both items. She didn't even bother bringing her phone and discarded her vehicle four hours north. She could be anywhere in the United States by now with my daughter. Red fire flashed before my eyes as I realized this was a thought-out plan Kyla had carefully constructed. This plan must have taken months to formulate.

My cockiness had me positive that when I located the tracking device's location, I would've located my girls. I just knew I would bring them back home, but this journey to finding them was just beginning. This search might be extended, but I wouldn't stop until I located my two girls.

Chapter Five

Kyla

Bria and I had been living in South Carolina for an entire month. Living in South Carolina was a breath of fresh air I did not realize I needed. If only I had dared to leave years earlier. Truth be told, I would've saved myself years of abuse.

Bria had already adapted to her new daycare. Every day on the short drive home, Bria would tell me how much she liked her new friends at school.

Back in Florida, Bria could only go to daycare three days a week. Bria was upset as she enjoyed being around other kids throughout the day. Brad had always said since I was not working, there was no reason for Bria to go to daycare five days a week. I had always wanted to work full time, but Brad would not allow it. It was clear he wanted me to depend on him. It was nice to prove to myself that I did not need him. If only he could see the woman I had become without his help.

Occasionally, Bria would ask me about her dad. She wondered where he was and why he didn't move with us. The best explanation I could tell a four-year-old was that her dad needed some alone time without us around. That statement would stop the question from being asked for a while before she would ask again.

There was never a second of the day that I was not on high alert. At all times, I looked over my shoulder whenever I was walked of the house or whenever I was in public. Living in fear was not the ideal lifestyle I had planned, but we were not clear yet. I would do everything in my power to keep us safe, though.

Sabrina and I connected more each day when we had our breaks from serving our tables. I could say she had become an incredible friend that I never thought I needed until now. Brad made sure that during the five years we were together, he isolated me from everyone except his parents. It was not too difficult for him to accomplish since I knew none of my birth family. The only individuals that I could even consider family besides Brad's parents were my foster family. Unfortunately, I lost all communication with them. I had even lost contact with Amy, the girl I had considered my best friend for several years.

Amy had moved into the foster home when I was twelve years old. She was thirteen at the time and a year older than me. When she first moved in, she was quiet and did not utter two words to anyone. She was soft spoken, and I knew she was like me. Amy and I shared bunk beds. She slept on the top bunk, and I slept on the bottom. One night before bed, I started a conversation with her about a TV show in our room. Turned out we were both fanatics over the TV show. We were inseparable from that night going forward. We became separable when Brad moved me out of foster care when I was three months pregnant. The day Brad moved me out was the last day I saw or heard from Amy. The decision to leave was not made by me. It was done by force. They would not allow me to stay in the home much longer for fear that I would start showing. They did not want my choices to influence the younger girls negatively.

My other coworkers were great to chat with in passing. I loved the quiet environment I had moved my daughter to, and I could not have asked for a better turnout of moving as quickly as we did.

Walking out of the locker room on Tuesday morning, I turned on the coffee machines as I did a light wipe of the counter. Sabrina walked out from the back and took the chairs off the tables before she wiped them down.

"Is it fine if I ask you a question?"

"Ask away." Sabrina had my undivided attention, and I was ready for anything.

"How did you get the weekends off? I've been working here for years and have never had an entire weekend off."

Shrugging my shoulders, I wiped my hands on the apron wrapped around my waist. The scent of coffee intensified as the coffee brewed. "I am a single mom, and I don't have any family in the area. So I don't have anybody to watch my daughter on the weekends."

If she knew why I was there, I knew she wouldn't pry.

"You must have done something to Kelsey. You are special, though, so I see why." Sabrina tossed her straight strawberry blonde hair over her shoulder to glance at me and smile.

I returned a smile as Scott walked out from the back.

"Hey, ladies," he greeted us as he waved at us.

"Hey, Scott," Sabrina and I sang in unison.

"Oh my, what beautiful music to my ears."

His response caused us to laugh.

All three of us talked as we continued to prepare the shop for the customers to file in.

Even though Meg's was a stand-alone, hole-in-the-wall coffee shop, it was clear the company was doing great in the financial area. In the past month, there was never a time when there was not a full house in the cafe.

The first hour of the day flew by as I served up steaming cups of coffee and tasty pastries. I had regulars I saw every day. It was awesome having conversations with them.

"Good morning, Mr. and Mrs. Smith." I approached their table with a smile.

"Good morning," they chorused as they focused on me.

"Are we having our usual two medium decaf black coffees and two plain bagels with lite cream cheese?" I asked them, pen and pad in hand.

The adorable, gray-haired couple nodded. "Yes, please," Mrs. Smith acknowledged.

"Your order will be up shortly." I scribbled the order down on the paper pad as I walked to the counter to deliver the order to Scott.

I headed to my next table, where a man dressed in a purple long-sleeved dress shirt and black dress pants sat alone.

"Good morning. Welcome to Meg's. What can I start you off with to drink?"

The man's eyes browsed over the menu before he took the time to glance up at me. Once he looked at me, his blue eyes widened. Our gaze locked for a few seconds. I had the chance to take in his handsome features. He had sparkling blue oceanic eyes, faint blonde stubble on his chin, and short, blonde-cropped hair.

He tore his gaze from mine as he took

another glance at the menu. "May I have an Americano?"

"Of course. I'll go put your order in now."

I walked away from the table, trying to shake my head clear of the man that grabbed my attention.

After putting his order in, I had the chance to visit my other tables. I took some orders, dropped off drinks and pastries, and cashed out customers.

"Enjoy your breakfast, Mr. and Mrs. Smith," I said after I delivered their coffees and bagels to their table.

"Thank you, Tiffany," Mr. Smith said as they ate breakfast.

"My pleasure."

I smiled before I walked away.

I went to the counter, where the Americano waited for me. Steam swirled from the top of the mug, alerting me to how hot the liquid was.

I walked the mug to the table. "Here is your Americano. Would you like to order anything else?"

Our eyes locked together again for a moment before his eyes flickered back to the menu. "I would like your recommendations on the pastries. Which one do you think I should try?"

I thought for a few moments. Over the last few weeks I had worked, I was given a chance to try all the pastries.

"The blueberry muffins are to die for," I admitted.

I first tried the blueberry muffin a week into my work, and I fell in love. So, I treated myself to the amazing pastry once a week as a job well done.

"I'll take one."

"Coming right up," I replied, scribbling on my notepad.

I turned and walked away when he stopped me, saying, "Excuse me."

"Yes?" I turned and looked over my shoulder, right into his eyes.

"What is your name?"

"Ky... Tiffany," I corrected myself.

I wanted to kick myself for the screw-up I had almost done on my name.

He smiled. He revealed an alluring set of straight white teeth. "I just wanted to tell you that you are breathtaking."

My heart responded by picking up its pace in my chest. I smiled as I looked around the cafe. I was surprised by his openness.

"Thank you."

I headed off to deliver the order.

Walking to an empty table, I stacked the plates on top of each other. I pocketed the tip left for me, and relief flooded my entire body. I was working and providing for my child.

It felt great.

Sabrina walked by, carrying two coffee mugs. "Behind you," she called out before she smiled and winked at me.

I continued my rounds, dropping off the

blueberry muffin before I went over to Mr. and Mrs. Smith, who were just finishing their breakfast.

"How is Chester doing?"

Chester was their pet chihuahua, who they talked about all the time. He was a white chihuahua which was rare to come across, but they had searched near and far to find him.

"He is doing well. Good as ever." Mrs. Smith beamed as Mr. Smith handed me his credit card. I entered his card into the portable credit card machine.

"She has that dog spoiled rotten," Mr. Smith added.

Mrs. Smith playfully squatted her husband's hand. "I'm not the only one spoiling him, Robert."

I laughed at their cute couple banter.

My heart ached though. I had longed for the love that I witnessed they shared these past few weeks. I yearned for that love from a young age. Since I never was loved by my birth family, I thought the only love I would ever find was love from a companion. I had found that in Brad when I turned eighteen, and he moved me out of foster care, but I was wrong. The love I found out that I needed was the love that I shared with my daughter. Storge love at its finest.

"Do you two have anything special planned for today?" I asked.

I handed Mr. Smith his credit card back.

"We are going to tour a museum today."

Mrs. Smith beamed as she clasped her

hands together.

"Well, I hope you two enjoy the museum."

"Thank you. We will take pictures and show them to you."

Mr. Smith pushed his hands against the table to assist in helping him stand up.

"I am looking forward to it. I will see you two tomorrow morning."

"Goodbye, dear." They chortled as I walked away.

I approached the table where the man was eating his pastry. "Tell me you are enjoying the blueberry muffin."

He was mid chew when I approached, but he nodded in approval. He waited until he had swallowed the food before he used a napkin to wipe away any crumbs.

"You were right. These blueberry muffins are killer."

"I'm glad you enjoyed it." I reached into my apron. I pulled out his bill and sat it on his table. "Whenever you are ready, I can take your payment."

He reached into his pocket and pulled out his wallet. He handed over a twenty-dollar bill and stated, "You can keep the change as a tip. Only if you do one thing for me."

I raised my eyebrow. I was not sure what this man was going to ask.

"What is that?" I asked, suspicion in my voice.

"Ask me what my name is."

I took a step back, shocked by his request. That was not what I expected to come out of his mouth. Yet, relief washed over me as his request was the best I could have ever expected from a stranger.

"What is your name?"

"I'm Ryan." Ryan stuck out his hand, waiting for me to place my hand in his.

I looked around the coffee shop. The clink of glass grabbed my attention. After a few moments, I placed my hand in his. He cradled my hand with care before he kissed the back of my hand.

"It's nice to meet you, Ryan," I responded. The kiss on the back of my hand was soft, causing a small flutter in my heart.

"It's nice to meet you, Tiffany. You will see me around. I hope you enjoy the rest of your day."

With that finishing statement, Ryan stood and towered over me by several inches. I stepped back a few feet, intimidation attempting to creep up on me as I craned my head to look at him. Flashes of Brad towering over me flooded my brain. I shook those thoughts away. Once those flashes dissipated, I watched Ryan proceed out the door and disappear while my heart tried to figure out what had just happened.

Chapter Six

Kyla

"Come on, Bria," Emily said as she grasped Bria's tiny hand.

I watched as Bria followed behind Emily.

Sabrina and I were sitting on a wooden bench at one of the local playgrounds in town. The smell of spring was in the air as the temperature warmed up. We were watching our daughters walk toward the toddler playground. It was Saturday afternoon, around three, and the park was not too busy, just two other families. It was a nice, bright, sunny day, and we thought it was a perfect day to get together so our daughters could play and get to know each other.

"I am so glad we set up this playdate." I watched them run up the steps leading to the slide. Bria's pigtails bounced with each step that she took.

"I am too. Emily and I don't go on too many playdates," Sabrina informed me.

"How come?"

"I don't have many friends in this area. Let alone friends with children."

"What about her friends from daycare?"

"We go on one playdate, but a second one is never set up," she responded as she ran her fingers through her hair.

"Did you grow up in the area?"

Sabrina nodded. "I did. Emily's daycare is the one that I went to when I was younger."

"Were you born in Branchville?" I asked.

We talked during work, but we never had the chance to sit down for more than ten minutes and have a heart-to-heart conversation.

"Yes, a full-blooded South Carolinian," she stated, her voice confident.

"You must like small towns," I said as a woodpecker flew nearby.

Sabrina shrugged as she twisted the gold diamond ring on her wedding finger. I had never noticed the ring on Sabrina's finger until now. "I always dreamed of moving to a bigger town, but that was before I had Emily."

A gentle breeze drifted by, wafting Sabrina's apple shampoo scent in my direction. "How come you never followed your dreams of moving?"

"My husband is established in a decent job here. But, knowing his love for the role, I don't foresee us moving anytime soon."

Our eyes locked onto our daughters, who were running around and giggling with each other. The sight warmed my heart, watching Bria have fun with someone her own age. She could never have playdates back in Florida. At Brad's request, she was only allowed to go to and from daycare three days a week. No playdates were allowed under any circumstances.

"I did not know you were married."

Sabrina ran her fingers through her hair. "I have been married a little over four years now. My husband's name is Julian."

"Is Julian Emily's father?"

Sabrina nodded. "Yes, he is. We got married after Emily turned a year old."

"Where did you meet Julian?" I loved hearing love stories. Even though my love life had come to a screeching halt, it didn't mean I didn't want to hear about successful love stories.

Sabrina smiled, her braces making an appearance. "We met at a local grocery store. He was behind me in the checkout line, and I had forgotten one of my grocery bags in the store. He chased me down once he checked out, and we began talking from there."

"Sounds like love at first sight."

"You could say that. We went to the same high school together and didn't even know it," she added.

"You never seen each other before you met in the store?"

She shook her head. "I don't remember seeing him in high school. To be honest, I was so focused on my studies, dating was the last thing on my mind," she admitted.

Dating was the last thing on her mind, but it was the first thing on my mind. I couldn't wait to receive the love I always desired, but I fell for the wrong man. He started out as the perfect gentleman. He treated me like a princess one day, and then a switch flipped, and he turned into a monster. He was the type of man that wanted to control my every move.

"Are you dating anybody?" Sabrina asked.

"Not at the moment."

"Did your relationship end when you moved here?"

"Yeah, you could say that."

A chorus of giggles came from our daughters. We looked at them, and they held hands, spinning in circles.

"Is Bria's father in her life?"

I took a slow, controlled breath as I looked around the park. Every time I thought of Brad, fear tingled in my veins. It was as if hearing his name or even thinking about him would summon him to come out of thin air and attack. The last thing I wanted was to be at the end of his wrath again.

"He has been for her entire life until these

past two months," I admitted, the truth lingering on the tip of my tongue.

Sabrina locked her hazel eyes onto mine for a brief few seconds before she placed her eyes back on our daughters. They were climbing through a maze, holding hands.

"Did he not want to be in Bria's life?" she asked.

"He has always been in Bria's life. But, after a few years, I realized that his being in her life would only hinder her childhood."

"Why do you say that?"

I took a deep breath and exhaled. The shame I had been holding inside for years was about to surface. However, I trusted Sabrina enough to keep this information to herself, so I thought it best to tell Sabrina why we had moved.

"Bria's father is abusive."

Sabrina gasped as she threw her manicured hand over her mouth. Her hazel eyes widened with terror, trained solely on me.

"Brad did not abuse Bria," I rushed out in a small voice.

"He abused you," Sabrina stated.

I nodded. "He abused me often. Mentally, emotionally, and physically."

Sabrina tore her eyes away from me. From her profile, I could see her eyes filling with tears as she took deep breaths to stop them from spilling onto her cheeks. "No one should ever have to deal with that."

Hearing Sabrina mutter those words

confirmed what I had known for several years. Deep down in my heart, I knew I shouldn't have had to deal with the abuse. I didn't want to deal with the abuse. I just didn't have the resources to react. "I decided to deal with the abuse for five years. Brad wouldn't allow me to work. Brad took care of all our needs."

"What does Brad do for a living?" Sabrina sniffled after her question.

I trained my eye on the lone wallflower blossoming. I could relate to that wallflower on many levels. "Brad's family owns a multi-million-dollar company that he owns a third of." Bria and Emily were working on a little puzzle attached to the playground. "There was not one thing in this world that Brad could not provide for us. Do you know how difficult it is to be told every single day that I could never survive without him in my life? That I will never amount to anything without his support?"

Sabrina shook her head. "I don't know, and I cannot imagine it."

"I suffered the great price of it all, and that was the abuse." I took another deep breath, willing myself to continue. "Six months ago, I decided enough was enough. I would rather live paycheck to paycheck to care for Bria and have her in a safe environment. Anything would be better than being provided everything and scared for our safety."

The words spilled out with no effort. Relief flooded me when the words left my mouth, lifting a burden off my chest.

"You mean your safety?" Sabrina added, placing her hand on mine.

"My safety," I whispered to myself.

Brad would yell at Bria, but he had never struck her. I doubted he would ever lay a hand on her. But he did everything he could think that would cause harm to me.

Sabrina wiped a lone tear that escaped her eye and fell onto her right cheek. "Where is your family?" The emotion that Sabrina displayed showed me how much Sabrina cared about me. Finally, I could trust Sabrina and I had not had that opportunity in many years.

"I'm not sure. I have lived in foster care for as long as I can remember. I never met any of my family."

"Have you ever considered trying to locate your family?"

"The thought has never crossed my mind. But, I might consider it soon."

I looked down at my hands in my lap, my eyes narrowing on my fingernails that looked scruffy.

"I must admit, you're amazing. How could you have gone through such a difficult upbringing?"

Sabrina wrapped her arm around my shoulder, rubbing my arm with affection.

I leaned my head on her shoulder. "I like to say it was the cards that life handed me. But I wouldn't change a single thing," I admitted.

"I knew when I met you that first day that there was something special about you."

She turned her body, and we hugged.

"I felt the same way," I reassured her as I rubbed her back.

"I am so glad we have developed a friendship."

"It is a refreshing feeling."

When we broke apart, she said, "I support you 100% for doing what you are doing for that baby girl of yours."

Our girls came running over to us. They were smiling wide with rosy, red cheeks and were out of breath.

I handed Bria her water bottle, and she took a few sips before she handed it back to me.

"Mommy, Emily is my best friend," she exclaimed, excitement radiating off her little body.

"I'm so glad Emily is your best friend," I responded, running my fingers on her frizzy pigtails.

"Can we keep playing?" Emily asked her mom after she had taken sips of her own water.

"Of course."

Bria and Emily ran away back to the playground, giggling.

Looking over at Sabrina, I noticed her eyes were still red.

"Stop feeling sorry for me. That's the last thing that I need from you. The only thing that I need is a friend." Turning to face Sabrina, I hugged her tight. "I have gotten away. I survived my abuse."

Sabrina nodded. "I know. I just can't fathom how anyone could cause any type of harm to anyone. But you handled it, and it has only made you ten times stronger."

"Bria is my strength. She is why I am still here and will continue to be here."

After our heartfelt conversation, we switched the conversation.

"So, are you going to tell me why you don't have many friends in the area?" I joked, trying to lighten the mood.

"All of my friends decided Branchville was too small, and they moved to bigger towns."

"If you could move anywhere in the United States, where would it be?"

Sabrina tapped her manicured finger on her lip as she thought for a few moments. "Hawaii."

"Why would you choose the Aloha state?" I asked, interested in her answer.

"I would love to live on the beach 24/7," she said. "How about you?"

"I'm exactly where I want to be. I have had my fair share of big towns to last a lifetime."

We continued chatting as we watched our daughters enjoy each other's company.

Finally, I had a friend after five years. The feeling was something I had not experienced in a long time. I did not want to lose this feeling ever again.

Chapter Seven

Kyla

"Good morning, Sabrina," I called out as soon as I entered the cafe.

Sabrina was always the first to arrive at work in the mornings as she was the head waitress. She was in charge whenever Kelsey was not in the office or away for any reason.

Kelsey was off all this week.

"Good morning, Tiffany."

I informed Sabrina of my real name on the day we spent at the park. She promised to continue calling me by my fake name to ensure my safety. Walking over to Sabrina, I wrapped my arms around her and hugged her tight.

Every single day when Sabrina and I would see each other, we would always hug each other.

"How are you doing?"

"I am great, and yourself?"

"Wonderful as ever."

The weight that had been sitting on my shoulders had been lifting little by little each day. I felt better as each day passed by.

I headed to the locker room to put up my items.

"Hey, Tiffany," Scott called out as I approached my locker. His locker was located two over from the right of mine.

"Hello, Scott."

"How was your night?"

I worked on my locker combination. "It was good. After dinner, Bria and I put together a puppy puzzle last night."

"That sounds like it was fun."

"It was fun. How was your night?"

"My night was great. I went on a date."

"Tell me more." I was excited.

"I will tell you all at the same time as soon as you are finished here," he responded as he walked past me and headed out front.

After putting my bag into the locker, I headed out to the front, where Sabrina, Scott, and our other coworker Chloe were all standing around talking. Chloe was responsible for all the wonderful pastries we served daily.

As soon as Chloe saw me walk into the room, she turned her attention to Scott. "Tell us all about the date."

I leaned my hip against the counter as I waited for the story to unfold.

"Her name is Vanessa. I arranged for us to meet at the movies. She was five minutes early, which we know I am a huge stickler for." He looked at each of us before he continued with his story. "She was what I expected. Our chemistry through text and phone conversation was the same in person."

"Awweee," Kelsey, Chloe, and I cooed in unison.

It was nice to hear positive stories from Scott. He was nice, and we all wanted him to be happy.

"Are you two official yet?" Sabrina asked.

"Not yet."

"How long have you two been talking?" I asked.

"Two months."

"When are you making it official?" Chloe asked.

Scott laughed as he threw his hands up in the air. "You ladies are killing me with the questions. I plead the fifth. Just know I am taking it slow. I will let you know all the details down to the exact date and time I do it."

"So, what movie did you two see?" Chloe asked.

"Yeah, was it anything good?" Sabrina chimed in.

All of us had a small conversation about movies that were showing in the theater that we wanted to see as we made the coffee shop ready to open.

Five minutes before six, Chloe headed back to the kitchen area to warm the oven. We continued prepping the coffee shop for the crowd we would be getting.

After a few busy hours, my new regular, Ryan, entered the coffee shop. Today he wore a light-yellow dress shirt with gray dress pants.

He sat at his usual table in my section and reviewed the menu.

Walking over to his table, I greeted him. "Hello, Ryan."

"Hello, beautiful." Ryan smiled.

He tugged on his bottom lip with his teeth as we stared into each other's eyes. That action alone distracted me from what I was doing.

Ryan stared at me as I stood frozen in place, doing nothing. I was sure by his expression he liked what he saw. He definitely had an effect on me.

I shook my head, trying to clear the daze that I was in. "Do you still need to look at that menu?"

Ryan looked up at me as he placed his hands on the table. "Why do you ask?"

"You have ordered the same thing for the past month and a half."

I scribbled down his usual order of an Americano and a blueberry muffin.

He rubbed the stubble that was on his chin.

"Maybe I branched out and want something different."

"Hm, I doubt that."

I did not think he would go out of his comfort zone and choose something different.

Ryan smiled as he laughed. "How are you doing today?"

As nervousness bubbled up, I tapped my pen on my thigh. "I'm doing well. How are you?"

"Amazing now that I am seeing you."

A smirk touched my lips. Ryan had been flirting with me since he became my regular customer a month and a half ago.

"Why is it amazing to see me?"

"You are the most beautiful woman I have ever seen."

I smiled at the sweet words he said. They were foreign words to my ears.

"That is so sweet of you." I looked at his hair. "Did you do something different with your hair?" Something looked different about him today.

"Yes. I had my hair cut yesterday."

"Your hair looks nice."

"You think so?"

"Of course. I wouldn't dish out a compliment if I didn't mean it," I said as I pushed my pen into my pocket.

"Thank you."

"It suits you. I will go put your order in."

"Thank you."

He closed the menu that he held in his hand.

"You're welcome. Your order will be up

shortly."

I turned around to walk away.

"Wait... Tiffany," Ryan called out, stopping me dead in my tracks.

He had called me beautiful since after our first interaction, and my name sounded foreign, rolling off his tongue.

"Yes?" I turned and looked at him.

"Would you like to go out with me someday?"

Confidence came off him in waves as he waited for an answer.

His question startled me a bit. I wasn't used to anyone besides Brad showing interest in me. Brad made sure anyone we encountered was never interested in me just by how he acted.

An all too familiar scent invaded my nose. My eyes scoured the entire cafe. With caution, I took in all the faces of the customers in the shop. The walls were closing in on me as my breathing intensified.

Brad's face flashed before my eyes, bringing me to a time that was all too vivid.

I stood in the local hole-in-the-wall grocery store less than three minutes from the house I shared with Brad. I was in the meat department line to get a specific cut of meat for Brad's dinner that evening.

"Next in line," the butcher called out.

I stepped up to the counter. "Can I have twenty ounces of prime rib," I asked.

"Coming right up."

The butcher went to get the meat behind the

counter.

"Excuse me, miss," came from behind me.

I turned, and a man in his late thirties stood behind me in line. He held the weekly ad in his hand that could be picked up at the front of the store.

"Yes?"

"I just moved here not too long ago. This is my first time shopping here. How would you say their meat quality is?" he asked me.

"Their quality of meat is superb. I come here all the time for our groceries. My boyfriend adores the prime rib."

"I better be able to cut it with a butter knife for these high prices," the man joked.

I laughed as the butcher went to cut the meat. All the items' prices were on the higher end. There was no way I could ever afford these prices if I paid for the food with my own earnings.

Within seconds, searing pain radiated through my upper right arm. Gasping in pain, I looked down. The scent of Brad's new favorite soap wafted into my nose. Brad's hand was wrapped so tightly around my arm that the back of his hand went from its normal tan tone to ash white.

"Brad, you are hurting me," I cried out in a whisper.

I was in pure distress, and Brad was the root cause. I tried my hardest not to draw attention to myself.

"Shut up," he growled, speaking in a low

voice right into my ear.

The growl caused my eardrum to ache.

"Hey, man. You should let her go."

That response came from the man asking me about the meat quality.

I frantically shook my head at the man attempting to defend me. Anyone defending me would only worsen what punishment was done behind closed doors.

"Shut up before I mop the floor with your ass," Brad threatened loudly.

At that point, everyone within fifty feet glued their eyes on us. We were the store's only focus of attention, and it made me uncomfortable.

Brad yanked me by my arm as he led me toward the store's exit. I was so embarrassed as I saw all the sorrowful eyes aimed at me. Everyone stared in shock, but no one else tried to intervene. In a way, I appreciated no one trying to help, but I could only stay strong for so long.

The hot heat blanketed me as we walked out of the air-conditioned store and into the blazing Florida heat. We were only seconds from approaching Brad's SUV.

"How could you be such a whore?" Brad exploded as he threw my body into the side of his vehicle.

My back smacked into the vehicle hard. The pain emanated through my upper back. "I did not do any—"

"Shut up," Brad interrupted me.

He reached into his front pant pocket for the

car keys...

The sound of glass shattering rattled me out of my memory.

My heart pumped out of my chest as I looked around. The cafe had gone silent as Scott shouted, "Sorry."

I turned my attention to Ryan, who looked at me with concern as the chatter in the shop started up again.

"Um, I have to go," I said.

The words tumbled out of my mouth at record speed. Training my gaze on the door leading to the back of the shop, I ran with only one destination in mind. I had to get out now.

Within seconds, Sabrina was on my heels, comforting me. "Are you okay?"

I had run into the locker room and thrown myself into a chair. I placed my head in my hands, trying to calm myself down. "I don't know."

"Did Ryan say something out of line to you?"

Taking a few deep breaths in, I shook my head. "No, he did nothing wrong."

"What's wrong then?"

"I swear I smelled Brad."

Sabrina squatted down in front of me. She lifted my head out of my hands, so we were at eye level. She moved the bang out of my eyes. She placed her hands on my shoulders and made me look into her eyes. "Brad is not here."

"Are you sure?"

She nodded. "I have watched every single person who has entered. Keep calm, please."

It's official. I was losing it. "I smelled his favorite scent. He is here. He has to be here." I pointed a shaking finger towards the front.

Realization danced in Sabrina's eyes. "It was not Brad, I promise."

"Are you sure?"

"Yes. A man in his early forties just walked past me. He walked towards the restroom. He wore one of those fancy expensive colognes. You said Brad had money, so maybe they wear the same cologne."

I continued taking controlled breaths as I attempted to subside my raging heartbeat. Relief flooded me as I repeated that Brad was not there. It was just another man that favored the same products. I was safe. I was not in harm's way. I shouldn't be afraid.

"Brad cannot and will not hurt you anymore. You must believe that."

After Sabrina talked me down from the panic attack, I wrapped my arms around her and hugged her tight. She rubbed small circles into my back as her apple scent swirled into my nose. Once I had calmed down enough to function, I walked back out front. I apologized to all my customers for stepping out for a few minutes.

When Ryan's order was ready, I placed his coffee and pastry on the table.

"I'm sorry if I made you uncomfortable." He gave me a heartfelt smile.

The apology I received shocked me and was unnecessary, especially coming from him.

I placed my hand on his. "No, it was not you."

He looked down at my hand on his. I went against my better judgment with that movement and removed it, regretting it immediately.

"Are you okay?"

"Yes, I just had a panic attack."

"I am sorry to hear that. Do you have panic attacks often?"

Genuine concern was written all over his features. He cared, and I knew he wasn't pretending.

"Not as often as I used to. Thank you for being concerned."

For five years straight, I had panic attacks at least once a month. This was my first one in a few months.

He picked up his cup and blew on his steaming Americano.

"Would you like to go out with me someday?" he asked again.

I thought for a few moments before I answered. "I'm not sure if I'm ready to date yet."

My sudden split from Brad was still fresh. The wound was still raw and sensitive. I just wanted to focus on Bria for the time being. Our mother-daughter bond was most important to me. A relationship would come in due time when and if it felt natural.

"That's fine. I respect your decision. How about your phone number?"

He took another sip of his Americano.

I contemplated the pros and cons of agreeing

to a phone number exchange. As I stared into Ryan's blue eyes, I nodded.

He smiled as he pulled his phone out of his pocket. I rattled my phone number off, and he sent me a text.

"Happy now?" I joked.

He nodded, his smile never leaving. "Happy as I will ever be right now."

Chapter Eight

Brad

The footage that could track Kyla's location was out of reach, which pissed me off. If only the security guard knew what it was like not to know where the love of your life and daughter was.

Vince, my buddy from high school, had come with me to pick Kyla's car up from the tow yard. It was hard getting into her car and driving it without her being in the passenger seat.

I walked into our bedroom, and my eyes settled on our king-sized bed. Kyla always made sure the bed was made without a single imperfection before she did anything else when we would get up first thing in the morning. Right now, the bed was a total wreck. The comforter and the sheets were thrown all over the bed, and it further hurt my heart that she was not there to make the bed perfect as she had always done. I walked over to her side of the bed. I stared down at the nightstand where her phone sat. It had not been touched since she had placed it there, but I had no other choice at this point. I had to do whatever was necessary to track down my family.

I powered the phone on as I sat on Kyla's side of the bed. Once the phone came to life, a picture of Kyla and Bria smiling into the camera was on the lock screen. I caught myself smiling at the picture. It pained me how much I missed those smiles.

I swiped my thumb across the screen. The screen requesting for the password to be entered popped up. Automatically, I entered our anniversary. When the phone did not unlock, my eyebrows scrunched together. That was the agreed password to both of our phones, and Kyla could never change it, no matter the situation. I entered Kyla's birthday, and the lock screen stared back at me, taunting me. I entered Bria's birthday, followed by my birthday, and the lock screen would not disappear.

Frustration grew as I huffed and threw the phone onto the bed beside me. The force of the throw caused the phone to bounce a few times before it settled on the bed.

I balled my fist up as I grew angry. Why did Kyla change the password? What was she hiding in the phone? What was the password? I tried every single significant date that I could think of. I sat there contemplating and racking my brain for the next password attempt, I thought about the day I came home from work. Kyla and Bria were gone.

I knew Kyla and Bria were not home when I arrived, as Kyla's car wasn't in the driveway. It was a strange occurrence as there was a set schedule in place. Kyla was always home with Bria by the time I arrived home. Dinner was usually twenty or thirty minutes from being done. By the time I walked into the house, I would have a shot of whiskey that Kyla had prepared. I would take a steamy, relaxing shower to wash away the stressful day before I would sit at the dining room table with my dinner plate waiting for me. That day when I came home, the house was too still for my liking. There was no TV playing in the background. There was no aroma of food in the air. There was not even a hallway light left on for me.

Picking up the phone, I keyed in the day Kyla and Bria left. When the phone unlocked, my heart sank into my stomach. I went to the messages to see who she had been in contact with the last few days before she left. My parents and I were the only three people she had been texting. Checking the contact list, the same three names were listed. I went into the history of Kyla's searches, and I was shocked. Kyla had cleared out every single last search she had ever done on the phone. I couldn't locate any beneficial information on the phone that I could use.

Standing, I threw the phone across the room with all the strength I could muster. The phone hit the wall with a hard thud, shattering the screen.

I went into my nightstand and grabbed my bottle of whiskey. I took two gulps before I thought about Kyla's financials.

My next attempt to track her would be to go to the bank to see the last time she had used her debit card and where the transaction had taken place.

My thoughts were everywhere as I drove to the bank five minutes from my house. Were Kyla's bank statements going to tell me the information I needed to locate her? Or would this be another dead end I couldn't use to my advantage? Would I regret allowing her to have some privacy in at least one aspect of her life? I hoped not.

I waltzed into the bank, the door closing behind me as I looked around. The bank was close to being empty. Two bank tellers were working, and two people in front of me were being helped. Standing in line, I looked around at the bank's internal structure. As each second passed, the more impatient I became.

"Next in line," the bank teller called out as the older woman walked away from the counter at a slow pace.

Walking up to the counter, I looked at the name tag on the woman's maroon shirt.

"Hi, Kate. I was wondering if you could help me?"

I spoke in a sweet tone while smiling warmly.

She smiled as she tucked her short, brown hair behind her ear. She revealed a string of silver studs. "What would you need help with?"

"I need to know the last transaction on an account."

"I can only provide you with that information if your name is on the account," she replied in a monotone voice.

I scratched my chin. "I know my name is on the account. I don't have the account number, though. Can you check it for me?"

"Of course." She clicked a few keys on her computer, asking me for personal information.

"Your name is on the account, Mr. Robertson. How may I help you?"

"I need to know where the last transaction took place."

Kate clicked the mouse a few times. Her eyes scanned the screen before she looked at me. "The last transaction was a little over four hours north."

"Can you tell me what type of transaction it was?" I asked as the air conditioner inside the building kicked on. The cool air hit me from above, and I shivered involuntarily.

"It was a withdrawal out of an ATM."

"How much was withdrawn?"

"Fifteen hundred dollars." Kate smirked as she placed her arm on the counter and leaned against it. "I have a suggestion. Why don't we finish this up and go out to lunch afterwards? I take my break in ten minutes."

I ignored her comment. "Can you tell me how long ago this transaction took place?" I had no time for games. I rattled off question after question. Only one thing was on my mind. Finding Kyla and Bria.

"It was two months ago."

"Wait. Two months ago? Are you sure there is nothing more recent?"

I couldn't help but feel dumbfounded.

"No more activity since then," she stated as her eyes flickered to the computer screen before she looked back at me.

I exhaled a deep breath.

"Thank you," I grumbled as I turned and walked towards the bank exit, full of anger. Pushing the door open, I raked my fingers through my matted hair.

Kyla went out of her way to pull money out of the account I had allowed her access to. That account should have only been used for daily and emergency purchases. Now that account had been wiped clean.

Kyla pulled a fast one on me. The more details I got from the trail she left, the more my chances increased at locating my family. I had to keep digging no matter how hurtful the information was that I gathered.

Chapter Nine

Kyla

Bustling around the house, I did my regular Sunday morning cleaning routine. It was my weekly task, and I stuck to it, so there was no need for a deep clean. The only change I had made was that my weekly morning cleaning routine used to be done on Wednesday mornings per Brad's request. My cleaning time had also shrunk from three hours to thirty-five minutes because of the intimate and small house.

I looked over my shoulder at Bria sitting on the couch watching a fun, educational show on

TV. She giggled right before she took a sip of water. Smiling, I continued to mop the living room.

Wringing out the mop, I thought about how different my life would be if I had not grown up in foster care. Granted, my upbringing in foster care was not the worst. The foster carers had instilled manners I used every day. I also had Amy in my life, which made it more manageable not to have a biological family.

How did I end up living in foster care? How old was I when I was placed in the system? Was it my mother's or father's choice? Was it a mutual agreement for me to be placed in foster care? Did my mother do it without my father's knowledge? Did my father do it without my mother's consent? Were my mother and father still alive? Did I cross their mind daily?

Where was Amy? We had lost all contact when I was forced out of the system. Amy and I had promised to keep in touch, but with Brad's hand in things, that had never happened. I wished I could somehow find her, but I didn't know what information to use to locate her.

"Mommy, can I have a snack?" Bria asked, breaking me out of my thoughts.

"Of course. What would you like to snack on?"

I had just finished mopping, and the floor was drying.

"Pretzels."

Walking into the kitchen, I placed half a serving of pretzels in a bowl. I took Bria her snack as I returned to the kitchen to remove the clean dishes from the dishwasher.

After I finished putting the dishes in their respective locations, I went into the living room. I sat on the couch next to Bria as I opened up a book. Feeling playful, I reached into Bria's bowl, grabbed a pretzel, and threw it into my mouth.

"Hey." Bria stuck her tongue out at me playfully.

I giggled at her silly reaction as I turned the page of my book.

My phone sounded. I pulled it out of my pocket as I closed my book to see that Ryan had texted me. Every day since I had given Ryan my phone number, I would get texts from him regardless if he had come into the coffee shop for his usual. He would either text me a good morning or a good afternoon text. After we went through how we were doing, he would ask a question designed to learn more about me, which I appreciated. He wanted to get to know me for me. I had already learned that Ryan was a thirty-year-old with an older sister who he adored. He had a Bachelor's Degree in Information Technology. He was employed with a large energy company as a Chief Technology Officer. I told Ryan that I had a daughter I was raising by myself. Turned out he loved kids and said he could not wait for the day when he could meet Bria.

Ryan: Good morning beautiful.
Me: Good morning.

Ryan: How are you doing this sunny Sunday morning?

Me: I'm doing well. How are you?

I placed my phone beside me on the couch cushion.

"Mommy, where's daddy?"

My heart pounded in my chest. The question came out of the blue. It irritated me how much I allowed Brad to put fear into my life even when I hadn't seen or heard from him for a few months. However, I couldn't bring myself to have any irritation from Bria asking about him as he was her father. I looked over at her. Her eyes were focused on the TV.

"He is still at our old home," I replied.

"Is he going to move to our new home?"

My phone sounded again, letting me know another text had come through.

My heart went out to Bria. She was hopeful and expecting Brad to come back into our lives. I knew she must miss him. He had been in her life every day since she was born. She was too young to understand the distance apart was for our safety. One day she would understand the purpose of this situation.

"I don't think so."

I glanced at the new message on my phone. I closed my book and placed it on the end table. Reading the book was not in the question if I would engage in a full-on conversation with Ryan.

Ryan: I'm great since hearing from you. What is your favorite color?

Me: Pink. Let me guess, your favorite is blue?

I smirked as I waited for his response.

Ryan: You are incorrect.

I laughed as he didn't tell me his favorite color.

Me: Are you going to tell me, or do you want me to guess again?

Ryan: My favorite color is yellow.

Shocked, I replied quickly.

Me: I would never have guessed in a million years that your favorite color would be yellow.

Ryan: I'm not the typical guy you encounter every day.

I smiled at his reply.

Me: I will be the judge of that.

"Mommy, when can I play with Emily again?" Bria asked as she looked over at me.

Bria and Emily had two play dates at the park since we had moved, and they enjoyed playing with each other. During their last play date, Sabrina and I had difficulties separating them. We had to pry their little hands and fingers off each other as they cried their eyes out while holding each other tight. They did not want their play date to end, and we promised to get them together soon.

"Soon. How does me and you having a play date now sound?" I asked as my phone sounded again with a text.

"Yay." Bria cheered as she clapped her little hands together.

I texted Ryan quickly that I was taking Bria to the park and would chat with him later. I went to the kitchen and packed a bag with drinks and snacks. Bria and I headed out the door, walking hand in hand.

As we got into the car, my heart felt light in my chest as I enjoyed Bria's smile.

This was what I worked hard every day to see.

Chapter Ten

Kyla

"Are you sure she won't be too much trouble for a few hours?" I asked Sabrina as I stared at myself in the bathroom mirror. I wore a pair of dark blue skinny jeans that showed off my curves, a red blouse, and a pair of silver high-heeled wedges that made my legs look long. Dangling from my ears was a pair of silver earrings complimenting my attire.

Ryan and I had been conversing on the phone and texting for several weeks. Ryan's personality was like no other I had ever met.

Whenever I would hear my phone jingle, a bit of excitement and nervousness coursed through me. Excitement because I had never been given this much positive attentiveness. Nervousness because there was a small chance in my mind that Ryan might turn out to be just like Brad. Brad started our relationship on the right path, but he changed after time had passed. After much thought and consideration, I concluded that it would be best to give in to Ryan's request for us to go out as friends. I looked forward to seeing Ryan outside of the coffee shop.

"Bria is such an angel. This get-together for them is long overdue." She stood in the bathroom doorway of my home, talking with me while I got ready to go out. At the same time, she watched Bria and Emily, who were in my living room playing with Bria's dollhouse.

"How much do I owe you for babysitting?" I adjusted the bang in front of my eye until it looked perfect.

Sabrina rolled her eyes. "I wouldn't charge you a penny. I just want you to have a great time tonight."

"Thank you. How do I look?" I walked past Sabrina and out of the bathroom. I did a runway model stride before I turned and struck a pose.

"I see a confidence, hot momma in the flesh." She whistled as she smiled.

Chuckling, I grabbed her into a tight, heartfelt hug. "Thank you so much. I owe you one."

I walked over to where Bria and Emily played

in front of the TV. I kissed Bria's head, and I pinched Emily's soft cheeks.

"I will be home no later than ten." I approached the door.

"Have fun but not too much fun," Sabrina called out to me.

Opening the door, I peeked my head outside. There were no sudden movements or shadowy figures I could make out in the calm darkness.

Once I was positive the coast was clear, I headed outside into the night. The air had a touch of coolness, a slight shiver traveled through me as I locked the house.

After driving north for twenty minutes, my GPS instructed me to make the next right. As I approached my turn, I zeroed in on the tomato and garlic placed on the pylon sign next to the restaurant's name. Smiling to myself, I parked in the first parking space I could find. Ryan arranged for our first get-together to include my favorite cuisine.

Pulling the sun visor down, I checked myself out one last time. I did a quick survey of the parking lot. I exhaled when I noticed no one watching me or following me. As I stepped out of my car, I could see Ryan standing in front of the restaurant entrance. This was the first time I saw Ryan outside his work clothes. He wore a pair of black jeans, snug on his hips, a yellow shirt that showed off his muscular frame, and a pair of black Jordans. In his right hand was a red rose.

"Hello, Ryan."

I approached him. His attention was focused on his phone, so he didn't see me coming. He looked up, and his eyes landed on me. His eyes danced over my body before his eyes met mine. He flashed his handsome smile. My heart did a slight flutter in my chest.

"Hello, beautiful. You look amazing as ever."

Ryan held out the rose.

I took the rose, brought it to my nose, and inhaled the delicate scent. I appreciated his generosity and thoughtfulness.

"Thank you." I twisted the rose between my thumb and index finger. That one gesture alone was greater than any possession Brad had purchased me in the years we were together.

Ryan opened the door to the restaurant. Walking in, I approached the hostess stand and Ryan joined me. Italian music played in the background as the delicious aroma of garlic filled my nose, causing my stomach to growl on cue.

"Reservations for two."

"What is the name of the reservations?" The hostess tapped on the tablet that she held.

"Walker."

The hostess grabbed two menus. "Right this way."

The hostess walked us through the dining room area, which had low lighting, and was filled up with guests as the night progressed. She guided us to a booth in the far corner of the room. Ryan and I slid into opposite sides of the booth as I placed my purse next to me on the seat.

"Your waitress will be with you two soon. Enjoy your dinner."

She smiled before she walked away.

I opened the menu, and my eyes widened when I scanned over the prices. I kept my mouth shut. Ryan had chosen the restaurant, so he knew the price range.

A tall, thin woman with brown hair pulled into a tight bun approached our table. "Welcome. My name is Sylvia, and I'll be your waitress this evening. Can I start you off with something to drink?"

She placed two sets of silverware on the table.

"Can we try the wine special of the week?" Ryan looked up from his menu at the waitress.

She smiled as she wrote on her pad of paper. "Coming right up."

She waltzed away with an extra sway in her hips. Ryan was oblivious to the action. I laughed under my breath. Whenever Brad and I would go to dinner, he was alert to the flirtation thrown his way. He always rubbed it in my face that I was not the only woman interested in him. I hoped and prayed that he took advantage of those interested women so he would leave me alone. Due to my horrible luck, that never occurred.

"Is this your first time coming here?"

I continued to browse the menu as I waited for his answer. I was spoiled for choice, completely undecided.

"No. I usually come here twice a year on

special occasions. However, this is my first time in about a year."

"So this is a special occasion?"

I tore my eyes away from the menu to look at him.

He looked at me, and we made eye contact. A smile pulled on his lips. "Yes, it is. Before long, you will know why."

Sylvia returned to the table with a tall bottle of wine and a basket of fresh bread. She popped the cork on the wine bottle and poured us each a glass full of wine before placing the bottle on the table.

"Are you two ready to order?"

"Yes, we are."

Ryan closed his menu.

"Ma'am?" she looked at me, pen in one hand and pad of paper in the other.

"I will have chicken marsala with mashed potatoes."

I closed my menu.

"I will have the veal parmigiana with a side of broccoli," Ryan ordered.

Sylvia smiled as she walked away from the table.

"Shall we make a toast?" Ryan asked.

He raised his wine glass in the air.

I raised my wine glass at his request for a toast to be made.

"I want to toast this wonderful new friendship we have developed. The new friendship that I hope will turn into something more in the future,"

Ryan added.

"Something more in the future?" I raised my right eyebrow.

"Of course. You are a one-of-a-kind woman."

I smiled, matching the smile that touched Ryan's lips.

We clinked our glasses together before we both took sips from our wine glasses. The exquisite, sweet grape taste danced on my tastebuds. It was my first time having wine, and the taste was delightful.

"I am pleased you agreed to go out with me." Ryan took another sip of his wine. "It took a lot of convincing."

I went into the basket of bread and grabbed a slice. He had no idea the type of convincing that went into my decision. When I left Brad months ago, I had sworn off getting to know any man. I feared making male friends or falling in love with another abusive man. For my sanity, I didn't have the mental stability to deal with more abuse. Ryan had shown me he was the complete opposite of Brad. Taking a bite of the warm goodness, I closed my eyes and moaned in satisfaction.

Ryan laughed at my reaction. "Is it delicious?"

"Delightful."

Ryan went into the basket of bread and took a bite. He nodded in agreement. "I forgot how amazing their bread was."

"I can see why you eat here."

Ryan nodded.

Ryan waited until he finished eating before asking, "So, where were you born?"

"I was born and raised in Miami, Florida."

"Miami is a big city."

"Too big, in my opinion."

"Did you move here because you were tired of big city living?"

He took another sip of his wine.

I nodded as I replied, "Yes, the change of scenery was what I thought was best for my family."

"Having your children at the center of your decisions is important."

Ryan's opinion showed me the type of man he was.

"Where were you born?" I asked.

"I was born in Charleston, South Carolina, but I grew up in this small town."

"With you being so successful with your career, did it ever cross your mind that if you went to a bigger city, you would have more opportunities?"

Ryan shrugged his shoulders. "I would have more opportunities, but I'm not the type of person for big cities. I prefer smaller, intimate areas."

I smiled.

"I can see why. Living here for a few months has felt more like home than living in Miami my entire life," I admitted as I took another sip of my wine.

I didn't want to live in another big city. I'd be content living in this small town for the rest of my life. It provided me with a state of comfort.

"Intimate cities are great," Ryan commented. "So, what hobbies do you enjoy?"

"I love going for walks. Dancing is a small passion of mine that I love, but I never did it as a profession. I just do it for fun with my daughter. I love being near bodies of water. Water seems to always put me in a relaxed mood."

"Why do you find bodies of water relaxing?"

He stuck his hand back into the basket for another slice of bread.

Looking into his curious eyes, I brought my glass of wine to my lips. I took a hearty sip before I sat my glass down.

"The atmosphere. The calmness of the water. It has always put me at ease," I answered.

Many times back home, when Brad and I were not getting along, I would just get in my car and go to the beach. Granted, it was only minutes from our house, but I would go just to clear my head and relax. The water had always calmed my mood to the point where I could imagine the life I had always wanted for myself. Due to the decisions made, I finally gave myself that life.

"I can understand that. Growing up, I always enjoyed my parents taking us on beach visits. The sound of the waves splashing on shore was like no other while I built sandcastles."

I smiled as Ryan recounted his memories. It amazed me to hear about happy childhood memories. I was ashamed that I never had the opportunity to grow up with parents and siblings as I had always dreamed of.

"What hobbies do you like?" I asked. Ryan had piqued my interest.

"Going to the gym. Going for a walk or a run. Watching and playing sports."

"Now I see where all the muscle comes from," I commented as I smiled.

Ryan flashed his breathtaking smile at me.

Ryan and I continued to make conversation as we ate our bread and drank our wine. Sylvia arrived at the table with our food after a short while.

She sat our food down in front of us. My eyes widened as I took in the presentation of my dinner. It was so beautiful that I didn't want to eat it. My eyes told me not to touch the food, it was too beautiful, but my stomach rumble said otherwise.

Picking up my knife and fork, I cut into my food. Once the first bite of my food touched my tongue, I fell in love. The taste of the chicken marsala was exquisite.

Ryan cut into his chicken. "Are you enjoying your dinner?"

I nodded in response as my mouth was full of food.

We continued to talk as we ate our meal.

After we finished dinner, Ryan paid the tab and tip. We walked out of the restaurant after I quickly examined the parking lot.

We approached my car.

"I had an amazing night," he said.

"I did as well."

I couldn't remember the last time I had gone on a date and enjoyed myself.

"We have to get together again soon." Ryan extended his hand towards me.

On instinct, I jumped back. My body smacked right into the driver's door of my car. The door handle dug into my lower back, causing immense pain. Flashes of Brad pummeling me flashed in my vision as I grasped the handle of my driver's door. I had a difficult time catching my breath.

"Are you okay?" Ryan's concern was written all over his face as his voice rose an octave.

"I don't know."

I brought my hand up to my chest, inhaling and exhaling as I tried to calm my beating heart.

"I was just going to hug you," Ryan stated.

My horrible vision started to clear away.

"I am so sorry."

My anxiety was through the roof. Ryan acted like a gentlemen tonight, but Brad had scarred me over the last four years. A lot of unraveling needed to be done for Brad not to have complete control over me. I needed to work hard for that.

"I hate I made you feel uncomfortable."

"It is not you, I promise."

"Can you promise me something?"

At a slow pace, Ryan grabbed my hands. I looked down at our entwined hands, the feeling of pure safety encompassing me for the first time in several years. The feeling was foreign, and I enjoyed every bit of it.

"What is that?"

I looked up to meet his eyes. It was too dark outside for me to enjoy the color of his eyes, but I was compelled to stare into them.

"When you are comfortable with me, will you let me know what is bothering you so I can help you?"

I nodded in agreement. The screech of car tires echoed in the distance, pulling our attention toward the street.

Once my breathing returned to normal, I wrapped my arms around Ryan's neck. I buried my head in Ryan's chest and inhaled the amazing scent of cologne that clung to his body. His muscular arms laced around my waist, and he held me firmly.

Being in Ryan's arms felt right.

I didn't want this night to come to an end.

Chapter Eleven

Brad

I stood at the kitchen sink, filling my glass with filtered water. I tossed two Tylenol into my mouth and gulped them down.

I had a raging hangover from drinking all day and night for the last few days. My head throbbed so badly that it felt someone had banged on my head with a bat.

My phone rang. I hoped and prayed it was Kyla calling to tell me she needed me. I looked forward to that call for months, and that call had yet to come through.

I cursed under my breath when I pulled it out of my pocket and I saw my Mom's name flash on the phone screen. Rolling my eyes, I contemplated answering the phone. I had avoided my parents since Kyla and Bria left for obvious reasons.

At the last moment, I decided to answer. I could not avoid my parents forever. Walking out of the kitchen, I went into the living room.

"Hello, Mom," I mumbled.

"Hi, Sweetheart. What took you so long to answer the phone?"

"My phone was not near me," I lied.

The truth was the phone never left my side. I was too fearful Kyla would call if she needed me, and I would miss the call. That was my worst fear.

"How are you doing?"

I plopped down in my lazy-boy chair. "I am doing okay. How are you and Dad doing?"

"We're good."

"What are you two doing today?"

"Right now, your Dad is out taking Max for a walk. I am watching TV."

Max was my parent's beloved Maltese they had since I was twelve. It surprised me the dog was still alive.

"It is a gorgeous day out. Why are you not walking with them?"

I ran my fingers through my hair. My tone came off as bitter. I would rather Mom be outside walking with Max and Dad than calling me. But I knew it was only a matter of time before Mom would ask about Kyla and Bria.

"I wanted to take some time out of my day to call my one and only son. I haven't heard from or seen you in quite some time."

"I know. I've been busy."

I was busy hunting down every clue I thought pertained to locating Kyla and Bria. Every clue turned up no beneficial information I could use to find them, which frustrated me.

"When are you, Kyla, and Bria coming over for dinner?"

"I am not sure," I replied.

"How are you not sure? It's been months since we had our monthly dinner night."

I inhaled a deep breath. I'd kept Kyla's and Bria's disappearance a secret from my parents. I had thought I would have the situation handled before questions were asked, and I didn't want them to worry.

"I don't know how to say this, but I need to tell you something."

"What is it?" she carefully asked.

"Kyla took Bria away from me."

"What do you mean she took Bria away from you?" Mom's response came out fast.

"Kyla packed up Bria one day, and I have not heard from them since."

Mom gasped. "What? How? When? Why?" Mom sounded worried and on edge. I could imagine her as she sat on the couch with her hand pressed against her heart.

"I have not seen them in three months."

Saying those words out loud made it seem even more real.

"Three months? Why didn't you tell us?"

"I didn't want you two to worry. You and Dad have enough to worry about with the business."

"Did you call the police?"

I exhaled as Mom's questions began to irritate me. Did she not realize the stress I had gone through these past few months? Did she not know I withheld this information so they wouldn't deal with the stress I had been dealing with? Every second of the day, every minute of the hour, every hour of the day. I was stressed enough to yank my hair from my scalp.

"I didn't tell you because I knew you would act like this," I growled.

I clenched my fist as my mouth watered. I craved the one thing that gave me my massive hangover.

"Did you call the police?" Mom repeated.

"I can't call them."

"Would you like to tell me why?" she inquired harshly.

Silence traveled through the phone. Mom had put the pieces together.

"Brad, I told you years ago to stop hitting Kyla," mom sniffled.

She was on the brink of tears, and I could do nothing to stop her from crying. I wanted to cry myself, but I refused to allow a tear to fall from my eyes. I had to be strong for her.

"I know."

"Why did you not stop?"

"I just couldn't control my anger."

I knew I was wrong for causing her agony, but I couldn't help it.

"Kyla loved you to the ends of the Earth."

"I'm aware."

There was a time when Kyla was head over heels for me. As the years went by, I noticed that the steam had sizzled out. I guess I should have blamed myself for that happening.

"All you had to do was stop hitting her, and she wouldn't have gone anywhere."

"I know."

I continued to agree with her. I didn't have the energy to argue with her in the mindset that she was in.

"So are you saying my only grandchild is gone?"

I had to pull the phone a few inches from my face as she cried.

"I'm doing everything that I can to find them." I thought for a second. "Without getting the police involved," I added.

I refused to get the police involved in the situation. If I did, I knew they would put out an amber alert for Bria. I couldn't risk that happening. I was certain Kyla would tell them about all the abuse she had suffered over the past few years. I was sure she had all the proof to lock me away for years. I couldn't go to jail.

"It's been three months. Your chances of finding them are slimmer as the days pass."

I knew what she said was right. My heart ached as she sobbed. Kyla's absence was the reason she cried her eyes out. I was mad at Kyla for the pain she caused Mom. For the pain she caused me.

I took a deep breath. There was one person I knew who had to know where Kyla was. As soon as that name came into my mind, I knew I had to make that call.

"Mom, I have to go."

"Why?"

"I will call you later."

"But..." Mom was mid-sentence before I hung up on her.

I went into my bedroom and grabbed my laptop. I searched Google for the person who I was sure Kyla had reached out to. I had not allowed her to communicate with her for the past five years. I was sure Kyla had contacted her the minute she walked out of the door to our home.

My fingers flew over the phone as I dialed the number. That number was associated with Amy, Kyla's old best friend. I placed the phone against my ear as it rang.

The phone rang three times before it was answered.

"Hello?" stated a soft voice.

"Hello. Is this Amy?" I asked in a calm, even tone.

"Yes, it is. May I ask who is calling?"

"This is Brad."

Silence lingered on the phone for a few

seconds.

"Brad, who?" Her voice dripped with a hint of skepticism.

"The Brad who dated Kyla."

The connection was so silent I pulled the phone away from my face to make sure the call was still active.

"Brad, why are you calling me?" she snarled.

The soft voice she had answered the phone with was long gone.

"It's nice to hear from you too, Amy."

I dished out the same attitude she dished out to me.

"Why are you calling me?" she repeated.

The annoyance in her voice was clear. It irritated me to my core how annoyed she was by me.

"Have you heard from Kyla?"

I hated going to Amy, but she was the only person I had known Kyla to be close with.

"I have not heard from Kyla in the past five years. Last I checked, I believe you are the reason for that."

I growled as my only hope of finding Kyla faded away.

"So, if you are contacting me about Kyla, there must be something wrong."

"Yes, something is wrong."

"What is going on?" Her voice softened.

"Kyla left me. She took our daughter with her three months ago, and I have not heard from her since."

"Kyla had a little girl?" Her voice was filled with surprise.

"We had a little girl." Last I checked, Kyla didn't create Bria by herself.

"What did she name her?" she asked.

"We named her Bria." Again, Amy excluded me, but this time she excluded me from naming Bria.

Silence settled on the phone. After what felt like an eternity, she finally spoke again.

"I am so glad she did it," Amy sniffled as her voice cracked.

"You are glad she did what?"

"I am so glad Kyla found the courage to leave you."

"How could you say that?" I fumed. I knew Amy was a horrible person, but I didn't think she was this terrible.

"You never deserved her," she ranted.

My blood boiled. "This call was a mistake."

"I would like to agree."

"I hope you rot in hell," I growled as I hung up the phone.

I left the bedroom and headed straight to the kitchen to my liquor cabinet. I grabbed a bottle of whiskey and took the top off. I brought the bottle to my lips and turned the bottle back. I lost the little sanity that I had. I did not know what else to do.

Chapter Twelve

Kyla

"Emily and Bria."

"Yes." Their voices blended in unison.

Sabrina wiped her hand on a dish towel. "Your snacks are ready."

She stood in the kitchen of her three-bedroom, two-bathroom home. The house was a generous size, and it was decorated with beautiful family pictures, paintings, and accents. Walking into the kitchen from the bathroom, I pulled a chair out and sat at the island.

Emily and Bria ran into the kitchen. "No

running, girls." Sabrina handed them a plate with cut-up strawberries and grapes.

After the girls called out a thank you, they walked out of the kitchen, balancing their plastic plates.

The sound of the front door opening and closing echoed throughout the kitchen. Within seconds, Julian walked into the kitchen. He was dressed head to toe in his work attire. Julian was an industrial engineer at a local manufacturing company.

"Hello, honey." Julian approached Sabrina and kissed her on the forehead.

"Hello, Tiffany," Julian waved at me.

Sabrina beamed. "Hey, babe."

I waved back. "Hello, Julian."

My phone chimed. I grabbed my phone out of my pocket and noticed that Ryan had just texted me with the location of where we were to meet in twenty minutes. Ryan had planned for us to have another outing together. I looked forward to hanging out with him again.

"That is Ryan."

I stood up.

Sabrina smiled as Julian walked out of the kitchen.

"I want you to have an amazing time this afternoon."

"I will. I promise."

I walked over to Sabrina, and we hugged.

"Call me if Bria is too much to handle."

Sabrina brushed my comment off. "Bria is a

doll. Enjoy yourself, and you better not worry."

For the first time in months, I strutted out of Sabrina's house with a calm nature around me. My nerves were not on edge, and I was not scared. I was finally comfortable in public without looking over my shoulder.

As soon as I was in my car, I texted Ryan that I was on my way.

Driving down the road, I passed by the place that provided me with my new life. I was so thankful for Meg's Coffee Shop. It was why I could go to my peaceful home every afternoon. The reason Bria and I was able to call our little house a home. The small town of Branchville changed our life for the better.

I approached the hole-in-the-wall ice cream shop on the right-hand side of the road. Ed's Gourmet Ice Cream was a stand-alone building that I noticed had a large crowd. It was located next door to a local park. I parked my car next to Ryan's silver Audi sedan.

Ryan leaned against his car. He wore a blue T-shirt, black jean shorts, and a pair of dark blue Jordans. In his left hand was a red rose. As soon as I turned my car off, Ryan closed the small distance between our vehicles. He opened my car door with his free hand.

"Hello, beautiful."

"Hello."

I beamed as I stepped out of my car. I placed my hand over my heart, and I smiled. Ryan spoiled me with a rose every time we got together.

"You look captivating as ever," Ryan complimented.

"Thank you."

Ryan closed my car door. I slid my hands across my loose-fitting coral halter dress to smooth the fabric.

"You look amazing as well."

"Thank you."

Ryan handed me the rose.

Clutching the rose, I inhaled the delicate, light scent as a smile bunched my cheeks.

Stepping forward at the same time Ryan did, we reduced the space between us. Ryan wrapped his arms around my waist as I wrapped my arms around his neck. The scent I became all too familiar with filled my nose as I enjoyed the feeling of Ryan's arms wrapped around me in a tight embrace.

"You feel perfect in my arms," Ryan said against my ear.

That statement alone caused a thrill to go through my body.

"I hope I am the only woman you are saying this to."

My knees got weak. Thank God for Ryan holding onto me so tight, or I would be hitting the ground right about now.

"You are the only one, and I mean that."

When my knees became strong again, I broke the embrace. Ryan caused these unfamiliar feelings, but it was spectacular to feel.

"The ice cream here must be great."

I managed to change the subject. How I felt for Ryan started to scare me.

"We will be the judge of that. This will be my first time trying it."

A few families and couples stood in line, waiting to place their orders or waiting for their orders to be ready.

Ryan and I approached the line.

"How have you been doing today?" Ryan asked.

"Good. Bria and I hung out with Sabrina and Emily all morning."

"You two must be really close."

We took two steps as we moved up in line.

"We are. I didn't have too many friends back home."

"How come?"

I shrugged my shoulders as I sugarcoated the truth. "I have always been an introvert."

"There is nothing wrong with being an introvert."

"Are you sure about that?"

Growing up, I always had an issue blossoming out of my shell and socializing.

"Of course. All you need is an extrovert to bring you out of your shell," Ryan stated as the line continued to progress.

"So which introvert would you try to bring out of their shell?"

Ryan looked over at me, and he flashed his charming smile. "Perhaps the beautiful woman standing next to me."

Butterflies fluttered in my stomach as I found myself smiling back at Ryan.

Ryan and I approached the order window.

"Welcome to Ed's. What delicious scoop do you want to try?" the teenage girl chirped cheerfully as she tucked a stray piece of blonde hair behind her ear.

"I will have a scoop of butter pecan on a cone," Ryan said as he pulled his wallet out of his pocket. He looked at me to give my order.

"I will take a scoop of strawberry on a cone."

Once Ryan paid and we received our ice cream, we started walking the park's path and began eating the ice cream.

Ryan took note of how much I enjoyed taking walks. That was thoughtful. Nobody had ever taken the initiative to consider what I wanted.

"This ice cream is great," I said.

The wonderful taste of strawberries danced on my tastebuds, and I was in sugar heaven.

"Yes, the best I've had," Ryan agreed.

As Ryan and I walked through the park, we observed the natural scenery we were blessed to experience. We were surrounded by Sabal Palmettos and Oak trees. The idyllic Hydrangeas that had blossomed ranged from pink to blue hues. A bird chirped in a nearby tree.

"If you had the opportunity to use a time machine for an entire day, would you go back in time or into the future?" Ryan asked.

I thought for a moment as I licked my ice

cream cone. His question surprised me as it was not expected. It was somewhat random, to say the least. Would I rather go back in time and ignore Ryan's advances in school? Or would I rather go into the future and get a peek at what my life would be like in several years?

"I'd rather see what the future holds."

If I had gone back in time and changed one decision, Bria would not have been born. I couldn't imagine life without her. She was the reason I still had breath in my body.

"I agree with going into the future. There is nothing I have done in my life that I feel I need to change," Ryan answered.

"What's been the biggest mistake that you've made?"

I took our conversation to a deeper level. It was a necessity to know if Ryan had different layers to him.

"Allowing my career to take control of life."

Ryan continued to eat his ice cream cone.

"What did you learn from that mistake?"

As Ryan and I continued walking on our path, a squirrel chased another squirrel right in front of us. The squirrels played their own version of tag, barreling over each other as they rolled into the grass.

"I have learned to put my career on the back burner. Life is too short to focus all my time and attention on my job. I take time for all my relationships now," Ryan clarified.

The honesty that radiated off him amazed

me. I would have never guessed there was a time when his career was the number one priority in his life.

"That is amazing. Being able to support yourself is a necessity, but learning how to put your relationships front and center is hard work," I stated.

"What's been your biggest mistake?"

Two birds sat in a tree nest high off the ground. They chirped to each other, catching my attention.

"I tend to give a person too many chances even when they don't deserve it. But, since I moved here, I have learned it is okay to put myself first."

The truth in my statement sent involuntary chills through my body.

"It's not just okay to put yourself first. It is a requirement."

Hearing those words come out of Ryan's mouth solidified my decision. I had no choice but to put Bria and myself first and leave Brad for good.

"What motivates you the most?" Ryan looked over at me, waiting for my answer.

"That is an easy question. My daughter Bria, she is the reason I work so hard." The thought of Bria always seemed to make me smile. "Where does your motivation come from?"

"My parents. They have always encouraged me to be the best I could be in whatever I did."

"It must've been amazing to have that type of

encouragement in your life."

I looked down at the ground and I noticed our feet were in sync.

"I'm sure your parents must have motivated you somehow."

A bee buzzed by in our path, traveling on its merry way to find a flower.

I glanced over at Ryan before my eyes reached the ground. Telling people about my life was difficult. I was embarrassed that I didn't have the normal upbringing that most children experienced.

"I don't know anything about my parents," I admitted as we approached a garbage can.

Ryan and I threw the remainder of our cones away.

Silence lingered in the air after those words left my mouth.

"Are you serious?"

We halted in our tracks. Ryan turned, and he gave me his undivided attention.

Nodding my head, I looked away from him. I felt embarrassed.

"Or anything about my family, for that matter. I grew up in foster care for as long as I could remember."

"I am so sorry for bringing them up. If I had known... me and my big mouth."

Looking up to meet Brad's eyes, sorrow was buried deep inside them.

"You don't need to apologize to me."

"I can just tell it's something you are not

proud to share."

"I would have to agree with you on that."

"You shouldn't be embarrassed, though, not with me. I can see you are doing well for yourself, considering you are doing it all on your own without any support."

"I do it all for my sweet girl."

Taking a deep breath, I exhaled as two bicyclists passed us on the path. My nerves relaxed.

"Have you ever thought about trying to locate your birth parents?"

He placed one of his hands on my upper back.

Nodding, I relaxed further that there was no judgment.

"The thought has crossed my mind, but I'm unsure if I'm ready. What if I find my parents and discover they just don't want me? What if I was a burden, and they thought life would be easier if I didn't exist?"

"It could be any number of reasons for you to end up in foster care. Think of the positives."

"You think so?" Ryan's statement made me feel hopeful.

"Of course. Please let me know if you ever want to locate your family. I would be more than happy to help you start the process."

"Thank you," I whispered. Smiling, a multitude of emotions swelled in my heart. I had never known in my entire life what it was like for a man to show me he cared about me. The feeling was foreign. I didn't know how to deal with the emotions that ran through my heartstrings. Tears burned the back of my eyes as an overwhelming feeling settled over me.

"You don't have to thank me. I would give you the entire world if I had the strength and capability to do so."

Ryan's arms snaked around my lower back. I wrapped my arms around his neck. I allowed my body to relax in his arms as he held me tight against his firm body, my cheek pressed against his chest. Inhaling my new all-time favorite scent of Ryan's cologne, my body relaxed. I had not felt this comfortable in so long. It felt great, and I didn't want this feeling to ever end.

Chapter Thirteen

Kyla

Five outstanding months had passed since relocating to South Carolina. The eight-and-a-half-hour distance from the city I had once called home all my life seemed like a foreign country a million miles away. If Brad was looking for us, he had not located us or found any possible way to contact us. These past five months without Brad were Heaven on Earth, and I did not want this feeling to end.

Bria had shown ample maturity since we moved to our new town. I chalked it up to Bria being able to thrive and blossom in an abuse-free environment. Bria had stopped asking about Brad, which was great.

The doorbell rang. The sound echoed throughout the house.

I put the last clean plate up that I had taken from the dishwasher.

"Bria, I would like you to meet someone," I sang as I walked towards the front door.

"Who is it, Mommy?" Bria ran into the living room.

"Mommy's new friend."

I looked through the peephole.

Ryan stood on the other side of the door. He wore a pair of tan khaki shorts and a black T-shirt. In his left hand was a red rose.

"Come open the door."

Bria swung the door open. She looked up as she stepped back a few feet.

Ryan presented an award-winning smile as he walked into my house.

He trained his attention on Bria.

"Hi, pretty girl."

He spoke in a soft tone.

"Hello." She waved her hand as her eyes flickered over to me.

"What is your name?"

I closed the door behind him. He had squatted down to the floor and gave Bria his undivided attention.

"Bria."

She smiled warmly, showing off her front

teeth.

"Is it fine if I stay for a little bit?" he asked her.

Bria nodded before she turned to look at me. "As long as you are nice to my Mommy."

My heart broke into a million pieces. It was pieced back together as Bria smiled at me. She was the reason that my heart still had a beat.

Ryan's facial expression softened as he looked over Bria's head at me. I forced a smile. I had not expected those words to come out of Bria's mouth. However, I knew her statement had brought a few questions to his mind that he would ask me by the end of the day.

Bria had begun to turn around when Ryan said, "Bria, I have something for you."

She stopped as Ryan pulled out a purple bracelet from his pocket. My heart warmed as Bria's eyes widened with excitement. I had told Ryan a while back that Bria's favorite color was purple and that she loved bracelets. He slipped it onto her right hand as she looked up at me.

"Can I have it, Mom?"

"Of course, Sweetie."

"Yay."

She jumped up and clapped her hands.

"What do you say about the bracelet you just received?"

"Thank you."

Ryan stood up from his squatted position.

Bria squealed as she ran over to me and hugged me tightly.

I ran my hand over Bria's frizzy ponytail as

her small body settled into my arms. Being a mom was the best feeling in the world, especially to for such a thoughtful little girl.

Bria ran off to her room.

I turned my attention to Ryan. He wrapped his arms around me and pulled me into a warm embrace. I placed my arms against his chest, loving the feel of his arms around me. Once we broke away from our hug, Brad handed me the rose.

"Hi, beautiful."

"Hello. Thank you for the rose. It's gorgeous."

"It's my pleasure." Ryan stuffed his hands into his pant pockets as he looked around the living room.

I walked to the dining room table. I had purchased a decorative, light blue colored single bud vase from the local thrift store in town. It was in the middle of the dining table. I replaced the old, wilted rose that Ryan had given me when we went to the movies and replaced it with the new stem.

"Bria," I called out.

"Yes?" She walked out of her room, wearing her new bracelet.

"Would you like to play outside for a little bit?"

"Yes." Bria ran to the back door and opened it.

"You did not have to buy her anything." I lead Brad to the backyard.

Over the past few months, I had set up the backyard with furnishings. Two lounge chairs and a waterproof Bluetooth speaker were placed under the shaded, covered area. A table with four chairs and a patio umbrella off to the right side of the yard. I had purchased Bria a sandbox that sat in the middle of the yard. Along with her sandbox, she had several colorful accessories that she could use to play with. It was the least I could do since I took Bria away from the ocean. We sat in the lounge chairs as Bria picked up her red shovel. Sitting at an angle, I could look at Ryan without taking my eyes off Bria.

"I know I didn't, but I wanted to."

"Thank you."

My body was warm inside, and it wasn't from the summer heat.

"This is a very nice place that you have here."

"Thank you. It is a rental, but the landlord is awesome. When something needs to be done, it is done immediately."

Bria now had her blue bucket, shoveling sand into it.

"The neighborhood seems so quiet and relaxed."

He reached his hand over to my shoulder and rubbed it in a slow, circular motion.

"Private too. I never hear my neighbors next door. I only hear them when we get our mail outside, and they spark a conversation."

I shut my eyes from the comfort of the shoulder rub.

"You will have to visit me at my house one day. I live a few miles outside of town."

I opened my eyes and looked into his eyes.

"I might have to take you up on that offer soon."

He nodded.

"Seems as if Bria is very protective of her Mommy."

Ryan started the conversation I knew would spark from Bria's comment.

I nodded as I broke our eye contact.

"She really is. She's a great daughter."

"Is Bria's father in her life?" Brad asked.

I took a deep breath. I was comfortable with Ryan but wasn't ready to have that conversation with him yet. It was hard to admit my difficulties in a previous relationship with a potential love interest.

"He used to be in her life."

Ryan stopped rubbing my shoulder and focused on me.

"Where is he now?"

Clearing my throat, I looked down at my hands in my lap.

"Could we talk about that some other time?"

Ryan nodded. I could see the worry in his eyes, but I knew he wouldn't pressure me.

"Of course, we can. I am so sorry for bringing him up. I never want to make you feel uncomfortable."

I smiled as I looked up to meet his eyes. His understanding meant everything to me.

"Thank you."

"So, I remember you telling me you like

dancing."

He smiled. I loved how he changed the direction of the conversation when he became aware of my discomfort.

I laughed. "Correction. I love dancing," I stated with confidence.

I turned my speaker on, and I connected my phone.

When Bria heard the distinct sound of the Bluetooth connecting, she stopped shoveling sand into her bucket. She looked at me with a toothy smile and dropped her shovel and bucket.

I turned on one of the latest pop songs that Bria and I enjoyed.

Bria ran over to me with rapid speed, kicking up the sand that was in her sandbox. She grabbed my hands, and we danced to the beat of the harmonious music.

Whenever music played, all my worries seemed to dissipate away. It was one of my favorite coping mechanisms.

Ryan sat back in his chair and watched us dance. The smile that he had on his face never left.

"Dance with us," Bria pleaded.

Ryan shook his head. "I can't dance."

"How can you say no to that face?" I asked him.

Ryan and I looked at Bria's face. She stuck her bottom lip out and gave puppy dog eyes.

"Okay, okay."

Ryan stood up. He walked over to us, and he

danced. Ryan's admission of being unable to dance was proven true as he was offbeat. It was one of the funniest sights I had seen in a long time.

As song after song played, all three of us continued to dance.

After a few songs passed, Bria returned to her sandbox. Her mind was occupied as she built a sandcastle.

Ryan grasped my hands in his, and we moved closer to each other. There were only mere inches in between us as we danced.

"Tiffany."

I looked up to meet Ryan's eyes. Whenever he called me by my name, I knew the next statement that would come out of his mouth was heartfelt.

"Yes?"

"Can I tell you something?"

"Of course. You can tell me anything."

"I care deeply for you," Ryan admitted.

As soon as those words left Ryan's mouth, it confirmed we were experiencing the same feelings. I had never thought I would consider trusting another man.

"I care for you as well."

Ryan and I stopped dancing.

My eyes locked with the mesmerizing eyes I had grown to adore these past few months. Time passed as our gaze intensified, enjoying the moment.

"You are making it so difficult for me not to

stare."

"Why do you say that?"

"You are the most gorgeous woman my eyes have ever landed on."

The words that came out of Ryan's mouth were a magnificent symphony to my ears that I did not want to end anytime soon. I wanted an encore to follow.

"You aren't so bad yourself."

I appreciated the handsome, perfectly man standing before me.

Ryan grinned, his ecstasy touching his eyes.

"I have never wanted to kiss someone as much as I have wanted to kiss you."

Ryan's eyes flickered to my lips, lingering for a few seconds before his eyes met mine again.

"Well, what's stopping you?"

An electric tug pulled on my heartstrings as Ryan raised his hand to caress my face. The warmth radiating off his hand caused my body to give off an unexpected shiver. Suddenly, our faces moved toward each other. A hint of spearmint drifted into my nose right before Ryan's soft lips collided with mine. Fireworks exploded inside my body as my heart jumped out of my chest from pure happiness. Time seemed to have come to a complete stop as our lips moved in sync for what felt like an eternity that I did not want to ever escape. Ryan kissed my lips and my soul with a heart full of passion. This was a feeling I had not ever felt, and I did not want it to ever end.

"Ooh. Mommy is kissing someone that is not Daddy," Bria yelled.

Ryan and I pulled apart, and we turned to look at her.

She giggled as she pointed at us before she resumed working on her castle.

Ryan and I looked at each other and laughed.

"I guess the mood is ruined now."

I continued to laugh at Bria's comment.

"I wouldn't say that," he responded.

"Why not?" I raised my eyebrows slightly.

"I've been meaning to ask you something for some time now. I believe that it is a perfect time."

"You can ask me anything."

Every bit of truth was in that statement. Ryan had my undivided attention.

"Will you be my girlfriend?"

Exhilaration wrapped itself around me as I felt light as a feather. I pinched myself on the arm to make sure I was not stuck in a dream. When I felt the discomfort from the pinch, I nodded.

"Yes, I will be your girlfriend. You have to be okay with us moving slowly, though."

"That's fine with me."

Ryan grasped my face in his hands and placed his lips on mine. Our lips locked together for a few seconds before we separated. My eyes fluttered open as Ryan leaned forward to kiss my forehead.

If only time could stop when I was in his arms.

Chapter Fourteen

Brad

My vision blurred as I took another swig of whiskey. The only thing that I could do right now was stay drunk. If I was not drinking my sorrows away, my mind would wander to the horrific things I knew Kyla was doing now that I was no longer there to protect her. I didn't doubt that she had already cheated on me. How could she betray me?

The social media sites that I helped Kyla create had been deleted. I had done several Google searches trying to pull up Kyla. I swore it was as if she had disappeared off the face of the Earth because I could not find anything. Kyla had done a great job of hiding. The planning that went into her and Bria's disappearance was remarkable. Never in a million years did I think Kyla had the strength and courage to leave and stay gone for so long. I had underestimated her.

The clink of billiard balls hitting one another plucked me out of my thoughts as I coughed. The cigarette smoke that lingered in the building affected me. I looked at the bartender and she stared at me with narrowed eyes.

"You are done drinking. You need to pay your bill."

I pulled a fifty-dollar bill out of my wallet and threw it on the counter. I raked my hands through my hair as I managed to walk out of the bar and into the fresh air. Thank goodness for the fresh air.

I dialed a number I had memorized for the past two weeks as I made my way to the parking lot. The phone number rang a few times before the call was answered.

"Justin Dowling, private investigator. How do you need my services?"

"Hello, Justin. My name is Brad, and I need your help to find my girlfriend and daughter."

"How long have they been gone?"

"They disappeared over five months ago, and all of my searches have come up empty."

I staggered as I passed by a silver minivan. I reached my hand out to balance myself, so I would not fall over.

"Do you think their disappearance was by forceful measures, or they disappeared on account of their free will?"

"Free will."

"Are you sure?"

"Yes, I am. There is no doubt in my mind." Why did this investigator question the information I provided him?

"Well, you have come to the best private investigator in the state of Florida."

"I'm glad to hear you say that," I admitted as I approached my SUV.

"I can locate your girlfriend and your daughter. My prices are not cheap, though."

"Money is no object for me. I just need my family back."

"I'll have your family in a few months max, 100% guaranteed."

"When can you start looking for them?"

"As soon as I receive money."

"I can meet you in four hours," I responded as I pushed myself into the backseat.

Four hours gave me more than enough time to sober up.

"I require 75% of my fees upfront before starting the search. The other 25% will be paid once I have their location."

That pleasing statement was music to my ears.

Chapter Fifteen

Kyla

I parked my car in front of the grand, two-story cobblestone house. The exterior of the three-bedroom, two-in-a-half bathroom house was tan with dark brown trimmings. The landscaping was pristine. The lawn was well taken care of, green and vibrant. The trees on the property were trimmed. Ryan's house was on four acres, fifteen minutes out of town.

Ryan opened his front door and stepped out. To my surprise, he wore a pair of black gym shorts and a gray T-shirt.

We had been dating for a month and a half. The relationship was a breath of fresh air. It was amazing not to have to try so hard. I saw Ryan every day as he continued to come into the coffee shop for his Americano and a blueberry muffin. Today was my first visit to Ryan's house. I had worked up the courage to take that next step of visiting his house.

Stepping out of my car, I tucked a piece of my hair behind my ear.

I opened the back door of my car, and I got Bria out.

Hand in hand, we walked along the dark brown paved pathway. We walked up the five steps that led to the front door.

Ryan held the door open wide.

"Hi, Ryan." Bria waved her tiny hand at him.

He squatted down and hugged her.

"Hi, Bria."

She walked past him and into the house as if she had been there a million times.

"Hello."

I wrapped my arms around his neck.

"Hello, beautiful."

He grabbed me around my waist and kissed my lips sensually.

"Your lips are so soft," Ryan whispered as he looked into my eyes.

"Thank you."

I winked at him as I walked into the house.

The living room had gray furnishings and was kid friendly. The walls were adorned with extravagant paintings and photography of natural scenery, such as lakes, sunrises, sunsets, and forests. Placed several feet from the couch and loveseat was a large flat-screen TV. This house didn't look like a single man in his early thirties lived there by his lonesome.

Ryan closed the door behind us.

Bria had already sat on the loveseat. She placed her headphones over her ears. Immediately, her mind was absorbed in the educational program I had installed on her tablet.

"Can I give you the tour of my grand abode?"

"Of course."

Ryan led me to the kitchen and dining room area that was located off to the right of the front door. The kitchen was adorned with dark gray appliances and cabinets. The countertops were a lighter shade of gray. The dining table for six was an elegant black set.

"Here is my kitchen and dining room."

"This is so nice. I hope you'll make me an amazing dinner in this kitchen someday."

"I can foresee that happening soon."

Ryan led me upstairs to the second floor of the house. The first door on the left was the bedroom that Ryan used as his home office. Right across the hall was a separate bathroom. The second door on the left was a guest bedroom where Ryan had a queen-sized bed, a flat-screen TV mounted on the wall, and two end tables. The second door on the right was Ryan's bedroom. Ryan opened the door. A king-sized bed with a bright yellow comforter was in the middle of the room. There was a flat-screen TV, two end tables, and a lazy boy chair. Off to the left was a bathroom that contained a jacuzzi bathtub.

"Your favorite color has shown up," I joked as I looked over my shoulder.

"I keep the color limited to my bedroom. So not many people see it unless they are invited to my room."

Ryan allowed that comment to sink in before he shut the door.

"How many people are invited here?" I asked him.

"Not many, but I can't wait to have you all to myself in that bed."

He winked at me as he flirted.

I smiled.

"Your house is stunning."

We walked down the hall and downstairs. I walked over to a painting with a low-hanging tree suspended over a calm lake. I studied the intricate details.

Ryan approached the painting.

"Thank you. I love collecting art."

That was an admission that I was not aware of until now.

I made eye contact with him.

"Every day, you surprise me with yet another great quality you possess."

"I'm not the only one in this relationship with great qualities."

He dragged his index finger along the back of

my neck.

"I'm alright," I responded, not even confident with my answer.

Hiding my identity was not a great quality, and the truth threatened to come out. I walked over to the couch and sat on the plush material. Bria laughed, her attention still focused on her tablet.

Ryan shook his head no as he walked over and sat beside me.

"You are not just alright."

"Why do you say that?"

I looked into his eyes. I was not ready to hear the answer but braced for his response.

"Your personality is incredible. You have a heart of gold. You are one of the most trustworthy individuals I have ever met in my entire life."

Hearing the word trustworthy come out of Ryan's mouth made my heart plunge. His eyes sparkled as he talked so highly of me. I dropped my gaze onto my hands folded in my lap, feeling shameful. If only Ryan knew that the identity he had grown to know these last several months was all a complete lie.

"I have to tell you something."

It was a secret I couldn't keep to myself any longer.

"You can tell me anything."

Ryan grabbed my hands and rubbed them.

"I have not been honest with you."

My eyes were focused on our hands in my lap.

"You have not been honest about what?"

Moving his right hand from my hand in my lap, he lifted my face up with his index finger. Staring into his eyes, comfort wrapped its warm arms around my body. I had nothing to be afraid of.

Ryan was nothing like Brad.

"My name is not Tiffany."

Ryan's eyes widened, but his attention never wavered. "What is your name?"

"My name is Kyla."

Ryan took a deep breath as he stood. He paced the living room area as he ran his fingers through his hair. Silence settled among us as I sat on the couch, unable to move, fearful of Ryan's response. It felt like an eternity had passed before he decided to respond.

"What was the point in lying to me about your name?"

"I did not want my past catching up to me." I stood and approached Ryan, where he stood by the entrance to the kitchen.

"What are you saying?"

I took a deep breath as I knew the last five years of my life would unravel right before my eyes.

"Anybody could have searched for me by my name and located me here."

"Are you telling me you moved here because you were running away from someone?"

I nodded. "It was in our best interest if we stayed under the radar."

"Who are you running away from?"

"We are on the run from Bria's father. Also known as my ex from hell."

"Did Bria's father abuse the two of you?" he asked.

"Only me, thank God."

I couldn't imagine what I would've done if Brad had laid his hands on Bria. If that were the case, I doubt I would be standing in Ryan's house. I'd probably be behind steel bars doing twenty-five years to life.

"Now I understand why Bria made that comment the first time I came over."

Ryan grabbed my hands, the sincerity vivid in his eyes.

"Brad was careless when he did what he did to me."

I couldn't even bring myself to say the word abuse. I no longer wanted to claim that part of my life. But I survived my abuse, and I never wanted to look back.

"So, Brad has no idea where you are?"

I shook my head. "One morning after he left for work, I packed Bria up. We left, and I never looked back."

"No wonder you kept your identity a secret."

I led Ryan over to the couch, and we sat. Ryan rubbed my hands with the pad of his thumbs in a circular motion. I cherished the actions he took that caused me to relax. I appreciated it.

"I was fearful he'd locate us," I said.

"Are you still terrified after all of this time?"

I nodded. "It is hard to relax. I still fear that he might find us. But I know that he is searching for us. I can just feel it."

Ryan's eyebrows scrunched together. His tone lowered as he looked over at Bria. I was thankful she had her headphones over her ears so she couldn't hear our conversation. "How long have this abuse been happening?" His face softened.

"Five years. I am not proud to have stayed that long, but I had to do what was financially suitable so Bria did not suffer."

My eyes flickered over to a gorgeous sunset photo before I looked into Ryan's eyes.

"You don't have to explain yourself. Knowing the person I have grown to care for, I know you did it because you had no choice. Not because you wanted to."

"He was why I had a home when I was put out of foster care."

"Why were you put out?"

"I conceived while living there and was no longer allowed to stay."

I looked over at Bria. The aura radiating off her was pure innocence.

"When did the abuse start?"

Ryan folded his arms across his chest. It was clear the situation I came from bothered him.

"It started right before Bria was conceived. I thought the small pushes and the grabbing of my arm would stop. Unfortunately, it only worsened over the years, so I was wrong to believe it would ever stop."

"It hurts my heart you had to go through that. It hurts me that any woman has to deal with that."

"I'm glad I managed to get out. There is no telling if I would still be alive if I had not made my escape when I did," I admitted.

"You are such a strong woman to have escaped. I don't condone abuse in any shape or form. Just know, I will protect you and Bria with my life."

Hearing those words come out of Ryan's mouth further intensified the affection I felt deep within my heart.

Ryan stroked my face before he gave me a soft, tender kiss. Once his lips left mine, we smiled at each other.

Expressing my gratitude, I stated, "I can't believe I was lucky enough to have found you."

"If you want to get technical, we found each other. I remember the day I saw you for the first time. That was the first day I ever saw a goddess."

"Being compared to a goddess is amazing. I've never heard that compliment before," I cooed.

"That is because you've never been with a real gentleman."

"That is true."

I couldn't help but agree with him.

"Is there anything else you want to share with me?" he asked.

I shrugged my shoulders as I removed my bangs. "These bangs are not real."

Ryan stared at me with admiration in his eyes. "Just when I thought you couldn't get more beautiful."

Ryan swooned as he kissed my forehead. He grabbed a red rose from the coffee table and handed it to me. Red roses were divine, but forehead kisses gave me life.

Chapter Sixteen

Brad

"Thank you for coming over, sweetheart."

Mom's voice rang out as I walked into my parent's magnificent kitchen. My parent's house was twice the size of mine, with four bedrooms and three bathrooms. The house smelled of one of my childhood favorite meals growing up. The meal included chicken florentine, fresh steamed green beans, and garlic mashed potatoes.

"You don't have to thank me, Mom."

Approaching my Mom, I wrapped my arms around her petite frame and hugged her tight. My mother had a fragrance on that I had been accustomed to since I was a baby. The scent brought back unforgettable memories from several years ago, causing me to smile.

"I just wanted you over for dinner."

"I am so happy to be here for dinner."

That statement held a lot of truth. It had been months since I had dinner with my family, and I was not going to allow anything to get in the way of spending time with them.

"I miss you so much."

Mom stirred the green beans before she turned off the heat.

"I miss you too. Where is Dad?"

I went into the alcohol cabinet and pulled out a bottle of whiskey.

"He's walking Max. He should be back here in any minute."

I went into the cupboard and pulled out two rock glasses. I put two ice cubes in the glass from the ice bucket on the counter and poured the glasses full of whiskey.

The front door opened and closed. Max's nails hitting the floor made a distinctive sound as he made his way into the house.

"Hey, Dad."

He made his way into the kitchen.

"Hi, Son."

His eyes zeroed in on the drinks in my hands.

"Thanks for my drink," he said.

He took the glass from my hand and brought it to his lips. I was told I was his twin from a young age. As handsome as my father was in his late fifties, I knew I would keep my attractive features for a long time.

I sat my drink at my spot at the dinner table.

Mom carried the pan of green beans to the dinner table, and I followed suit by taking the bowl of mashed potatoes and the pan of chicken florentine.

We all sat at our usual spots at the dinner table. Dad sat at the head of the table, mom sat next to him on his right side, and I sat next to him on his left side. It pained me that the seat next to me did not have Kyla, and the seat next to mom did not have Bria.

We passed the food around the table family-style as we filled our plates up with delicious food.

"How have you been doing, Sweetheart?" Mom asked before she ate a green bean.

"I've been okay. How have you two been?"

"We've been fine," Mom answered for them both.

Dad took over the conversation as he cut into his chicken. "We would like to discuss something with you."

"What is it?" I continued eating.

"Your work performance has been declining," Mom said before she sipped her ice water.

"It has harmed our business," Dad explained.

My heart dropped into my stomach. "Are you serious?"

Mom and Dad nodded, worry etched into the wrinkles on their faces.

"We understand the stress you have gone through trying to find Kyla and Bria," Mom began.

"But you must find a way to separate your personal life from your work life," Dad finished.

Grabbing my glass of whiskey, I took a hearty sip.

"I'm so embarrassed," I stated.

I couldn't believe I had allowed my issues at home to pave the way for my work performance. I was disappointed.

"Don't be embarrassed. We are your parents," Mom said in a comforting tone.

Dad spoke. "We just need you to focus on work while you work and handle your personal issues when you clock out at the end of the day."

Nodding my head, I took a bite of chicken florentine.

"Is there any news on Kyla and Bria yet?" Mom asked.

"I couldn't find anything on my own, so I had no choice but to hire a private investigator."

"Any updates from the private investigator?"

Dad raised an eyebrow, waiting for an answer.

"Not yet, but he is the best of the best."

"That's awesome. I cannot wait to see my grandchild. It's been too long," Mom said.

A slight quiver was in her voice.

"You'll see her before you know it."

My statement oozed with the confidence that I lacked inside. They didn't need to know that though.

"Just promise us one thing." Dad had a stern look on his face, which usually indicated he was serious and meant business.

"Promise what?"

"You will tell us if and when the private investigator contacts you."

He sipped his whiskey while his eyes were trained on me.

"Are we clear?" Mom gave me a stern look.

"Why?" I did not know where this conversation was headed.

Dad took a bite of chicken florentine.

"We know how you are when it comes to Kyla. We do not want you to find her and Bria alone."

"We are looking after her well-being and your own," Mom clarified.

"I am not going to hurt her."

I was irritated with the major turn the conversation had taken.

"We just want to be present when you get the information from the private investigator. We don't want you trying to track down Kyla by yourself."

I would not argue or attempt to reason with my parents when their minds were already made up. Deciding to save my sanity, I agreed with them.

"Okay, I will let you two know."

"Thank you, Sweetheart." Mom smiled, pleased with my response.

"Thanks, Son," Dad replied, giving me a smile that was not shown often.

Growing up, Dad always gave me tough love while Mom was the one to baby me. So getting a smile from my Dad meant he was proud.

We ate while we had light conversation. Deep down, I felt horrible for lying to my parents, but I didn't want them to worry any longer. I would deal with Kyla myself, whether my parents wanted me to do it or not. They would have to deal with that fact when the time came.

Chapter Seventeen

Kyla

"I believe I'm ready," I stated.

My heart thumped hard in my chest. I never imagined after all these years, I would be able to say that with confidence.

"You know this will change your life, right?" Ryan looked over at me.

Nodding my head, I agreed. "I'm hopeful this will change my life for the better."

"Well, let's do it."

Ryan and I sat at my dining room table. Bria wasn't home, she had a playdate with Emily and

Sabrina. My eyes feasted upon the red rose Ryan had just given me. On the table sat Ryan's laptop. Opening his laptop, the screen came to life. Ryan typed away on his computer. He clicked the enter key, and the website I had dreamed about for weeks appeared on the screen.

A large tree with several branches appeared. I read through the testimonials at the bottom of the screen. As I read through each one, my hope of finding a family member intensified.

Ryan clicked on the bright green find button. Another screen popped up explaining the process.

"So we have to enter all your known personal information into this form." Ryan pointed at the screen.

"Oh my goodness," I gasped.

"What?"

"It says there is a 90% chance I'll be able to find a relative within a few months."

I felt a mixture of excitement and nervousness.

"Isn't that amazing? You might know who your mother and father are in a few short months."

Ryan moved the laptop, so it sat in front of me.

"I hope so. I wonder if they have been looking for me all this time." I entered all my information into the system.

"It's a possibility. There is no way you will know until you connect with them."

My fingers stopped halfway through typing in my birthplace. "What if they have no interest in finding me?"

Doubt set in, my anxiety trying to rear its ugly head.

Ryan placed his hand on my arm. "Please, don't start thinking like that."

"What if I am part of that 10% that doesn't find their family?"

Uncertainty made its way into my mind, crowding my better judgment.

"Kyla..."

"But..."

"No buts," Ryan interrupted me as he shook his head. "We will stay positive that you will find a family member. Please relax."

Ryan rubbed my arm as I took deep breaths to calm my nerves.

Once I calmed down, I returned to filling out the information. I reviewed all the information I had entered, ensuring I had answered everything to the best of my ability.

I moved the cursor over to the submit button. My hand hovered over the touchpad as a raft few life events flashed before my eyes. Being in foster care from as young as I could remember. Wearing clothes that were two sizes too small. Not having a warm meal to eat every night.

"You can do it."

Ryan's encouraging words gave me all the motivation to submit the form.

A message popped up on the screen after I

clicked submit.

Your information has been received. Once we have all the essential information gathered, someone from Tree Branch will contact you to share the wonderful news. Talk to you soon.

A multitude of emotions bombarded me as I reread the message.

"I can't believe I just did it."

Taking the first step to locating my family was the best decision I could have ever made. It was a journey I had wanted for many years. I just never had the chance to accomplish it until now. Brad always told me that the only family I needed was his family. He never thought it was important for me to locate my birth family. He would always say negative things about how my family had given me up at a young age and that I should just forget about them. They didn't love me enough to keep me. So why was I going to go through the trouble to find them? He was fine with me continuing with the life he had provided, but I was never okay with that.

"I can only imagine how significant of a step that was for you," Ryan said.

He exited out of the browsers, closed his laptop, and grabbed my hand. Together, we stood, and he led me out the door to my backyard. The humid air wrapped its arm around me.

"I didn't do it just for me. I did it for Bria. She has only known Brad's family. I could never complain about Bria having his family in her life. Truth be told, they treated her like the princess she is. I would just love for her to get to know my family."

Ryan reached for my other hand. He brought my hands up to his face, and he placed soft kisses on the back of my hands.

"To be honest, I have never met anyone as selfless as you."

Ryan looked up at me, locking his eyes with mine. The gaze in his eyes was of pure sincerity.

"Why do you say that?"

I searched for the answer hidden in his eyes but could not unscramble the answer.

"Your main concern is what benefits Bria. You always put yourself last."

"As a mother, every decision I have ever made has been with Bria's best interest in mind."

"She is so blessed to have you as a mother."

"You really think so?"

Those thoughtful words caused me to smile.

"Of course. I'm blessed to call you my girlfriend."

Ryan leaned in and kissed on my forehead.

"Thank you. Can I tell you something?"

"You have more secrets?" Ryan raised his eyebrows high.

"No." I laughed. "I just want you to know how much you have helped heal me these past few months."

"Kyla, I..."

"No, you don't understand," I interrupted him. "You have managed to help reset all the damage that Brad did to me over five years. You have done that in months, and there is no way I could ever repay you for that."

"I'm glad you have allowed me to be a part of your healing journey."

Ryan wrapped his arms around my waist and held me close as I laid my head on his chest.

"I'm not sure where I would have been without your moral support."

Ryan drew away as he caressed my chin. His eyes searched deep into my soul as a fire was set off inside me.

"What are you thinking about?"

Ryan shook his head. "Nothing in particular. I'm just admiring the astounding woman that is my girlfriend."

"Your girlfriend sounds awesome."

"She is awesome. You should get to know her," Ryan commented, making us both laugh.

"In all seriousness, the safest place I've ever known is right in your arms."

Ryan drew me into his arms as he stroked my back. I placed my ear to his chest so I could hear his heart beating. That was a beautiful sound of life.

"Kyla, I love you," Ryan proclaimed.

My heart performed a somersault as my breath halted in my chest. I was terrified to feel that intense, passionate feeling for Ryan. I had never had that type of love for anyone besides Brad. That love for Brad had dissolved within two years of that relationship. Hearing Ryan say those words made me aware that our feelings had always been mutual.

"I love you too, Ryan."

I had not spoken such true words in a long time.

When Ryan's lips found mine, I closed my eyes. My heart and soul were invested in this relationship. It felt great.

Chapter Eighteen

Brad

Sitting down my empty glass that had contained whiskey, I looked around the bar. The pungent smell of cigarette smoke was thick in the air. A light haze of smoke floated throughout the small, crowded bar. The smoke caused my eyes to become irritated. Country music blared from the speakers around the room's corners as the sound of billiard balls hitting one another rang out. "Do you want another round?" the bartender asked me.

I nodded.

Heavy hands dropped down hard on my shoulders. Pushing myself to a standing position, I turned around with my fight stance ready. I was prepared for anything that might be coming my way.

"Calm down, buddy," Joe called out.

He had lifted his hands above his head in surrender.

"Sorry, Joe."

I relaxed my stance. We shook hands before we pulled each other into a tight bear hug.

Joe has been my best friend since ninth grade. His family had moved to Florida from New Jersey because his father had accepted a job opportunity. We had been inseparable since the first day we met in English class. Joe was enlisted into the army at eighteen, one month after we graduated. It was hard saying 'see you soon' to my best friend, but I knew he had to follow his dreams of protecting our country. He served for four years before he returned to Florida and got a fantastic job working for the state.

"How have you been doing?" he asked.

We sat at the bar. The bartender came over and filled my glass.

"I'm dealing. How are you?" I took a sip of my drink.

"I'll take a shot of vodka," Joe called out to the bartender.

He placed his attention on me. "I'm great. It's not like Brad to just be dealing."

"I have a lot going on right now." I wrapped

my hand around my glass.

"Must be. The guys haven't seen you in months. They have been worried about you. I have been worried about you."

The bartender gave Joe his vodka, and he took a sip.

I felt bad as I had been missing out on our once-a-month sporting events. We would either host the events at each other's houses or host at different bars in our area. Once a year, we would travel to the stadium and watch in person.

"I want to apologize for my absence."

"You don't have to apologize to me."

"Thank you."

A burden lifted off my chest. I knew Joe, of all people, would understand.

"Are Kyla and Bria still gone?"

I nodded as a song I favored from a young child came through the speakers.

"I hired a private investigator a little over two months ago."

"I can't believe she has stayed gone for this long."

"Tell me about it."

I took another sip of my drink.

"How do you think she is managing to survive without you?" Joe asked.

All my friends were aware of how I took care of Kyla and Bria. They knew Kyla had it made with me since she didn't have to work, and I took care of all the financial burdens that came along the way.

"I'm not sure."

A slim manicured hand landed on my left shoulder. I turned, and a blonde with green eyes stood behind me.

She pulled the empty bar stool back that sat next to me. In a seductive manner, she sat down.

"Hi, handsome," she purred, focusing on me.

"Hello."

I did a quick once-over of her. She was beyond gorgeous with wavy, ash-blonde hair that stopped right above her ample breasts. She had striking sea-green eyes that could stare deep into your soul. The woman wore a pair of light blue high-waisted jeans and a white halter crop top blouse that stopped right above her pierced belly button that accentuated her breasts.

The woman captured the bartender's attention.

"The usual."

Within seconds, the bartender popped the top off a Busch Light beer and had it in front of her.

"Thank you, darling."

She brought the drink to her lips and tipped it back.

"You must be a regular here," I said.

"I am. I don't believe I have seen you here before. What is your name?"

She spun a piece of hair around her index finger. Somehow, she made that one gesture seem ravishing.

"Brad."

I glanced over at Joe, who winked at me before he smiled. "What is your name?"

"I'm Kate."

"It's nice to meet you, Kate."

I took another sip of my drink.

"Brad, what do you say we get out of here and go back to my place?" she asked as he went into her purse and pulled out lipstick.

She opened the lipstick up and applied a thin layer of red lipstick to her scrumptious lips.

I took a big gulp of my drink, a burning sensation warming the back of my throat. It took everything in my bones not to take Kate up on her amazing offer. Closing my eyes, I took a deep breath.

"That sounds like a wonderful offer, but I must decline."

Kate's gaze intensified as she reached into her purse and pulled out a ripped piece of paper.

"Here is my phone number if you change your mind."

I clutched the piece of paper tight in my hand. Kate leaned over and placed a wet kiss on my left cheek before she grabbed her beer and walked away.

"What in the hell was that?" Joe asked with wide eyes before he took a sip of his drink.

"Me turning down a woman?"

"Hell, yes. She was smoking hot." Joe attempted to locate Kate in the bar with his eyes.

I tossed the piece of paper over to Joe. "You can have her if you want her." My voice was monotone.

Joe picked up the piece of paper and examined it.

"Why didn't you take her up on her offer?"

"She's not Kyla."

My eyes zeroed in on a bottle of liquor behind the counter.

"Didn't you say Kyla left you?"

Nodding, my mind pondered what Kyla could be doing now. How did she not need me? Kyla needed me for the last five years. How did Bria not need me? She was my baby girl, and I was her father. Did Bria even miss me? Perhaps Kyla had someone new in her life, and he pretended to be Bria's father. Did she ask about where I was? Did she even ask about me? Or did she forget about me these several months that she had been away?

"Then why are you so hell-bent on her?" Joe took another sip of his drink.

A low growl rumbled in my chest as I looked over at Joe with outrage in my eyes. Within a quick second, I was on my feet with Joe's shirt collar balled up in my hands. Joe's eyes widened with disturbance as our faces were only mere inches apart.

"Don't you ever question me about my decisions," I sneered.

"Calm down, Brad," Joe warned me sternly.

Joe knew better than to make any sudden movements.

"Hey, you. Get the hell out of this bar. There

is not going to be fighting in here," the bartender yelled as he pointed at me.

Giving Joe a hard push in the chest, I released my grip on him.

I stormed out of the bar into the still night air. Taking deep breaths, I raked my hands through my hair. Why would Joe question me on the best thing to have ever walked into my life?

My phone sounded. Looking around the empty parking lot, I pulled the phone out of my pocket. My heart beat wildly when I saw Justin's name on the screen.

"Hello, this is Brad," I said, heading towards my SUV in the parking lot.

"Hey Brad, this is Justin. Do you have time to talk for a few minutes?"

"Yes, I do."

Approaching my vehicle, I unlocked it and slid into the driver's seat.

"So it took a lot of investigating, but I located Kyla and your daughter Bria."

Letting out a sigh of relief, I was grateful that the several months of not knowing and sorrow were coming to an end.

"Where are they?"

"That information will be provided once I have my remaining 25%."

"Where can I meet you?"

My SUV roared to life.

"Meet me in the parking lot of the grocery store on the Avenue."

"I will be there."

Hanging up the phone, I unlocked my glove box. I pulled out my emergency envelope full of cash. I fingered through the bills before I backed out of the bar's parking lot. As I pulled out, I saw Joe coming out of the bar. He waved his hand to get my attention, but only one thing was on my mind. Getting the location of my girls. I drove to the grocery store, my eyes landing on Justin's black Acura sedan.

Stepping out of my SUV, I approached Justin. I handed over the envelope full of cash. He opened the envelope and fingered through the bills. Once his counting resulted in complete satisfaction, he gave me his attention.

"Using the pictures you provided me started out as rather difficult."

"Can you further elaborate?" I asked as Justin leaned his body against his car.

"Kyla has bangs now."

"Wow. Are you serious?" I could only imagine what Kyla looked like with bangs. I was never a fan of bangs so she could never get them. She had made changes since she left me.

"Yes, it stalled my investigation for about a week."

"Well, are they still living in the United States? Or did she take my daughter to another country?"

"They are living in a town called Branchville. Branchville is in South Carolina."

"I always imagined she would've gone farther than just South Carolina." It was great to know my family was only two states over and not in another country.

"She did abandon her vehicle at that shopping mall. She purchased an older, silver Honda from someone she interacted with online."

I shook my head in disgust. I could not believe the information that I received.

"How was I unable to find any information on her when I did my investigations?"

"Well, you're not a professional." Justin pointed out the obvious in a slick tone that I did not favor. "That is where my expertise comes at an advantage. Kyla managed to hide under the radar."

If Justin was not providing me with the information I needed, I would have given him a piece of my mind. Instead, I responded, "Well, how did she manage to do that?"

"She has not been using any social media since she left."

"So, you are telling me that she's been hiding in plain sight since she has not been using social media?"

"I didn't say that. She has been going by a fake name to disguise herself. I am sure she took that route, so you wouldn't be able to find her if you had decided to search for her."

"What name has she been using?"

"She has been going by the name Tiffany Franklin."

Tiffany Franklin. Nodding, it became clear that Kyla had outsmarted me. Never had I imagined Kyla would go by a fake name. Never would I have considered trying to search for her by using another name. I could not believe Kyla had changed her appearance.

"I need you to provide me with their new address. I'm planning to make a surprise visit."

Chapter Nineteen

Kyla

Maneuvering through the maze of tables in the coffee shop, I delivered my favorite regulars, their medium decaf black coffees and plain bagels with lite cream cheese.

"Thank you, dear," Mrs. Smith stated.

"Can you two try your coffee for me? I want to make sure it's not too bitter like it was yesterday."

Mr. and Mrs. Smith took careful sips of their coffee. "It's perfect," Mr. Smith commented. Mrs. Smith nodded in agreement.

"Perfect. Enjoy."

Walking past one of my other tables, I observed an empty coffee mug. Grabbing the mug, I went behind the counter where Scott had just finished making a fresh pot of caffeinated coffee. I poured my customer a fresh mug of coffee and delivered it to the table.

"Thank you."

She glanced at me before she went back to reading the book that was in her hand.

"You are welcome."

I did a quick scan of the book cover, which piqued my interest.

"If you don't mind me asking, how do you like that book?"

The customer closed the book to give me a full view of the book. "So far, it's a phenomenal book."

"What is it about?"

"An abused woman that decides enough is enough. She packs up her child and is determined to start another life."

My heart skipped a beat. That book sounded just like my old life. "I hope she succeeds," I responded when I could find my voice.

As I was about to attend another one of my tables, hands were thrown over my eyes. Excitement entered my body instead of terror. Spinning around in a 180-degree circle, I removed the hands from over my eyes to see that Ryan stood in front of me. He wore a gray suit with a light blue tie.

"Hi, beautiful." Ryan wrapped his arms around my waist, pulling me into a warm embrace. His scent filled my nose, causing me to relax.

"Hello, handsome." Our lips locked as the familiar scent of spearmint floated around me. "Go ahead and take your seat. I'll have your order up in a minute."

"I'll take my order to go this morning."

"How come you are not staying?"

"I have an important meeting I have to attend." Pulling his phone out of his pocket, he checked the time. To my surprise, the screen contained a picture of us on one of our dates. "It starts in forty-five minutes."

"I hope your meeting goes great." I led Ryan to the counter. Scott waved at Ryan before he went to make his Americano.

"Thank you. I am nervous."

"You have no reason to be nervous."

Placing Ryan's muffin in a plastic container, I handed it to him.

"Hey, Ryan," Sabrina said as she smiled. She walked by, carrying two coffees.

"Hey, Sabrina." Ryan turned his attention to me. "Our investors are coming this morning, so it's a big deal."

"There is no doubt in my mind that you will wow those investors with your hard work and dedication."

"Thank you, beautiful."

Scott poured Ryan's Americano into a paper

cup and walked it over to him.

"I can give you words of encouragement all day but I know you will do great," I said.

Ryan thanked Scott for the drink. "I am going to head on to work. I'll call or text you later."

Ryan kissed my forehead. "I love you," he purred against my forehead.

"I love you too."

Ryan walked towards the door. I watched as he held the door open for an older man that approached the coffee shop door. The man walked into the coffee shop. He nodded as a thank you. My heart warmed inside as Ryan was always a true gentleman. It was not a facade he pretended to have only while in public.

"Someone is in love," Scott sang.

Turning my attention to Scott, I smiled. "That is true. I've never felt love like this a day in my life."

"You don't have to voice it."

"Why do you say that?"

"Tiffany, it's written all over your face."

"Are you and Vanessa in love yet?"

I had the need in my heart for everyone to feel the love that I could experience. It wasn't love itself that made me ecstatic. It was the person who I was in love with that made me experience those feelings.

"We've been dating for two months now. I believe I am, but I haven't had the nerve to voice it yet."

"Don't wait too long to tell her."

My phone rang.

Pulling my phone out of my pocket, an unknown number flashed across the screen. Taking a scan of my surroundings, I took a deep breath. I had not given this phone number out to too many people.

"Hello."

"Hello."

The voice was unfamiliar.

"Am I speaking with Kyla Williams?"

I sighed in relief as I realized it was not Brad's voice on the other end of the phone.

"Yes, it is. May I ask who is calling?"

"My name is Ashley, and I am calling from Tree Branch."

My heart pounded hard in my chest.

"Hello, Ashley."

I made a beeline for the front door.

"How are you doing today?" she asked, making small talk as I walked outside into the parking lot.

I walked down the sidewalk, so I was not in front of the doorway.

"I'm okay but hoping to be doing even better by the end of this phone call."

Enthusiasm oozed into my voice.

"All of us at Tree Branch hope the same for you as well. We do have some positive news to share with you."

"Did you find my mother or father? Did you find them both? I cannot wait to meet them."

I couldn't keep my excitement at bay.

Ashley gave off a chuckle over the phone.

"I'll explain to you how our services work first. Individuals reach out to us in search of family. We can only locate individuals who come to us hoping to use our services."

"Who were you able to locate?"

Anticipation ate at me as I watched a yellow car drive through the parking lot.

"We located your Aunt Liliana."

"Aunt Liliana," I whispered to myself.

I had no knowledge that I even had an aunt. The wonderful news was a symphony to my ears.

"Is she my aunt on my mother's side or my father's side?"

"Liliana is your mother's sister," she clarified.

Delight washed over me as I could not stop myself from smiling.

"Where does Liliana live?"

"She lives in Washington, Seattle."

My enthusiasm sizzled. Meeting my aunt in person was not going to happen. She was on the other side of the country. There was no way I could afford to take time off from work to take such a trip at this time.

"Are you still there?" she asked as I had not responded.

"I'm here."

The defeat set in that I would not be able to see my aunt in person, but I was still looking forward to at least chatting with her over the phone or on video chat.

"Are you busy the first Saturday of next

month?"

"No, why do you ask?"

"I have already spoken with Liliana before I called you. She wanted me to confirm if she could fly to South Carolina so you two can meet face to face."

My mouth dropped open. I could not believe Liliana had already planned to meet me before I received a call about her.

"That would be perfect."

My voice cracked with those four words, on the verge of tears. It was difficult to believe I would meet a family member in less than a month.

"With your verbal consent, I will provide your aunt with a phone number to contact you. After that, it'll be your responsibility to keep in contact with her."

"You don't have to worry about that. There is no way I am losing contact with my family ever again," I reassured her. However, waiting for such an extended amount of time to meet a family member, I would not take this opportunity for granted.

"Liliana will be reaching out to you soon. Congratulations on your wonderful news. We would love to hear from you and hear how your first meeting goes."

"Thank you so much, Ashley."

Hanging up the phone, I did a victory dance. This had to be a similar feeling that people experienced when they won the lottery.

Sending Ryan a text to call me after his meeting, I headed back to the coffee shop. Nothing could bring my mood down.

Chapter Twenty

Kyla

My phone jingled. Reaching my hand into my pocket, I pulled it out while keeping one hand attached to the steering wheel as I answered the phone.

"Hey."

"Hey. Where are you two?" he asked.

"We are about ten minutes away."

"Okay, good. I just wanted to check to make sure you two are fine."

"Sorry, we are running late. Sabrina and I just could not stop talking."

"You don't have to apologize. I know all too well how you and Sabrina get when you two get together."

"Thank you for being so understanding. Bria and I will see you soon."

Ending the phone call, my eyes flickered to the rearview mirror to look at Bria.

Bria looked out the window, watching nature pass by as her head bobbed to the music that played through the speakers.

"Are we almost there, Mommy?"

"Yes, we are, Sweetie. Only a few more minutes."

Within a few miles, we turned off the highway and onto a single-lane road. Up in the far distance, I could see Ryan's car pulled over on the shoulder of the road. As I parked behind Ryan's car, he appeared. He wore a pair of khaki shorts and a red shirt from a path between a range of trees.

We got out of the car as Ryan approached us. Bria ran up to Ryan as he squatted down, and she jumped into his arms. He rubbed her back as she wrapped her arms around his neck and hugged him. Making my way over to them, I kissed Ryan.

"What is this place?" I looked around. Nothing more than trees was visible.

"You will find out soon enough. Come, follow me."

He led the way down the path.

Following Ryan and Bria, we walked from

where Ryan had just come from. We walked a quarter of a mile through the forest before the forest opened up to a spacious clearing. In the middle of the clearing was a picnic basket that sat on a blanket with two totes. Off several feet away was a picturesque calm lake outlined by an array of flowers.

"Oh my goodness." I admired mother nature displayed before me.

"What do you think?" He placed Bria on the ground. Bria ran over to the totes and rummaged through them.

"This place is spectacular." I was in complete awe. "How did you find this place? It's in the middle of nowhere."

"Someone I had met a while ago told me about this place. I had to come to see it for myself."

Bria had taken out wooden blocks from the totes, and she played with them.

"That someone is a genius and has an eye for serene locations. I wonder how they found this place."

"He is a painter. He finds the unique locations to do his paintings. Come follow me."

Ryan took my hand and walked me about fifteen feet away. He placed me in front of him and pointed his finger over my shoulder into the distance. "What do you see?"

Squinting my eyes, I saw what he pointed at. It was a low-hanging tree that was suspended over a calm lake.

"Is that the inspiration for the painting in your house?" I looked over to where Bria was. Her mind was still occupied by the blocks.

"Yes, it is." His voice boomed with confidence.

"Do you know the painter?"

"No. I attended an art gallery a while back to purchase some paintings. I fell in love with that image."

"It is a phenomenal image."

"After I purchased the painting, he found me right after, and we had an extensive conversation about his painting."

"Is he an emerging artist?"

Ryan nodded. "He just started in the industry. His talent and expertise are mind-blowing."

I agreed with him. "If he is in the early stages of his career and painting such intricate detail, he will create masterpieces. I wonder how he found this place. I haven't seen anything more scenic than this."

Ryan shrugged his shoulders as he stuffed his hands into his pocket. "That must be one of the pros of being an artist. Traveling and finding the perfect image to create."

"If only I could've been born with artistic genes."

"Perhaps you were," he began. "You won't know until you meet with your aunt."

"Even if my aunt were to tell me my mother or father was a maestro, it has been proven it skipped a generation."

"Don't ever doubt your capabilities. You are more than able to become anything you never thought was possible. You just have to set your mind to it."

"Somehow, you manage to make the doubt that I have go away."

"I'm glad I can do that." Ryan took his hands out of his pockets. "Now, you have to do something for me."

Looking over at Bria, she pulled out a container of bubbles. She found the jackpot that would keep her mind engaged. "What is that something?"

"I would love to capture a picture of you lounging on that tree."

I looked over at the tree again before I looked at him. "Are you serious?"

"As a heart attack. My desire to capture this moment in time might seem all too selfish. My favorite place and my favorite woman."

I smiled as I looked down at my outfit. "I would love to, but I am not dressed for such a picture."

I wore a pair of dark blue jean shorts and a gray T-shirt.

"You always look amazing, no matter what you are wearing."

Bria ran in front of us, blowing her bubbles.

"Okay."

Ryan walked Bria back over to the picnic set up. "Can you play right here until Mommy and I do something?" he asked her.

"Yes." She sat and focused on blowing as many bubbles as possible.

Ryan returned to me, and we walked over to the tree together.

"Please be careful," he said.

He assisted me with getting on the tree. Once I was comfortable, I maneuvered my body to lean back on my elbows and strike a pose.

"How is this?"

"Stunning."

He snapped pictures of me on his phone. Confidence radiated off me as I moved my body into a few more poses. I felt like a supermodel on a photo shoot.

After several minutes of taking pictures, Ryan helped me off the tree, and we walked over to where Bria sat. She had several bubbles floating in the air and was on her way to making more.

"Are you two ready for lunch?" Ryan asked.

"Yes." I sat on the blanket.

"Not right now. I'm blowing bubbles," Bria murmured as she brought the wand to her mouth and blew more bubbles.

"Yes, right now. You can blow bubbles later."

Bria pouted as she put the wand back into the container. She sat on the blanket, her arms folded across her chest. The pout disappeared when I handed her my phone.

Ryan sat next to me. He pulled out sandwiches, chips, and water bottles from the basket. We started eating and talking while Bria watched videos.

"Where did your love of collecting art come from?" I took a bite of the turkey sandwich.

"My mother always had an eye for the arts." A butterfly caught our attention as it traveled right between us. "She used to take us to a museum twice a month. Art galleries that were hosted by her friends for charity."

"Did you favor art at a young age?"

Ryan ate a few of his chips. "Heck no. My mother had to drag me to all the museums and art galleries. When I turned sixteen, it all changed."

"Do you and your mother still do those activities together?"

"Every now and again when our schedules don't clash."

"What do your parents do for a living?"

"My mother is an accountant, and my father is an anesthesiologist."

"You come from a family of success." I took a sip of my bottled water.

"I wouldn't go to that extreme. My parents did work hard to get to the positions that they are in, though."

"It must be such an accomplishment to work hard to gain success all on your own."

"Where are you going with this?" He gulped down some water from his water bottle as he eyed me.

"Brad's success was handed down to him. He didn't put in extra hours and sweat. Just because he is an only child, he is set for life."

"Well, that is what happens when you date a trust fund baby." His response was followed by a slight chuckle as I ate my sandwich.

Raising my eyebrows, I swallowed the food that was in my mouth.

"Are you joking right now?"

I was taken aback by his response.

"What do you mean?"

I rolled my eyes as I sat my sandwich down, sarcasm in my posture. "It is mind-blowing for you to sit in front of me calling someone else a trust fund baby when you grew up with a silver spoon in your mouth."

"Just because my parents worked hard and provided me with a life where I didn't have to worry about hunger does not classify me as having a silver spoon in my mouth."

I took a deep breath. His response to not having to worry about his next meal hit me hard. I glanced over at Bria, who was occupied in the video she watched. As she brought the sandwich to her mouth and took a bite, I could tell she was not even aware of an argument. I wanted to keep it that way.

"That house that I live in was purchased with all the finances I earned on my own." Ryan raised his voice an octave higher.

"Are you expecting me to give you an award and congratulations for taking care of yourself? That is what you should do when you become an adult and have real-life responsibilities."

Irritation was clear in my voice.

Ryan laughed as he scratched at the hair on his chin.

"I cannot believe the words coming out of your mouth."

"What is so funny?"

"The turn this conversation has taken is hilarious."

"I wish I could laugh right along with you, but I find nothing that was said funny."

"I cannot believe you mentioned real-life responsibilities."

He wrapped his sandwich up, and he looked into my eyes.

"This statement comes from the woman who decided to stay in an abusive relationship for five years because she was afraid of those real-life responsibilities."

Ryan spewed words out of his mouth that was laced with venom.

My heart skipped a beat right before it shattered into a million fragments. Searching the eyes of the man I fell in love with, I could not find a single emotion as my entire world was utterly destroyed. The back of my eyes burned as my throat formed a lump of emotion I could not swallow. As a tear fell onto my cheek, I pushed myself up to stand.

"Bria, it's time to go," I choked out as I held my hand out to her.

"I'm not done with my lunch yet," Bria said.

Ryan stood up.

"I will make you some food when we get

home."

"I don't want to leave. I want to play with the bubbles."

Bria pouted as her lip trembled.

"She can take the bubbles with her," Ryan suggested.

"Bria, you can play when you get home." I ignored his comment entirely. "Now let's go," I said, trying to maintain a stern voice, but it shook with a sob.

"Kyla..." Ryan began as Bria took my hand, and we walked in the direction of the car.

"I don't have anything else to say," I responded.

"You can't walk away from me like this. Please hear me out."

He continued to follow us.

"I must go. I suggest that you don't follow."

Picking Bria up in my arms, I walked to the car. Looking once down the path, Ryan stared at me as he stood several yards away. Another tear fell from my eyes as I slipped into my car and drove off, leaving the broken pieces of my heart behind on the forest ground.

Chapter Twenty-One

Kyla

"It is great to see you."

Sitting down on the lounge chair right next to Sabrina, I handed her a chilled glass of freshly squeezed lemonade.

"You see me almost every day," Sabrina pointed out as she laughed.

"That is true. I guess I meant to say that we can never just sit down and talk for hours on end with no interruption."

"If only we could get paid to just talk."

She took a sip of her lemonade.

"I would be more than willing to work overtime every day for that."

We looked out in the yard where Bria and Emily played in her sandbox. Bria shoveled sand into the bucket Emily held.

"There is a way for us to get paid just to have conversations."

"How so?"

I took a sip of my lemonade. I looked over at Sabrina, ready for her to announce her grand idea.

"We could become co-hosts of a TV talk show."

I tapped my finger on my lips. "What a wonderful idea that would be but…"

"But you are too chicken to talk in front of a million people," Sabrina finished for me.

"It's called being an introvert."

We both laughed at my comment.

"Well, let's convert you into an extrovert."

"If only it were that simple."

I took another sip of my lemonade.

"I can picture us talking about the latest gossip all day." She ran her fingers through her hair.

"Such as what styles are considered in and what styles are last season?" I suggested.

"Which celebrity decided to elope over the weekend?"

"What music is on the top ten charts this week?"

"Exactly. We would find enjoyment in

discussing all those topics."

"I can't help but agree with you."

"You know we would be amazing at it," she stated as she sipped her lemonade.

"Only one thing is stopping us from having that dream come true."

"What?"

"We aren't even close to being qualified for that job."

"How are you so sure?" she asked me as we watched the girls build a castle.

"Remember when I told you about Amy?" Sabrina nodded. "She and I used to watch talk shows. In most cases, they only look for individuals that have obtained a degree."

"Darn it." Sabrina thought for a few moments. "Wait, if we are famous, I'm sure a degree wouldn't matter."

"Yeah, I agree with you. There is only one problem."

"What is that?"

"We are not famous, and I doubt we ever will be."

"Well, it's best to come to terms with that. Getting paid to talk all day won't be happening."

She let out a sigh of disappointment.

Sipping on my lemonade, silence settled upon me.

"What are you thinking about?"

Looking over at Sabrina, I shrugged my shoulders. "Just what it would be like to be on a TV show as a host."

"If you were a TV host, what question would you want to ask?"

The girls ran over to the table and drank some of their water.

Staring off into space, I went deep into thought.

"What is a common experience for many people you've never had the opportunity to experience but would love to experience one day?"

Sabrina nodded as the girls went back to their castle. "That's a good question."

"Well, I would love your honest answer."

Sabrina smiled as she tucked a piece of hair behind her ear. "Hmm. I would have to say I never was adventurous."

"How come?"

"As we both experienced, we became mothers at a young age. You know as well as I do how difficult it is to have time to do what you desire. There was no time for partying. No time to just pack a bag and leave for a week. There was only time to be a mommy to my precious baby girl and a wife to my husband."

"It's never too late to experience that adventure. Hell, I would love to experience it with you."

"One day, we will have to make plans. So, what would your answer be?"

A few moments passed. "College."

"College?" She raised an eyebrow.

"Yes. In high school, it was always suggested that

college was the pathway to success in life."

"Do you believe that is true?"

"I'm not sure. I just know I always wanted to experience that success, but I never had that opportunity."

"You do know it's never too late to go to college?"

I nodded. "I know, but it would be too difficult to do now. Working full-time and taking care of Bria is all I can handle right now."

"I understand. Remember, if you ever decide to take that step, you are more than capable. You are intelligent and gifted. You can do anything that you set your mind to."

"Thank you for the encouragement."

"Anything for my best friend."

Sabrina took a sip of her lemonade before she smiled at me.

"I'm dying to know what question you would ask if you were on a talk show."

"Who do you wish you could get back in contact with?"

I looked over at Sabrina with a smirk on my face.

"Did you even think about your question?"

Sabrina laughed as she shook her head.

"This is not the first time I've thought about what I would want to ask if I were on a talk show."

"It seems as if your lifelong goal is to become a TV host."

"Yeah, it is one of my goals. Stop avoiding my question. What would your answer be?"

"Well, the obvious answer would be my family, but I don't recall ever having contact with them. So, my answer would have to be Amy. I'd love to know how she was doing, how her life had changed since the last time we saw each other five years ago."

"I would love to reconnect with Sidney."

Sabrina bent over as she scratched at a spot on her leg.

"Sidney was your best friend from elementary school, right?"

"Yes. We didn't have cell phones back then, so keeping in touch was not possible."

"Have you ever thought about looking Amy up online?"

I twiddled my fingers. "That has crossed my mind, but I am not too sure she would even want to talk to me."

Sabrina reached over and rubbed my shoulder. "I'm sure she would love to hear from you."

I shook my head. "I allowed Brad to prevent us from speaking to each other."

"You cannot blame yourself for that separation. You did what you had to do to survive, and I never want to hear you blame yourself again."

I smiled as I nodded. "So, are you going to try to find Sidney?"

Sabrina shook her head. "There are too many Sidneys in this world to even attempt a search without a last name."

As I was about to respond, my phone jingled. When I looked at the screen, I huffed as I put it back into my pocket without answering.

"Are you okay?" Sabrina asked as she raised her eyebrows.

"Yes, I am. I just don't want to talk to him." My eyes settled on Bria.

"Ryan?"

"Yeah. He calls every day. I am unsure why he is still calling when I have not returned any calls."

"I thought you two were back on speaking terms."

Shaking my head, I took a sip of my lemonade. "Not at all."

"Kyla."

"Yes?" I looked at Sabrina.

"It has been two weeks."

"I'm well aware."

Truth be told, I missed Ryan's voice. I missed his magnetic presence. I missed his muscular arms being wrapped around me, making me feel safe and secure.

"When are you going to have a conversation with him?" Sabrina tucked her hair behind her ear.

"I'm not sure."

Sabrina took a deep breath and exhaled. "I understand what he said was horrible. I am not excusing the choice of words. You have to look at the big picture. He has apologized to you nonstop. When do you think you'll be ready to talk with him?"

"It has been a long, agonizing fourteen days." I knew because I had kept count.

"Can I tell you something?"

"Of course, you can tell me anything."

"I am telling you this because I love you with all my heart. I only want to see you happy. Please don't allow your pride to stand in the way of your happiness."

I allowed Sabrina's words of wisdom to sink in. "I will invite him over later to talk."

Sabrina smiled as she rubbed my shoulder. "You won't regret it, I promise."

After Sabrina and Emily went home a few hours later, I took Sabrina's advice and invited Ryan over. It was time for us to sit and have a well-overdue conversation.

Within the hour, the doorbell rang. I smoothed my hands over my light-yellow shirt and dark blue jean shorts as I approached the door.

Opening the door, I looked at Ryan. He wore a pair of gray pants and a light blue shirt. Ryan smiled, which didn't quite reach his eyes.

"Hello," he said.

"Hi."

"You look beautiful as ever."

"Thank you. Come on in."

Ryan walked in as I closed the door behind him. He walked over to the couch and sat down.

Lingering near the door, I fumbled with my hands as I looked over at Ryan.

"Why are you being shy?" he asked.

"I'm not."

I forced my feet to make the brief journey over to the couch.

"I want to start this conversation by thanking you for inviting me to talk."

"There is no need to thank me. I have been avoiding this conversation long enough."

"Regret has been eating at me since those words rolled off my tongue."

I listened as I locked eyes with Ryan. Searching his eyes, they were full of the emotion they had lacked weeks prior. This was the Ryan I knew and loved with all my heart.

"You are one of the strongest individuals I have ever met in my entire life. I can't fathom how you dealt with your situation for five years. I am in no position to judge you for the decisions you made in your life. I'm sure Bria was the only thing in mind when you made those hard decisions. Will you forgive me for the horrible things I said to you?"

Taking the words in that Ryan said, I knew his apology was authentic. I nodded.

"Of course I forgive you."

A genuine smile reached Ryan's eyes as he wrapped his arms around me. placed my ear on his chest.

Inhaling his familiar scent, my body relaxed in the comfort of his arms. I missed listening to his heart's rhythm.

"It is only right for me to apologize to you."

"Apologize to me for what?" Ryan took my hand once our hug ended.

"For stating you grew up with a silver spoon in your mouth."

"It's fine. I was just grateful my parents provided me with the upbringing they did."

"We were both in the wrong that day." I looked up at him, spearmint wafting off his breath.

"It was torturous not hearing your voice." Ryan tucked a strand of hair behind my ear. His hand brushing against my ear caused my body to shiver. I missed his touch. Two weeks was a long time.

"It was agonizing not having your presence around me."

"I have never felt that alone a day in my life." His admission shocked me.

"You never needed to feel alone."

"Why do you say that?" He raised an eyebrow.

"Your work has been your companion until the day I came into your life."

Ryan smirked as he nodded. "That is what happens when no one has ever captured my attention as you have done."

"Are you saying I'm special?" My voice oozed with flirtation.

"You make me happy in a way no one else could even have the capability." He paused. "I'd like to say you hold a special place in my heart."

"Well, you aren't so bad yourself."

"Is that so?"

I nodded as I looked at his lips. "What is on your mind?"

I cleared my throat and brushed my thumb across Ryan's lip. "How I desire to kiss your soft lips."

"What is stopping you?"

Leaning forward with a bit of aggression, my lips crashed onto his. It was as if my mouth depended on his to survive. He grabbed the back of my head and held me against his body. I could not move, and I didn't want to. Boy, how I missed those lips.

Chapter Twenty-Two

Brad

I looked around the busy building that I was in as I sat in the uncomfortable black chair. Salesmen scuttled all around, attending to their customers that was willing to hand over large amounts of money.

Frank, my salesman, walked back over to the desk. In his hands was a stack of papers that he had placed in front of me.

"All you have to do is sign these documents on the highlighted areas, and you'll be all set with your new vehicle."

Flipping through the documents, I scanned over the significant information that most dealerships hid in the small print. Once satisfied with the information, I picked up the fancy blue pen and signed away.

"I will need the keys to the vehicle you are trading," Frank said, pointing at the keys I held onto for dear life.

Even though I had signed papers for a new vehicle, handing over the keys to my most prized possession was difficult. When I purchased it, I spent hours at this same car dealership designing the top-of-the-line vehicle I had envisioned for my first vehicle. Unfortunately, due to limited time, there was no time for all the customizations as I was on a mission. I wasn't trading Kyla's car in. I was hopeful she would want her car back once I found her and talked to her.

The salesman pried the keys out of my hands as there was no other option. The only way I would pull off stalking Kyla was to get rid of my black SUV, which she knew all too well.

Once the car deal was completed and I was the proud owner of a white BMW sedan, I walked outside into the afternoon brightness. I transferred my two packed suitcases to my new car.

"Congratulations on your new car."

"Thanks," I responded nonchalantly.

"Are you traveling somewhere?"

Stopping to look at Frank, I contemplated my answer. He looked as if he cared, but I knew it was because I just gave him a much-needed deal.

"Yes, I'm going to visit my daughter."

"I hope you enjoy your trip. Call me if you need anything or have any questions concerning your new vehicle."

"Thanks, Frank."

I closed the trunk of my car. Sliding into my new, unfamiliar car, I started it up. The cool air blasted out in full effect as I attempted to teach myself the improvements with the newer model.

Tapping the touch screen, I inputted Kyla's new address. An eight in a half hour's drive needed to be done. Relaxing in my seat, I turned my radio onto my favorite station. If I was going to make an eight-and-a-half-hour trip, it would be jamming out to country music.

As I navigated the highway, my mind pondered over the last five years I spent with Kyla. There were times I didn't treat her the best. I thought she would've realized that no relationship was perfect. But I couldn't fathom how she assumed anyone would treat her better than I had.

As my vehicle made its way out of the sunshine state and into the peach state, the day turned into night. I became more anxious as time passed by. I was much closer to seeing my baby girl and my girlfriend every second of the hour and mile of the hundred that was driven. It was a long time coming. To think I never married Kyla because I was fearful of being tied down to one woman for the rest of my life. I regret the decision now.

My phone rang, making sound travel throughout the vehicle speakers. The screen displayed Mom's name. I answered.

"Hello."

"Hello, Sweetheart. What are you up to?"

"I'm just out taking a drive."

My parents didn't need to know I would track down Kyla and Bria alone. They had made me swear to inform them when I had information from the private investigator, and I had neglected to do so. This was my battle to deal with on my own. I hated lying to them, but they gave me no other choice.

"When are you going to be back home?" Mom asked.

"I'm not sure yet. Probably in four or five hours. I can call you when I get back home, though."

A yellow and black striped sports car passed me, zooming by at an accelerated speed.

"Yeah, that would be great."

"Perfect. I'll chat with you later."

I was ready to get off the phone.

"Wait. Have you heard from the private investigator yet?"

"Not yet," I lied through my teeth.

"Oh my goodness. For the private investigator to take this long, there is no telling where Kyla could have taken Bria."

Mom's voice had a bit of worry in it.

"I'm hopeful we will hear something soon."

I tried to lighten the mood my mother had put herself in. I wanted to inform my parents of the wonderful news but had to make this trip alone. I created this mess I was in and would solve it alone.

"I hope so. Have a safe drive, and I will talk with you later."

"Okay. I love you, Mom."

"I love you too."

Ending the call, a feeling of guilt washed over me. I hated lying to my parents. I lied to them about minor occurrences, such as sneaking out of the house at sixteen to drink and party with my friends in our secluded hangout in the woods. I had never lied to them about anything major, but they had given me no choice.

Taking a deep breath, I pushed my guilt to the side. I was on a mission and couldn't allow the conversation with my mother to throw me off.

Reaching over, I turned my country music up louder than before. The past five and a half hours were a breeze as there was steady, paced traffic and no delays. I hoped the last three hours were going to be the same.

"In four miles, please get off on the next exit," the maps app instructed me.

My mood brightened as I was only a few miles away from my daughter and girlfriend. When I approached the exit, I made my way off the highway.

Even though nightfall had arrived and it was

dark out, it was clear how different Branchville was from Miami. Branchville was filled with open land that was lined with a multitude of trees. Miami was filled with tall, extensive buildings that sat on top of one another. This area was the opposite of what Kyla had known her entire life. What could have possessed her to move to a place like this?

Traveling another five miles north, I approached the street that Kyla and Bria lived on. The houses were spread out more in this area than I was used to. I was about to switch the lights off my vehicle when I remembered this was a vehicle Kyla was unfamiliar with.

"Your destination will be on the right," the maps app stated.

Turning onto the street, I did a quick survey of both sides of the road.

I looked at a small bungalow-style on the right-hand side of the street. I couldn't tell the house's color as it was too dark to make out. Sitting in the driveway was a light-colored Honda sedan. This house was where my baby girl and girlfriend were now living.

Traveling at the rate of a turtle in front of the house, I decided to pick up my speed to drive to the end of the street and turn back around. I did not want Kyla to look outside and become suspicious of a vehicle hanging outside her house. As I drove by a second time slowly, I could see the lights on inside the house. From the looks of things, Kyla didn't have company as only her vehicle was in the driveway.

It took every ounce of my being to wrench myself away. I pressed my foot on the gas pedal. I could not make my move now. I had to wait for the perfect time to bring my presence to their attention.

Driving back toward the highway, I headed to the small hotel I had passed. That hotel would be my new home for the duration of my stay.

Pulling into an empty parking space, I observed only two other cars in the parking lot. This town was very remote and did not receive a lot of visitors.

Stepping out of my car, I raised my arms above my body as I stretched. I walked into the front office, where a man in his forties attended the desk.

"Hello. What can I do for you?" the front desk attendant asked, lacking every bit of enthusiasm.

I handed over my credit card and stated, "I need a nice room. I will be staying for a few weeks."

The man took my card and typed away on the desktop with his two index fingers. My eyes zeroed in on the dirt caked under his fingernails. After a painstaking five minutes, the keypad lit up in front of me. I grabbed the stylus pen and signed. Once signed, he handed me a key card.

"Enjoy your stay."

Walking out of the front office, I grabbed my suitcases from the trunk. Approaching my room, I entered my key card into the door. Once the light turned green, I walked in.

The basic room was cheap, with a queen-sized bed, a sofa, a small flat-screen TV, and a table for two.

Sitting my suitcases on the couch, I unpacked my luggage.

Stripping out of my clothes, I took a steaming hot shower. As the hot water trickled down my body, my mind drifted to my family. It had been months since I had last seen them. I knew Bria had grown in that time. I couldn't believe I had missed so many months of her life.

Sending a text to Mom, I informed her I had arrived home late and was going to crash. I hated lying, but I had no other choice.

For the first time in months, I went to sleep without the aid of my whiskey.

A melodious tune interrupted the deep sleep my body had settled in. After I could gather my bearings, I realized it was the alarm on my phone. Reaching my hand to the nightstand, I dismissed the alarm. Sitting up in bed, I stretched. Today would be a great day. I would get a visual of my family, and I could not keep my excitement at bay.

Once washed, I dressed in black jeans, a black T-shirt, and a black baseball hat. I stuffed a blue T-shirt into my back pocket just in case. The goal was to draw no attention to myself.

Walking out of my hotel room, it was still dark at five in the morning. I had to get to Kyla's house before they left to note her every move and routine.

Within minutes, I slowed down as I turned onto the street.

The blinds were raised, and the lights were on inside the house. Kyla and Bria were still inside, perhaps getting ready. One room was decorated with purple butterflies all over the walls. That must be Bria's room. The other room didn't have any decorations on the wall. That room must be Kyla's. Now I had a possible visual of the house layout. Driving to the end of the road, I could turn around just in time to see the house was now dark. Kyla and Bria walked out of the front door. It was shameful Kyla got Bria up early in the morning. I would be pissed if I wasn't happy to feast my eyes upon my family for the first time in so long. I turned my lights off when she turned towards the front door. I attempted to blend in with the darkness as I didn't want Kyla to see my vehicle at a standstill right down the road. She turned around and took Bria's hand. I wished it was light outside as I couldn't make too much detail.

The headlights on Kyla's car came to life, and I could see the dashboard glow inside the car. A minute ticked by before she backed out of the driveway and drove down the road.

I allowed a few moments for her to go through the stop sign and make a left in the opposite direction of the hotel. Once she had completed her turn, I turned my lights on as I followed her at a distance. Kyla being the precautious driver she has always been, drove the speed limit and not a mile over.

Five minutes passed before Kyla put on her left blinker and slowed down. I glanced in the direction where Kyla planned to turn and saw the daycare center, presumably where Bria attended. The outside drop-off area was lit bright with lights, and there were five cars in the parking lot. A green Ford pickup truck passed by before she completed the turn. I allowed three cars to pass on the road before I completed the turn.

Kyla had already parked in the drop-off/pick-up area. I pulled into the parking lot, where I had a clear view of my family. Kyla opened the driver's door and stepped out. Under the light, I could see Kyla, but it was not the appearance I expected to see. Kyla had a bang over her eye, and she wore a pair of tan pants and a white collared shirt. She opened the back door, and within seconds, Bria got out and my heart warmed. I observed how Bria's hair had grown at least two inches as her pigtails hung longer than the last time I had seen her. She wore a purple t-shirt with a butterfly and a light blue skirt.

Kyla's mouth moved as she looked at Bria. I wished I was closer to hear what was said. Bria's mouth moved, and they laughed. Kyla grabbed Bria's hand and walked into the daycare.

As I sat in the parking lot, waiting for Kyla to come back out of the daycare, my excitement died down. This was the woman that I had taken care of for five years. This was the woman that I was in love with, and I couldn't ever see myself living without her. While I drank my sorrows away, Kyla pranced around town, living her best life. How could she have done me like this? How was she fine with me not knowing if she and Bria were safe?

Kyla walked out of the daycare. She tucked a piece of hair behind her ear before she sat in her car. Within moments, Kyla drove towards the exit of the parking lot. Trailing at a safe distance, Kyla turned her left blinker on. Once she turned, two cars passed before I made my way into traffic. Kyla traveled not even a mile down the road before she turned into a small shopping plaza. She parked next to a white Toyota sedan.

I pulled my car into a parking space on the far end of the lot, and I turned the car off. Kyla stepped out, carrying her favorite purse I had purchased her for her nineteenth birthday. She walked across the parking lot into a place called Meg's Coffee Shop.

Did Kyla work at a coffee shop? I knew she wasn't going inside for a cup of coffee. Kyla despised coffee with a passion. She could make a mean cup of coffee, but she would never drink it. Was that how she took care of our daughter? It surprised me Kyla had decided on this type of job for her career. She was such an introvert. There was no way I imagined she would take this career route.

I glanced at the time. It was five minutes before six. If Kyla worked full time, I had a long shift to sit through. The darkness changed to light as I sat out there for the next two hours. Occasionally, I took a stroll around the parking lot. Making sure to stay out of Kyla's view, I watched customers enter and exit the building.

Ringing sounded in my pocket. I pulled my phone out and let out an exaggerated breath. It was mom calling.

"Good morning," I greeted her, trying to sound cheerful.

"Good morning. How are you doing?"

"I'm good. How are you?" I watched a gray-haired couple holding hands as they entered the coffee shop.

"I'm fine. I am just calling to see why you didn't come to work today."

My mind scrambled for a good lie. "I took a vacation."

"A vacation?" Mom repeated as if she didn't hear me the first time.

"Yes, a vacation."

"Where is this vacation?"

"Mom, why are you asking all of these questions?"

"You are acting strange."

"I am not acting strange." A blue car parked next to me. A woman with curly, blonde hair that wore sunglasses stepped out of the car and walked towards the coffee shop. This coffee shop had plenty of traffic. Their coffee must be delicious.

"Why would you take a vacation while your family is missing?"

I rolled my eyes. I hated having to explain myself to my parents all the time. I was a grown-ass man. I didn't need to be questioned.

"I just needed to clear my head. I will be home soon."

Before she could respond, I hung the phone up and stuffed it into my pocket.

I took a deep breath. I only had the opportunity to see Kyla from afar. I needed to see the love of my life up close and in person.

Starting from the far end of the shopping plaza building, I would make my way to the coffee shop. I was bound to get an up-and-close visual of her. Once my feet touched the sidewalk, I walked casually. I slid a pair of designer sunglasses over my eyes as I trained my eyes on the coffee shop. That was the only destination in my peripheral vision.

As I approached the front of the coffee shop, I collided with a hard, sturdy object. As I looked up, I looked at a man dressed in a maroon dress shirt and black dress pants. He was a few inches taller than me.

He held his hands up in a defenseless manner. "I am sorry about that."

I grunted. "Sorry, I was not paying attention."

"It's cool."

The man turned around. He walked down the sidewalk before he entered the coffee shop. I took a deep breath as I approached the window.

Kyla had her back towards me as she stood at the counter. I watched as her arms moved before she turned around. She carried two coffee mugs and approached a table with a young couple. As I watched Kyla talk and smile with her customers, my heart softened and warmed all over. Kyla's beauty had me awestruck. It had been so long since I had last seen her, I had forgotten how beautiful she was. Even as Kyla moved on to another table visible from my stance at the window, I couldn't bring myself to tear my eyes away from her.

A strawberry blonde walked past her. She must have said something as she passed because Kyla turned in her direction. She replied before a smile lit up her face.

As Kyla turned her attention back to the customer she tended to, I ripped my eyes away from her beauty as I walked away quickly. I could not blow my cover no matter how much I wanted to stare at her beauty.

Chapter Twenty-Three

Kyla

My heart jumped out of my chest as all sounds around me ceased to exist. I was just informed of the news of Mr. and Mrs. Smith moving to Texas when I swore I had seen a black streak pass by on the sidewalk. My breath caught in the back of my throat as fear wrapped around me, attempting to suffocate me. I stared hard at the window, expecting the streak to come by once again.

Forcing my feet to move, I placed one foot in front of the other as I approached the door. I looked in both directions on the sidewalk, trying to find the culprit. There were only a few people in the parking lot, but none were wearing black.

"Beautiful," came over my shoulder as my ears recognized sound again.

Spinning around, I looked at Ryan. Ryan looked gorgeous in his maroon dress shirt that showed off the outline of his muscular arms and black dress pants.

"Yes?" I croaked out, my mouth dry.

Ryan's eyes flickered all over my face.

"Are you okay?"

I could hear the concern in his voice.

"I-I don't know."

Ryan took my hand.

"Tell me what's wrong."

"I believe I just saw Brad."

"Where?"

Ryan walked over to the door and looked around the parking lot.

"I-I don't know. He is wearing all black."

Ryan walked out of the coffee shop and into the parking lot. I watched as he walked around, trying to locate who I saw.

Ryan walked back into the coffee shop. "Brad is not here."

"How do you know? You don't even know what he looks like," I snapped.

Ryan looked at me, not even responding to my snarky remark. As I looked into his eyes, I felt remorseful. "I'm so sorry for the attitude. You did not deserve that."

Ryan grabbed my hand. He rubbed the pad

of his thumb into my hands. "It's okay. You do not need to apologize to me. I can see you're rattled."

"Yes, I do. You have been nothing shy of amazing to me. You did not deserve my lashing out. I am just so fearful Brad will find us at any moment now. I'm preparing myself for when that day arrives."

Ryan caressed my face with his hands as he made me look into his delightful eyes. "Do you remember what I told you the first day you visited my house?"

I smiled as the memory was vivid, even though months had passed since that day occurred.

"Of course, I remember. I'll never, ever forget it."

He smiled. "Tell me what I said."

"I'd prefer to hear it come from your lips again."

"I will protect you and Bria with my life."

Closing my eyes, my body relaxed. I had been so relaxed these past few months that my mind played major tricks on me today. Ryan wrapped his arms tight around my waist. Lips crashed onto my mouth as my eyes fluttered open briefly. Ryan had never kissed me with this much intensity before. I was surprised, but I enjoyed it.

"If only time could stop when I am in your arms."

"Would you be content with being in these arms for the rest of your life?"

“I would be content being in your arms for eternity,” I professed to Ryan before I gave Ryan a soft, teasing kiss.

The truth to those words spoken was raw.

Chapter Twenty-Four

Kyla

"Hi, Mommy."

Bria had just walked around the corner at her daycare when she spotted me.

"Hi, Sweetie."

I squatted down and wrapped my arms around her. I held her a bit tighter. An extra second longer. Bria patted my back with her tiny hand. The false sighting of Brad had put me on edge, but Ryan had managed to calm me down.

"How was your day at school?"

"It was great."

Once the hug ended, Bria and I held hands as we walked out of the daycare center. The sun shined bright, with no clouds in the sky. The air had cooled down as fall arrived.

"I'm glad you had a great day."

"How was your day?"

"It was awesome. Guess what, Bria."

"What?"

"It's Friday," I exclaimed as I opened the back door for Bria.

"Yay. What are we going to do this weekend?"

I slid into the driver's seat once Bria was secured and started the car up.

"Mommy will be busy tomorrow night, so you will spend some time with Emily." Bria clapped her hands and cheered in the backseat. "Tonight, Ryan wanted to take the two of us out."

"Where are we going?"

"It's a surprise," I said in a singsong tone as we left the daycare.

"Do you know what it is?"

I nodded. "Of course, Mommy knows. It's a surprise, especially for you."

"I love surprises."

Bria burst with excitement and energy.

Once we arrived home, Bria and I went into the house. We had two-and-a-half hours before Ryan came to pick us up.

Bria had talked about a movie she wanted to see for the past two weeks. The trailer kept showing on the TV channels that she watched.

Ryan told me last week that he would love for us all to go on a movie date. I had to agree, as Ryan and Bria were getting closer as the days passed. Seeing how great he was when he was around children was beautiful. He would make a fantastic father one day.

Bria and I showered. We dressed in matching purple rompers. Just as we put our shoes on, the doorbell rang.

I walk over to the door. Making sure it was Ryan on the other end of the peephole, I allowed Bria to do the honors of greeting our date for the evening.

Bria walked to the door and swung it open.

"Ryan!" She walked into his outstretched arms.

"Hey, Bria. How are you doing?"

"I'm good. Where are you taking us?" Bria asked, getting right to the point.

"Bria, don't be rude." I smooth my hand over her hair. "Be patient."

Ryan looked at me, and he smiled.

"Okay."

She shrugged her shoulders as she looked down at the floor.

"Sweetie, go to the bathroom before we leave," I said to Bria.

"Okay, Mommy."

She ran to the bathroom and closed the door behind her.

"Are you ready to go?" Ryan handed over a red rose.

"Ready as I'll ever be."

I wrapped my arm around Ryan's neck and gave him a quick peck on the lips.

As I pulled away to put the rose in the vase, Ryan grabbed me by my waist and drew me back into his arms. His body pressed against mine, he kissed me deeply. His kisses were so addictive I was positive I'd never be able to go without them another day.

Once the toilet flushing sounded, Ryan and I separated. As my eyes fluttered open, I could see him tug on his lower lip with his teeth seductively. Tingles shot through my body as I tore my eyes away from him to place the rose in the vase. Once Bria walked out of the bathroom, I locked up the house, and we loaded into Ryan's car.

"Where are we going?" Bria asked from the backseat.

I turned around in my seat to look at her. "If Bria is not patient, Bria won't get her surprise."

"Aww, no, don't be mean," Ryan cooed from the driver's seat.

"You have such a soft spot for her, don't you?" I said with a soft smile and a chuckle.

"Of course. Bria is my little sidekick." Ryan looked at Bria through the rearview mirror before he backed out of the driveway. "In ten minutes, you will see your surprise."

"Yay," Bria squealed at the top of her lungs.

Pulling my phone out of my purse, I handed it to Bria. "Here, occupy yourself with games. You are too chipper right now."

"The matching outfits are so cute," Ryan observed as he tapped his fingers against the steering wheel as he drove.

"Thank you. I ordered them online last week."

"Bria looks so adorable. You, on the other hand..."

Looking over at Ryan, I attempted to figure out why he didn't finish his sentence by the expression on his face. His face gave away nothing.

"On the other hand, what?"

His eyes flickered over to me before he placed his attention back on the road.

"You look too sexy," he whispered so Bria wouldn't hear. "Those long legs have me losing my mind."

"Stop it." I laughed nervously.

"It's true. If Bria was not in that backseat..."

I smiled as I knew what was on his mind when he didn't finish his sentence. Reaching over, I gave Ryan a playful hit on the arm as he flashed a smile.

"How was your day at work?" I asked as I looked forward and focused on the road.

Changing the direction of the conversation was necessary. Staring at the greenery we were passing, I appreciated its beauty. The leaves on the trees started their transition from green to a range of fall color hues.

"It was great. I received a raise today."

"That is such wonderful news." I gave his arm a comforting squeeze. "Congratulations. I am so proud of you."

"Thank you."

"It's great to see how you can still thrive in your career even though you took a step back."

"I'm grateful that I did. I would not have approached you if I had not."

I raised an eyebrow as I looked over at him. "Why do you say that?"

"I would not have pursued you if I had known I would not have had time for you."

"I respect that. When did you decide to step back from your career?"

Silence settled before he responded. "The second our eyes met."

My mouth dropped open out of pure astonishment. "Are you telling me I was your inspiration for putting your relationships before your career?"

"That is what I am saying."

He placed his hand on top of mine in my lap.

"I must admit, I feel special."

"You are special. In all honesty, I could not pass up the opportunity to talk to you."

"I'm glad you were persistent with me."

"I'm glad as well."

Ryan made a turn, and we pulled into the movie theater parking lot.

"Bria, look where we are," I said.

Bria looked up from my phone and gasped. "Are we at the movies?"

"Yes, we are. We are going to see that movie you said you wanted to watch."

"Yay! Movie time."

Bria beamed in the backseat as Ryan parked.

As soon as I unfastened Bria's seatbelt, she stepped out of the car and danced.

"She has inherited the great dance moves from her Mommy."

"With gladness, I take ownership of that."

Ryan and I laughed.

Ryan slipped his hand into my hand. "With gladness, I take ownership of you."

"I'm fine with that."

Ryan drew me into his arms and placed the softest kiss on my lips. This kiss felt like a feather had touched my lips before it disappeared. The kiss was a tease which I was positive he did on purpose.

"No kissy time. It's movie time."

Bria placed her arms in between our bodies. She pushed them outward, separating us to get much space between us. Stepping into the gap, she grabbed my hand and Ryan's. She led us to the booth where we were to purchase our tickets.

As Ryan asked for three tickets to the movie, I smiled. This was the life four months of intense planning resulted from. This was the life I created from starting over with no friends or family. This life resulted from a mother that wanted the best for her daughter and stopped at nothing to provide it.

"Mommy, can I have candy?" Bria asked me as we approached the concession stand.

Ana Denise

"You can have anything that you want."

Chapter Twenty-Five

Brad

Watching Kyla this morning up close almost blew my entire plan as my cover was almost blown. I never ran around a corner so fast in my life, but I had to do what was necessary. I had stripped the black shirt off as I threw the blue shirt on. I tossed the shirt into an open garbage bin as I removed the sunglasses. Pulling the cap farther down over my face, I walked through the parking lot, heading towards my car.

The same man I bumped into on the sidewalk had made his way outside and he looked around the parking lot. Why would he be outside searching the parking lot? He wasn't outside for too long before returning to the coffee shop.

I took a deep, refreshing breath when I threw myself into my car. My heart beat out of control. There was no more room for another error like I had just done.

Another error might result in Kyla packing up Bria and taking her farther away from me. I could not allow that to happen again.

After that near run-in, I decided to go visit a drive-thru fast-food restaurant for food. Due to not having eaten since yesterday around three, I was hungry. So, I had to replenish myself, so I could maintain my energy.

After scarfing down two sandwiches and a large black coffee, I went back to the hotel to freshen up. There was still a few hours left before Kyla was due to pick Bria up from daycare, and I wanted to be there thirty minutes before Kyla arrived.

Setting my alarm to go off forty-five minutes before Kyla would pick up Bria, I laid down on the bed and allowed and closed my eyes.

As I settled into a deep sleep, my phone rang. A low growl rumbled in my throat. I grabbed my phone off the nightstand. My eyes stayed closed as I swiped my thumb across the phone to ignore the call. Not even ten seconds later, the phone rang again.

Opening one eye, I saw Dad's name on the screen. My dad never called me, so I knew this conversation would not result in me getting any more sleep. I prepared myself for the worst.

Taking a deep breath, I answered the phone. "Hello, Dad."

"Hey, Son, where are you?"

"I'm on vacation."

"Son, you need to quit lying."

"I'm not lying." I huffed as I rolled my eyes. He would not let up on me. Why did I expect anything less from him?

"We know you would never take a vacation with Kyla and Bria missing."

"But I am, Dad."

I pushed myself up to sit in the bed. Taking a nap was out of the picture for me.

"Where are they?"

"I don't know," I answered as I became angry.

"We know that you have found them."

"Why would you think that?"

I walked over to my suitcase and grabbed my whiskey. I unscrewed the top and took a hearty sip.

"Just tell us where you are. We want to be with you when you talk with Kyla. We don't want you doing anything reckless."

"Listen," I began as the liquor warmed my throat. Lying was the last thing I wanted to do. I had already figured my excuse out. "I have to do this myself."

"No, you don't, Brad."

"Yes, I do."

"It's okay to need your parent's help

sometimes. When are you going to realize that?"

"I created this situation on my own. It's only right if I solve it on my own."

I took another sip before I tucked it into my suitcase. I refused to be drunk when I followed my family.

"Just tell us where you are, and we will be there in the morning."

"No," I yelled, surprising myself.

The other end of the line had gone quiet. I pulled the phone away from my face to make sure the call was still active. The call was active. Dad was just quiet.

"Who in the hell do you think you are talking to?" His voice was full of venom.

"I'm sorry."

"If you are not back in town by Sunday morning, there will be consequences."

"What consequences?" I asked.

"You will find out if you are not here by Sunday morning."

The disconnection sound echoed in my ear.

Pulling the phone away from my face, I put it in my pocket. Calls from Dad never resulted in anything positive, and this one was nothing less than expected.

Running my fingers through my hair, I grabbed my car keys and headed to my car. As I drove to the daycare, my mind went in a million directions. What were the consequences he referred to? Knowing Dad, he would disown me and never speak another one to word to me again.

Pulling into the parking lot, I parked in employee parking. Kyla's car pulled into the drop-off/pick-up area within minutes. She stepped out, walked inside, and immediately came out, holding Bria's hand. They got in the car before they made their journey to the house.

Driving a good distance behind, I knew where they were heading. Once I arrived at their house, I saw that the car was empty, and they had already gone inside. I drove around the block two times before I decided to park on an empty lot. From the lot, I could see Kyla's entire house.

Two-in-a-half hours passed before a silver Audi pulled into the driveway. My eyes narrowed as a man stepped out from the open driver's door. As he walked up to the front door, my jaw dropped. That was the man I bumped into on the sidewalk outside the coffee shop. The same man that looked around the parking lot. This man had to be Kyla's new boyfriend. Anger boiled in my veins. Hours ago, I bumped into the man I knew had screwed my girlfriend. If I had known then, I would have beat his ass to a pulp just for bumping into me.

The door swung open, and he squatted down. Seconds passed before he stood but did not walk into the house. What was going on?

Going against my better judgment, I started my car up. Driving towards the house, I went at a normal speed that would not draw attention to myself. As soon as I passed the front of the door,

I looked over to observe this man's arms wrapped around Kyla's waist. They were in a lip lock. Kissing. Outside. For anyone and everyone to see who passed by.

My stomach turned sour. My heart shattered into a million pieces as I kept driving. This was not the time to make my presence known. I had to stay undercover.

Circling the block, I came around the corner when they made their way to the stop sign in his car. Trailing at a distance, I followed them a few miles before we turned into a movie theater parking lot. I parked two rows behind them.

Kyla stepped out of the car and unfastened Bria's car seat. This guy had a car seat in his car for my daughter? Why in the hell did he have a car seat for my daughter?

Bria danced as the man stepped out of the car. He made his way over to the other side of the vehicle where Kyla and Bria were. Their lips moved in conversation. They laughed at the response before they talked more. Within seconds, their lips met again.

As I sat back, watching in disgust and utter sadness, I couldn't help but witness the chemistry. How did Kyla have such great chemistry with this man? How did she cut off all chemistry with me?

Bria stepped in between them and grabbed their hands. Bria led the way to the movie theater entrance.

Killing the ignition, I stepped out of my SUV

and made large strides up to the entrance. I would beat this guy unidentifiable and drag my family back to Florida. How could they walk into the movie theater like a happy family?

Was this man trying to be Bria's father? Did she call him Daddy? Did Kyla allow Bria to call him Daddy? Did she encourage it?

I came to a complete stop. This was not the time or place to make my presence known. There were too many witnesses, and my journey had just started. I had weeks, maybe months of following planned. Walking back to my car, I slid into the driver's seat and slammed the door shut. I yelled at the top of my lungs as I hit the steering wheel with my fist. I placed my head in my hands, taking deep breaths in and exhaling them. I knew making this trip would break my heart, but I didn't know this trip would shatter me. Broken was what I felt inside.

Broken was my new middle name, and I had no choice but to wear it with pride.

Chapter Twenty-Six

Kyla

A pylon sign containing a ship caught my eye from a distance. "Your destination is on the right," the maps app informed me.

Entering the parking lot, I looked around. What did Aunt Liliana look like? Did we share the same dark brown complexion? Did I have any features she had? Or would we look like complete strangers?

Pulling the sun visor down, I opened the mirror up. Since moving to Branchville, I had removed the bang from over my eye for the first time. I wanted Aunt Liliana to see me. The real me with no additives.

Stepping out of my car, I ran my hands over my navy-blue knee-length a-line dress to smooth out any visible imperfections. Approaching the restaurant entrance in my black wedge heels, I waltzed inside.

The smell of the ocean entered my nose, reminding me of home. I walked up to the hostess stand off to the left of the entrance. Standing at the podium was a small, petite woman with red hair pulled into a high ponytail.

"Welcome to Buoys. Do you have reservations?" the hostess asked.

"Yes, I do. Reservations for two."

"What is the name of the reservations?"

"Williams."

"Your dinner companion is already here. I will take you to the table."

My heart flipped in my chest as nervousness washed over me. My aunt was already in the restaurant.

I was seconds away from meeting her.

The hostess led me through the nautical-decorated restaurant. Walking by several tables and booths, we approached a table with a woman that had her back towards me. Her hair was pulled back into a formal bun.

My feet stopped in their tracks, feet away. The hostess looked back at me before she said, "Your waiter Richard will be with you two shortly."

She walked past me as Aunt Liliana turned in

her chair.

Taking a deep breath, I looked at my Aunt's face. If there was any doubt about us being relatives, it left immediately. We had the same dark complexion and similar facial features. She stood as my eyes met hers for the first time. The emotions that I experienced were etched into her facial expressions.

"Kyla," Aunt Liliana said, never taking her eyes off me.

"Aunt Liliana."

We closed the distance between us as we extended our arms. We grabbed each other into a tight embrace. I inhaled her scent and buried my face in my aunt's chest. It was a familiar scent, but I could not figure out where I had smelled it before. Salty tears streamed down my face.

"You are so beautiful."

Aunt Liliana held me outstretched in her arms. Her face expressed a multitude of emotions as it was drenched in tears. She smiled at me.

"So are you, Aunt Liliana. I see the resemblance in us."

"Honey, call me Aunt Lily."

She brought her hands to my face and wiped my tears away.

"Aunt Lily," I stated, doing as she had requested.

"You look just like your mom did at your age."

"Really?"

Hearing my aunt mention my mother warmed my insides. Nobody had ever mentioned my mother before. I had never interacted with anyone that I was aware of that even knew my mother.

"Yes, honey." She wiped more tears from my face. "Stop crying," she pleaded as tears continued to fall from her eyes. "You are making me cry."

"I can't help it. You are making me cry."

Aunt Lily and I giggled as we each couldn't stop crying.

Our waiter made his way over to our table. He looked at us and raised his eyebrows.

"Do you two need a minute?"

We looked at each other and shook our heads. "No, we're fine," Aunt Lily responded.

We walked over to the table, and I across from Aunt Lily at the dinner table. We grabbed napkins from the middle of the table and dotted our eyes dry.

"My name is Richard, and I will be your server. Are we celebrating anything special?" He looked back and forth between the two of us, waiting for an answer.

I looked at Aunt Lily, and she smiled. "Yes, we are. We are celebrating a reunion."

"Congratulations to both of you. Would you two like a complimentary glass of wine to celebrate?"

"I'll have water," Aunt Lily said.

"Water will be fine."

I sat my drenched napkin on the table.

"I will be right back with your water."

He smiled before he walked away.

"I can't believe this is happening."

I couldn't help but beam. This was such a heartwarming day.

"I know. I can't believe it, either. It has been a long time coming, honey. I've searched for you for a long time."

My eyebrows raised. "How long have you searched?"

"Since you were three years old."

Shock hit me as my mouth dropped open. "Since I was three?"

Aunt Lily nodded. "It is a long story to tell. Don't worry, I will tell you everything. Look at the menu, honey. I am paying for dinner, so order whatever your heart desires."

Following my aunt's suggestion, I picked the menu up and studied it in depth.

Our waiter came back to our table a few minutes later and sat our glasses of water in front of us. "Are you two ready to order?"

Aunt Lily looked at me, and I nodded. "We are ready. I will have the rainbow trout with a side of sauteed spinach."

Richard wrote the order down as he placed his attention on me. "I will have the mahi mahi over a bed of wild rice."

Richard smiled before he walked away.

I took a sip of water. I placed the glass of water back on the table and clasped my hands in my lap.

"So, who is older? You or my mother? Or is there another sibling I am not aware of?"

Aunt Lily smiled as she grabbed her water and took a quick sip. "It's just the two of us. I am older than your mother by three years."

"How does it feel being the older sister? I wouldn't know. I am an only child. Well, to my knowledge, I am an only child."

"Being an older child, I was always expected to have more responsibilities." She sat the glass of water on the table. "Which I did not mind. I loved taking care of my sister."

"What is my mother's name?"

"Her name was Kimberly," Aunt Lily responded.

"Was?" I whispered.

The look in Aunt Lily's eyes told me the linking verb was not a mistake. My heart dropped to my stomach as my tears burned the back of my eyes.

"I am so sorry, Kyla." Aunt Lily choked those words out as she struggled to formulate them.

Reaching for another napkin from the middle of the table, tears dropped from my eyes and onto my cheeks.

"Can you tell me what led up to her..." I trailed off.

I could not say the word death. I refused to say it.

"Our parents were older when they had me. My father was forty-five, and my mother was forty-two. Three years later, here Kimberly comes along."

"Why did my grandparents wait so long to

have you two?" I took another sip of my water as I dabbed at my eyes.

"In their younger years, they were focused on creating a stable life. They were ambitious. All they did was work hard for the successful future they envisioned for their family."

"Did you two get along with your parents?"

"Growing up, we were the picture-perfect family. Meals after Sunday morning service. Movie nights once a week at eight sharp, you name it. Everything went downhill when Kimberly went to high school."

Aunt Lily took a sip of her water as she fiddled with her wrapped silverware on the table.

"Why did everything go downhill?"

"Our parents were old-fashioned. They were not laid back in the least. Kimberly wanted to be free. She wanted to live life and express herself."

"My mother was rebellious?"

Aunt Lily smiled as she nodded. "She was a free spirit. That is what I loved most about her. She followed her mind, and she didn't allow anyone to change the way she thought."

"My mother sounded like a strong woman."

"She was very strong. Things took a negative turn when she was sixteen, though."

"What happened?" I was completely invested.

"Kimberly walked right off the school bus and told me she had thrown up during the second period. She had also said her period was late by two months."

"She was pregnant with me?"

"Ten weeks pregnant to be exact."

"Do you know who my father is? Is my father still around?"

Aunt Lily shrugged her shoulders. "Kimberly never disclosed to any of the family who the father was. I believe she kept him a secret so our parents would not find him and run him off."

My heart broke. I would never have the opportunity to meet my mother or father.

Richard walked over to our table. He carried our plates of food. He sat the plates in front of us. "Enjoy your meal, ladies. Please let me know if you need anything else."

With that finishing statement, Richard walked away.

Silence settled among us as Aunt Lily, and I ate our meal. The quality of the meal was excellent, cooked to perfection.

"Were you all living in Florida at the time? Is that how I was put into foster care there?"

Aunt Lily had just finished chewing the food in her mouth when she responded, "We never lived in Florida. We never even visited the state when we took our once-a-year family trips our parents took us on."

"Where did you all live at the time?"

"Washington. We were born and raised there. Kimberly was the only one that wanted to leave Washington."

"When did my mother decide to leave Washington?"

Aunt Lily took a deep breath. "Our parents found out when she was four months pregnant. Kimberly kept it a secret for as long as she could. You were growing, and she had the cutest baby bump," Aunt Lily stated as she smiled at the memory. "My parents gave her three months to get things in order before they kicked her out of the house. They disowned her, and it hurt my heart that they could treat my sister in such a way. They felt as if they failed at raising her," Aunt Lily emphasized with an eye roll.

It hurt me deep within my soul to hear what my grandparents had done to my mother when she was pregnant with me.

"Did she leave Washington by herself?"

Aunt Lily shook her head as she continued to eat.

"She had met a guy one day while walking through the mall. From what Kimberly told me, it was love at first sight. They both had the desire to live in Florida."

"He was fine with her being pregnant?" I raised my eyebrow, shocked out of my mind.

Aunt Lily nodded as she took another sip of her water before she ate more of her meal. "It shocked me as well. They left for Florida when she was seven months pregnant. I told her to keep in touch with me. At the time, I was enrolled in a local college full time."

"Were you at the hospital when I was born?"

"Of course I was. I would not miss the birth of my one and only niece for the world."

Smiling, I was grateful my mother had at least one support system in her life. It must've been difficult to not have her parents for moral support, but she had her older sister by her side.

"I came to visit four times a year. From what my sister always said, Kimberly and her boyfriend were doing good for themselves. He worked but was never gone from the house too long when I would visit and spend time with you all."

"How did I end up in foster care?"

"I was not aware, but sometime after your mother gave birth to you, she started experimenting with drugs," Aunt Lily began as I continued to eat my meal. "Her boyfriend sold them, but they were using them occasionally." Aunt Lily took a deep breath, and I reached across the table to squeeze her hand. "One night, when you were three, they decided to go somewhere. Her boyfriend was driving. They were high, and the car crashed. They both passed away at the scene. You were the miracle baby that survived."

Gasping, my heart dropped in my chest. I had mixed emotions hit me all at once. I was grateful my mother didn't just give me up because she didn't want to be in my life. I was hurt because my mother passed away before I could remember anything about her.

"If you don't mind me asking, why didn't you take over guardianship of me? Was that something you would have been interested in?"

"Of course, I wanted you, honey. That was

my desire once I received that devastating call about your mother. I planned to raise you as my own. The state would not allow me to. Due to your mother having drugs in her system, the state thought it was best to place you in foster care. I was nineteen with no income but willing to drop out of college and work full-time to care for you."

"You would've done that for me?"

She nodded as she smiled. "Of course. I have loved you since I found out you were in your mother's tummy. I tried to keep in contact with you, but they moved you between several foster homes, and they never provided me the opportunity to adopt you." Aunt Lily and I took a sip of our water. "When I was contacted weeks ago about you, I felt like my entire world was complete."

"Do you have children?"

Aunt Lily shook her head. "I married my college sweetheart Robert. We have been together for a long time, but we found out early in our marriage that I could never have children."

"I'm so sorry to hear that."

"Don't be sorry. The tough patches in my life have shaped me into the strong woman you see today."

Richard walked over to our table. "How is your meal?" he asked.

"It's wonderful," I said as I took a bite of my mahi mahi.

"Magnificent."

Aunt Lily took another sip of her water.

"Do you two need anything?"

"We will need the check in about thirty minutes," Aunt Lily responded.

Richard smiled and nodded as he walked away.

"So, do you have any children?"

"I have a four-year-old daughter. Her name is Bria. She will be five soon, and I am thinking about throwing her a birthday party."

"Of course, I'll be there," Aunt Lily blurted out.

I laughed at her forwardness. "I didn't even invite you yet."

"I know you didn't, but I have a feeling deep inside my bones that tells me we will be inseparable."

"The birthday party will be in a few weeks. I know you live in Washington, so it might not be viable for you to make that trip back here."

"I would travel this world a million times if it meant spending quality time with you and your daughter. I missed out on nineteen years of your life. I am going to be here for you the rest of them."

Taking a sip of water, my body relaxed. This meeting exceeded my expectations, and I finally had someone to call family. This will always be one of the best days I have ever experienced in my entire life.

Chapter Twenty-Seven

Kyla

Walking along the dark brown paved pathway to the front door, I adjusted my overnight bag that was on my shoulder. Opening the door, the aroma of fresh herbs met me right at the front door.

Ryan walked around the corner with a yellow apron wrapped around his waist. He wiped his hands on a dish towel. "Dinner will be ready any moment now."

"You look sexy in that apron." I flashed a

smile of gratitude.

Ryan struck a pose for me as he placed his hand on his hip, worthy of a runway. "If you are lucky, I might give you a chance to take a picture of me wearing it later."

He winked at me as he closed the door once I walked inside.

"That would become my new background for my phone."

"When do you ever see a man rocking an apron?"

"That might be common." The image danced in my mind. "You forgot to put an emphasis on yellow."

"When do you ever see a man rocking a yellow apron?"

"Never, but it's a wonderful sight," I said flirtatiously.

Ryan smiled. "Why don't you go put your things in my room? Dinner should be ready by the time you come back downstairs."

"Okay."

I walked through the living room, up the stairs, and into Ryan's room. I sat my bag on the bed, walked downstairs and entered the dining room.

In the middle of the table were four lit taper candles. Two plates of sirloin top roast with mushroom risotto sat on opposite sides of the table. Two wine glasses and a tall bottle of red wine sat unopened.

"Dinner is ready." Ryan pulled out the chair

for me to sit.

Sitting down, I stated, "This food looks amazing. I cannot wait to dig in."

"I hope you enjoy it. I don't ever cook extravagant meals as such for myself." He sat across from me and grabbed the bottle of wine. He popped the cork and filled our glasses.

I cut into my roast and ate a piece. My eyes rolled back in satisfaction.

"How do you like it?"

"All I can say is, you can cook for me whenever you would like. I will never object."

Ryan laughed. "I take it that you like my meal." He took his first taste of the risotto.

"Correction. I love your meal."

I took a sip of my wine before I continued to eat my food.

"I'm looking forward to you cooking with me."

"That would be an adventure."

"How so?" He picked up his wine glass and took a sip.

"I've never cooked with someone before," I admitted.

"Seriously?"

I nodded. "I've always wanted to but never had anyone to cook with."

I was in food heaven.

"We can cook together soon. Would you like that?" He asked?

"Yes, that would be great."

"Bria can join us in cooking, too," he added.

"Knowing Bria, she would make a huge mess

while singing her soul out."

"I wouldn't mind it all."

"Are you sure?"

Ryan gave me a knowing look. "I am in this big house by myself all the time. I enjoy the noise she tends to create."

Ryan's comment raised a question. I knew the answer in the back of my mind, but I needed him to voice it aloud.

"Have you ever thought about if you wanted children of your own?"

Ryan nodded. "The desire to have children has always been there."

"I kind of figured it was."

"Then why did you ask?" A smirk appeared as he continued eating his food.

"Clarification."

He nodded. "I always told myself I would only consider having children if I ever wanted to settle down. The thought of settling down started crossing my mind a few months ago."

He looked deep into my eyes as if he was on a search to find a treasure in my soul.

I grabbed my glass of wine and took a hearty sip. Even though Ryan and my relationship was going well, the thought of settling down put a bit of fear into my heart.

"How would you feel about meeting my family?"

I looked up from my plate of food and focused on Ryan. "I would love to meet them. I'm just..."

"You just what?"

Ryan raised his eyebrow as he took a sip from his wine glass.

"Nervous. Scared out of my mind. Anxious. Fearful..."

Ryan laughed as he raised his hand to cease my continuous word spew. "Why are you nervous? It is just my family," he clarified as he returned to eating his food.

"I know, but it's something about meeting the family of my boyfriend for the first time that puts me on edge, and they are going to hate..."

Ryan laughed at me as he placed his hand on top of mine. "You are rambling. Listen, you will be fine. I talk with my parents about you all the time. They feel like they know you already."

"Do they know I have a child? Are they fine with that?" I continued to eat my food.

"My parents are not judgmental. They were impressed when I told them how you are raising her on your own. They said they couldn't imagine raising a child on their own."

I smiled at the compliment. "It's not by choice, but I appreciate the kind words."

"So, what do you say?"

"I would love to meet your family. I'm just nervous."

"No need to be nervous. My parents will love you just as much as I do."

Ryan reached across the table and rubbed my hand, reassurance washing over me.

After we finished eating our dinner, I stacked the dirty dishes and carried them to the kitchen counter. I was about to load the dishes into the dishwasher when his hand touched my lower back.

"This night is not going to consist of you lifting one finger," Ryan whispered in my ear. The warmth of his breath on my ear sent chills down my spine.

"I would like to help you clean."

Ryan shook his head as he took my hand in his. "Don't worry about the dishes. I want you to follow me." Ryan led me out of the dining room and into the living room.

"I have to make a call to make sure Bria is being on her best behavior."

"Sabrina has it all under control. Just come here." He walked me to an area of the living room that was furniture-free. He picked up a remote and pressed a button. A slow beat played through the speakers around the room.

"Can I have this dance?" He placed the remote on the end table.

"Yes, you may."

He placed one hand on my lower back and clasped my other hand in his. He pulled me close as we danced to the slow beat of the melody flowing from the speakers.

"I never thought the day would come when you would dance with me by choice."

Ryan smirked. "I surprised the hell out of myself when I turned the music on." His response caused us both to laugh.

We stared into each other's eyes as we

danced through two songs. The moment was perfect. My future with Ryan flashed before my eyes as he kissed my forehead tenderly. I see myself walking down the aisle with Ryan. I see us having our first child together. I see us sitting in rocking chairs on the front porch as we grayed gracefully. The vision caused a heartfelt smile.

Ryan and I stopped dancing as he said, "I will be right back."

"Where are you going?" He walked towards the stairs.

"I have a surprise for you. Give me a few minutes to get it ready."

As Ryan traveled up the stairs, I walked around the living room. My eyes landed on a painting of a mountain overlooking a pond. If only I were as talented as the artist that created this painting. I would create astonishing work along with them and my work would be in houses worldwide. Walking over to a photograph, I admired the array of colorful lilies with a sunset in the background.

"Your surprise is ready." His voice came from a distance.

Making my way upstairs, I walked to the end of the hall where Ryan stood at the entry of his bedroom. As soon as I approached, Ryan stepped back, and I walked into the room. Red rose petals led from the bedroom door to the bathroom door. Rose petals were thrown all over the bed.

Turning around, I looked at Ryan. "Ryan,

what is this?"

"Happy six-month anniversary, beautiful." He kissed me on my forehead.

"I didn't even..."

"I know you didn't. All that matters is that I remembered. Go and find your surprise."

Turning around, I made a beeline for the bathroom. Opening the door, the smell of vanilla wafted into my nose as I observed the low-lit bathroom. Six candles burned on the vanity. The jacuzzi tub was filled with a mass of bubbles.

"Ryan, this is so amazing. So thoughtful."

Ryan rubbed my back. "Go ahead and relax. You have a massage planned in twenty minutes."

Ryan left the bathroom and closed the door, leaving me in privacy to get undressed and enjoy this magnificent bubble bath.

Stepping out of my clothes, I placed one foot in the tub. The water was at the perfect temperature. Situating myself in the tub, I relaxed as I closed my eyes.

A soft noise stirred out of my sleep. Moments later, a knock sounded on the door.

"Yes?"

My eyes were still closed.

I floated on a cloud, somewhere between being awake and being in a heavy daze.

The sound of the door opening floated into my dream. "Are you sleeping?"

My eyes fluttered open as I stared into a pile of bubbles. I turned to look at Ryan, and he smiled. I stretched as I raised my arms above my head.

"I didn't realize I had fallen asleep."

"Dry off when you are ready for your massage."

Once the door had closed, I stepped out of the tub and grabbed one of the two towels on the vanity. Drying off, I placed the wet towel in the laundry basket and wrapped the dry towel around me.

Walking into the bedroom, Ryan stood by the bed. In his hand was a bottle of oil.

"Receiving this type of treatment for only dating six months, I can only imagine what will come when we come across our one-year anniversary."

"In six months, you will find out." He motioned his hand towards the bed. "Go ahead and lay down."

I made my way over to the bed and laid on my stomach, maneuvering the towel to cover my lower half. Turning my neck toward Ryan's direction, I stared as he tugged the blue T-shirt he wore over his head and tossed it to the floor. I completed a grand tour of his chiseled torso right before he worked his magic.

Warm oil was drizzled all over my back. Strong hands kneaded deep into my back. As I watched his muscular arms flex and perform wonders, the tension and stress I dealt with for months loosened up, and I was set free.

"How does it feel?" Ryan asked as he worked on my left arm.

"Revitalizing."

"I'm glad you are enjoying it."

"It's hard not to. I've never had a massage before."

"There is always a first for everything."

Ryan walked over to the other side of the bed and worked on my other arm.

"I'm hoping you'll have a lot of firsts with me."

"There will be plenty of firsts. I can assure you of that."

Moments passed after Ryan stopped rubbing my arm. When silence settled in the room, I pushed myself up on my arms and rotated my body to sit on the bed.

Ryan stood near the bathroom. Placing his attention on me, his eyes dropped from my face to my chest. I looked down, and my eyes gazed at my small breasts that were on full display. Nervousness rearing its ugly head, I reached up to cover my breasts with my arms.

"No." Ryan approached the bed. He grabbed my hands and took them away from my chest. "I want to see all of you."

Ryan lowered himself before me until he was at eye level with my breasts. My breath halted in my chest as his tongue snaked out of his mouth and flicked my right nipple. My nipples hardened as he drew one into his mouth. Tugging on my nipple with his teeth, I moaned in satisfaction.

Ryan grabbed my chin, forcing me to look into his eyes full of blazing desire.

"Are you ready to make love to me?"

I nodded as I couldn't find my voice to respond.

Ryan reached his hand in between my legs, and a finger slipped inside me. Gasping for air as my eyes rolled to the back of my head, Ryan's mouth found my other nipple, tugging on it with the same intensity. My body was close to climax when all pleasure ceased to exist.

My eyes fluttered open. Ryan stood before me. A bulge imprinted in his pants as he unbuttoned them. In one swift movement, Ryan's pants were pooled at his feet as his erection sprung to action. He slipped his boxers off as he walked over to the nightstand. He pulled out a condom and slipped it on as he stopped right in front of me.

"I've been waiting for this moment since the day I locked eyes with you," Ryan said as he pushed me back on the bed.

The silky soft fabric of the bedspread made contact with my back.

"I hope it's everything you've been waiting for and so much more."

Ryan pushed my legs open and settled in between them.

Grabbing my hands in his, he pinned my arms over my head and kissed the length of my arms, collarbone, and neck before his mouth captured mine. His tongue trailed along the outline of my lips before it entered my mouth with force. Our lips and tongue danced to their own unique tune that they only knew.

When Ryan thrust into me, goosebumps rose all over my body as I shuttered with the initial shock of penetration. Pleasure built deep within my core as my back arched. I gazed deep into his burning eyes as Ryan pushed in and out of me. Our eye contact intensified, never wavering as his rhythm continued to pick up its pace. Ecstasy penetrated my soul as I gave myself to Ryan. A moan escaped from my mouth as Ryan kissed me.

Before long, rapture and pleasure rippled throughout my body, causing me to lose all control. I cried out, "Oh, Ryan."

Ryan continued his pace as I came off my climax high when his body jerked hard, and he grunted. His body fell onto mine, and I rubbed his back.

"That was damn amazing."

His voice was raspy.

"The best," I commented.

"I can't believe I waited all those months to get my first taste."

"Was the wait worth it?" I winked at him.

He pushed himself up on his arms to look into my eyes. "It was worth it."

"Why do I feel like there is a but coming up?"

Ryan smirked. "You know me so well." Ryan looked into my eyes. "But I can't go too long without being inside you. You rocked my world, and I think I might be a bit obsessed," he admitted as he kissed my forehead.

"Well, I guess it's safe to say that makes the

two of us."

After cleaning up, I walked over to the bed and slipped under the covers. Turning on my side, I closed my heavy eyes. Within minutes, Ryan slipped into the bed, and he wrapped his arms around my waist as he pulled me close. Sleeping in his arms was the safest and most comfortable place I'd ever known.

Chapter Twenty-Eight

Kyla

Deep breath in. Hold. Release deep breath. Pause. Deep breath in. Hold. Release deep breath. Pause.

"You have to relax," Ryan stated.

"Yeah, Mommy. Relax," came from beside me.

Looking over at Bria, I smiled as I gave her hand the tiniest squeeze.

"I'm nervous."

The only parents I had met were Brad's parents, but that was over five years ago. So, this was all new to me. Waters I wasn't expecting to experience for a very long time.

"Don't be. You will be fine. My parents are going to love you. Just as much as I love you."

We approached the immaculate, two-story colonial house on an acre of land in a gated community. The exterior of the house was a soft yellow with white trimmings. The landscaping was pure of any flaw.

We walked up the five steps that led to the front door. Being right at home, Ryan swung the door open without knocking. Stepping aside, Bria and I walked into the house as Ryan walked in behind us and closed the door.

My mouth dropped open in awe. The house oozed with elegance. There were pearl white furnishings throughout the living room. As expected, the walls were adorned with an array of extravagant paintings.

An attractive petite woman with an elegant low formal bun walked around the corner with a smile that could be seen a mile away. She wore a coral-colored long, flowing skirt and a white blouse tucked into her skirt.

"Hello. Welcome to our home."

She approached us as she waved before she wrapped her arms around Ryan.

"Hello, Momma." Ryan hugged his mother tight.

Once their hug ended, she directed her attention to me. "This must be the wonderful Kyla I hear so many great things about."

Nodding my head, I stuck my hand out. "It is so nice to meet you, Mrs. Walker."

"We hug around here, Kyla." She pulled me into a heartfelt hug, her expensive perfume surrounding me. My insides warmed as the nervousness left me. "Please, call me Amelia, pumpkin."

She squatted down and looked at Bria. "My, oh my. You are just the most adorable little girl that I've laid my eyes on. What is your name, cutie pie?"

"Bria." Her voice was strong and bold.

"It is so nice to meet you, Bria. I made homemade chocolate chip cookies. Maybe Mommy will let you have one or two after dinner."

Bria clapped her tiny hands in response.

"I hope you two eat pork."

She looked at me as she headed down the hall.

"Pork is great," I responded as we followed Amelia into the house.

"Come on in and make yourself comfortable at the dinner table. James and I are making plates now."

Ryan led us to a sophisticated white dining room table in its separate room. We sat at the table.

Ryan's parents carried plates of food into the room. I looked at Ryan's father. Ryan was the replica of his father. The only difference was that Ryan's father had salt-and-pepper hair and faint wrinkles around his eyes.

"Hello, Son." He looked at me and smiled, revealing a nice pair of teeth. "You must be Kyla."

"It is so nice to meet you, Mr. Walker."

He set a plate of food in front of me.

"Dear, call me James." He directed his attention to Bria and said, "This pretty girl must be Bria?"

Bria nodded as she smiled. "Nice to meet you."

"She must like you. She didn't speak but two words to me," Amelia commented as she sat in her chair across the table.

"What can I say? Everyone tends to love the old guy." James sat next to Amelia.

"Dad, you are not old," Ryan pointed out.

"My hair and my aching back say otherwise."

"Enough about your age James. Dig in, everyone. This is a new recipe that I put together for tonight."

My eyes widened as I looked at my plate.

"It is pesto-stuffed pork tenderloin with a side of asparagus and mashed potatoes."

Silence settled upon us as everyone started to eat their food. I cut Bria's food into smaller bites before I ate a piece of pork tenderloin. The meat blasted with flavor.

"How do you like it, Kyla?"

"It is delicious."

"Bria?"

Bria stuck up her thumbs as she chewed away on her food. "Yummy."

"Ryan?"

"Mom, you know how amazing your cooking is. Do I even have to comment on how delightful it is?"

Amelia smiled before she ate a piece of asparagus.

"Kyla, what do you do for a living?"

Looking over at Ryan, he gave me a reassuring smile. "I am a waitress at a hole-in-the-wall coffee shop."

"That is lovely. If you don't mind me asking, what is the name of this coffee shop?"

"Megan's Coffee Shop."

"I might have to stop by and get a cup of coffee someday. I've heard their drinks are perfect."

"Kyla wouldn't know. She doesn't drink coffee." Ryan said before he ate some mashed potatoes.

James raised his eyebrows as he took a sip of his glass of water. "You are the first person I have ever met that does not like coffee."

I laughed. "I hope you don't think I'm weird."

"Weird? Never. One a kind? Maybe." James gave me a warm smile.

"I can vouch for their coffee. I go there often," Ryan said.

"Are you sure it's the coffee that has you returning and not the beautiful girl serving it up?" James asked.

We all laughed.

"Kyla has a little bit to do with me going often, but the coffee is delicious."

"James and I will have to come by one day when we have free time and grab a cup." Amelia took a sip of her water.

"That is her way of saying we will never be coming by for a cup."

"James, why are you saying that?"

"Our schedules are always busy, and they never coincide," James pointed out as I ate my meal.

Amelia rolled her eyes with a smile as she focused her attention on me. "I will come by sometime soon for a coffee."

"I look forward to seeing you."

"So, how old are you, Bria?" James took a sip of his water as he waited for Bria to reply.

Bria looked up as she held up four fingers. "Four."

"Aren't you such a big girl?" Amelia asked.

Bria nodded as she ate some of her mashed potatoes.

"She will be five in a couple of weeks."

"Are you doing anything special for her birthday?" James asked.

"I am going to throw her a birthday party. I think I am going to host it at a park. Invite some of her friends from school."

"Isn't that wonderful? I remember having birthday parties when I was younger. I always had the best time," James replied.

"Would you two like to come?" Ryan asked.

"We wouldn't want to impose." Amelia cut a piece of meat before she put it into her mouth.

"We would love for you two to come."

"Tell us the time and place, and we will be there," James replied.

"I'll get those details to you two soon. So, Ryan told me about your careers. Can you tell me what influenced you to pursue your careers?"

"Growing up, math was my forte. I decided it would be best for me to crunch numbers for the rest of my life. Hence me becoming an accountant."

"I have always had the desire to help people. I wanted to get into the medical field and found an interest in anesthesia." James responded.

"If you two had the opportunity, would you have changed your career paths?"

"I would not change anything," Amelia said.

"I would become a Chippendale dancer."

"James," Amelia exclaimed as she dropped her fork on her plate. A loud clink sounded.

A laugh erupted from deep within me.

"Dad, you are something else," Ryan spoke up as he smiled and laughed.

"I'm only kidding," James called out. "I wouldn't change anything about my career choice either."

"You keep joking like that, Kyla will think you are crazy," Amelia voiced.

"Do you think I'm crazy?" He placed his attention on me.

Before I could respond, Ryan managed to turn the conversation around with a question.

"Sophia couldn't come into town to visit?"

Amelia shook her head before she took a sip of her water. "Her schedule has been busy. She never gets time to breathe outside of work."

"I was looking forward to meeting her," I said.

"You'll meet her soon enough. Once her schedule clears up, she'll make a trip back home for a visit."

"What does Sophia do for a living?" I asked as I continued eating my meal.

"Sophia is a fashion designer in New York."

"That is impressive. Now I see why she doesn't have time. She must be talented."

"You see this outfit I am wearing? This is one of Sophia's many designs."

"Her work is stunning. It takes an innovative individual to put out such an amazing creation."

"I'm not sure where she received her artistic abilities from," James stated.

"I agree. James and I are the farthest from artistic. That is the reason for our career choices."

"I wish I would've had the opportunity to choose a different career path."

"Dear, let me tell you something." James placed his attention on me. "I will tell you the same thing I told my children growing up. It is not always about your career choice. You could be a grocery store clerk, but as long as you can be the best you can be, you will be fine. Not everyone will be famous one day. Not everyone will make millions off a single deal. In your situation, be the best waitress that you can be."

Looking over at Ryan, he gave me a heartfelt

smile.

"I can't express how great it is to hear that. I have never heard that growing up. I've always been told that I must go to college to do something productive with my life."

"That is not true. I became a senior accountant, and I started at my accounting firm at the age of eighteen. No college under my belt."

"That was a very long time ago, though," James responded.

"Dad," Ryan gasped.

"James," Amelia exclaimed.

"It was a joke."

"It better be a joke. My Mom is far from old." Ryan took a sip of his water.

"Remember, just be the best you can be," James reiterated as he sipped his water.

Nodding, my nerves relaxed. Ryan's parents were more welcoming than I had ever expected.

"So, what do you like to do for fun?" Amelia placed her attention on me as she picked her fork back up.

"Spend time with Bria."

"Well, honey, that is a necessity. When you have free time, what best occupies your time?"

"I don't ever have free time. My time is spent with Bria. We get together with my friend and her daughter and have play dates on occasion. I pick up a book and read it if I have some uninterrupted time."

James and Amelia nodded in response.

"Well, I'm a sports fanatic. Anything that is

sports related, I am sold on it," James stated.

"I am the art fanatic, hence all the paintings in the house."

"I guess that is where Ryan's love for art and sports come from," I pointed out.

"That is correct." Ryan smiled his gratitude.

Once we finished dinner, Amelia called out, "Who's ready for chocolate chip cookies?"

"Me," Bria yelled out a bit too loud.

"Bria, use your inside voice."

"She's fine. She is excited, and she has every right to be. Plus, we haven't had this much noise in the house in a long time. It is a nice change. Once I put these dishes up, I'll bring a plate of them out for us all to share."

"I'll help you clean up." I stood, ready to gather the plates off the table.

"Dear, you are our guest. We don't expect you to help," James said as he stood.

"I'll help Amelia. You and Ryan relax. I don't mind."

Amelia and I gathered the plates off the table, and I followed her into the decorated kitchen. The aroma of chocolate goodness lingered in the air. As Amelia and I filled the dishwasher, Amelia looked over at me.

"Honey, can I tell you something?"

I responded, "You can tell me anything."

"Ryan gave us a vague explanation of what you have been through."

"He did?"

She nodded. "I just wanted to let you know that we think you are doing amazing as a mother with all you had to conquer."

"Thank you."

"No, thank you for leaving when you had the chance. Not everyone is given that opportunity." Amelia looked off into the distance as if she was deep in thought. After a few moments, she looked at me and continued to talk. "You can and will do something productive with your life." After the dishes were loaded, Amelia went into the microwave and grabbed the plate of cookies. The cookies looked perfect, crisp around the edges and gooey in the center. I followed her to the dining room, where James, Ryan, and Bria talked.

"Who's ready for cookies?" she called out.

Chapter Twenty-Nine

Kyla

"Thank you all for coming out this afternoon for Bria's fifth birthday."

Looking around, my eyes perused the huge crowd of children and parents that surrounded the decorated tables topped with a variety of food, beverages, and gifts. My heart filled with warmth as I located Sabrina, Julian, Emily, Aunt Liliana, Ryan, and his parents.

"This party means the world to her, so I would love for you to contribute to the fun she will have today. Refreshments are for all to enjoy. Let's have fun," I burst out as the crowd cheered and clapped.

"Thank you, Mommy." Bria beamed as her cheeks had a hint of rose to them.

"You don't have to thank me, sweetheart." I brushed my hand over Bria's ponytail and straightened the purple birthday sash across her body. "Go have fun with your friends."

Some of the crowd went over to the playground as their children ran to play, and some of the crowd fixed plates of food.

"This was such a great idea doing her birthday party at the park." Sabrina grabbed a bottle of water out of the cooler. Julian and Ryan were in the corner drinking soda as they chatted with each other.

"My place is too small to host all of her friends and their families."

"I wish I would've had your smarts. When we decided to have Emily's birthday party last year, we had it at our house. We spent hours cleaning the mess up." Sabrina playfully rolled her eyes. "Never again." She looked over to the playground before she looked at me. "Do you need me to help you with anything else?"

I shook my head and responded, "You have done more than enough. Thank you, Sabrina."

Aunt Liliana walked over and wrapped her arm around my shoulder. She pressed her face against mine as she squeezed my shoulder. Her perfume surrounded me. "You did amazing with the decorations."

"Thanks to you, Amelia, and Sabrina for helping me."

Sabrina smiled as she excused herself to walk over to the playground where our girls played.

"There is no way I could've done it without you two."

Even though Aunt Liliana lived in Washington, she promised to visit at least twice a month. There were special occasions when she would visit more often, such as Bria's birthday. She could travel often as she owned and operated her own cleaning business.

"There is nothing in this world that I wouldn't do for my niece and great-niece."

"That is wonderful to hear."

"It is wonderful to say. I can't tell you how long I have been waiting to say that."

"Can I ask you a question?"

"Ask away."

"How long have you been wearing that perfume?"

I tucked a piece of hair behind my ear.

"Since I was sixteen. This has been my favorite perfume for ages."

"Oh my gosh." I brought my hands up to my mouth as I gasped.

"What's wrong?"

"Is that the perfume you used to wear when you used to come to visit me?"

She nodded. "How did you know?"

"I remember your perfume," I choked out as

tears burned the back of my eyes.

"Don't cry." She pulled me into her arms and softly rubbed my back.

Burying my face into her neck, one flutter of my eyes caused the tears to fall from my eyes.

"Why are you crying?" She held me outstretched in her arms.

I took a deep breath. "There is a sense of déjà vu washing over me. This is the closest I'll ever feel to my mother."

"Oh, honey." Aunt Lily pulled me back into her arms. "I'm glad you can experience that feeling. Whenever you want to talk about your mother, by all means, I would love to sit and have a chat about her."

"Thank you."

Aunt Lily wiped my tears away. "Now, less crying. More mingling. Okay?"

"Yes, ma'am."

Following my aunt's advice, I composed myself. I made my rounds to the parents and talked with them. Working at the coffee shop helped me blossom out of my shell.

"Pumpkin."

Turning around, I faced Amelia and James. They were both dressed casually in a pair of blue jean shorts and matching blue t-shirts.

"You two look so adorable in your matching outfits." I walked over to give them a hug.

"Thank you, pumpkin."

"Dressing alike was Amelia's idea," James responded.

"Why is it only my idea?" Amelia looked over at James.

"You suggest it. I go along with it. Doesn't seem too much like it was my idea," James pointed out.

Amelia nudged James on the arm in a playful manner as an arm snaked around my waist. Moments later, a soft kiss was pressed to my temple.

"What are you all talking about over here?" Ryan took a drink from his soda.

"How your mother forces me to wear matching outfits with her."

"If it were by force, I'd have to hold you down and dress you myself."

In a joking manner, James responded, "I haven't said it hasn't happened yet."

"Playful banter is what thirty-three years of a happy marriage get you."

"It's a beautiful sight." Ryan rubbed small circles into my side.

"Yes, yes, it is. Growing up and watching it firsthand inspired me to find love as such."

As I was about to respond, Amelia clapped her hands as she hopped from foot to foot with a huge grin on her face.

"What's going on?" Ryan asked his mother.

"The gift that we purchased for Bria is to die for."

"Really? Now I am dying to know what you bought her."

"We bought her a karaoke machine," James

mentioned.

"I wanted to tell her." Amelia produced a faux sad facial expression.

"You took too long for my liking."

"A karaoke machine?" Complete shock took over.

"Yes. A karaoke machine. Isn't that such an amazing gift?" Amelia spun her diamond ring around her finger as she nodded.

"She will never leave that machine alone," Ryan commented.

"I know. She'll sing my ears off 24/7."

"She is more than welcome to come to sing our ears off at our house," James said.

"Are you sure about that?" I raised my eyebrows.

"Of course. We love having children around. For some reason, our children have yet to produce any for us to spoil to the ends of the Earth." Amelia threw a hint at Ryan as she winked at him.

Giggling, I looked over at Ryan. For the first time since I had known him, his cheeks had changed from their normal skin tone to a bright pink color. He was embarrassed.

"I trust you two. You can have Bria anytime you'd like."

"Woohoo." James cheered as he did his dance which caused laughter to erupt from all of us.

"Someone is happy over here." Aunt Lily's voice floated over my shoulder.

"Very happy," Ryan emphasized. "My father never dances."

After thirty more minutes of mingling, I called for everyone to join us around the table so we could sing happy birthday.

Bria ran over to the table, and I straightened her sash before she sat in front of the cake. Ryan lit the candles on the cake, and we sang happy birthday. Bria's face beamed with happiness the entire time.

"Make a wish."

Bria closed her eyes for a few seconds before she opened them up and blew out her candles. As soon as the candles were blown out, we cheered and clapped.

"Who wants cake?" I grabbed the cake cutter in my hand.

"Me," all the children yelled.

Chapter Thirty

Brad

Bria turned five today. She had grown up so much since the last time I held her in my arms and told her how much I loved her. That occurrence felt like years ago and had only been several months. Several. Long. Months.

Bria looked so beautiful wearing her blue romper and her purple birthday sash. The romper wasn't familiar to me, so it must've been a purchase done after the move.

As she ran around the playground laughing and having fun with her friends, it took every ounce of my being not to get out of the car and grab her into a tight embrace.

The hurt I felt deep in my bones was difficult to deal with. I had been in Bria's life since the day she entered this world. I was there for every single major milestone. I was there for every single birthday. Betrayal was thick in the air as I watched Bria's birthday party go on without my presence requested.

A woman that had facial similarities to Kyla wrapped her arms around her. Was that Kyla's mother? After all those years of being abandoned in foster care, I couldn't believe her actions. The system raised her, and after she took Bria away from me, she went on the journey to find the mother that didn't want her. She acted as if she had known this woman her entire life.

Shaking my head in disgust, I reached into my glove compartment and took one drink of my whiskey. I couldn't help but drink to this new revelation. My parents were not enough to make her feel loved; they did everything in their power to make her feel like their own.

I watched as Kyla bounced from parent to parent. She held plenty of conversations as I sat in my car in pure amazement. She had blossomed into an outgoing woman since she left me. What happened to the shy woman that I dated for five years?

I couldn't help but watch as she hugged a couple wearing matching outfits. They smiled at each other as if they were more than acquaintances. As I wondered who these people were, Kyla's new boyfriend walked over and wrapped his around her waist before her gave her a kiss on the temple. This must've been his parents, as he did have a noticeable resemblance to the man. They stood around and talked so casually. As if they were one big happy family with no care in the world.

If only I still had a big happy family to return home to. Due to not arriving home by my Dad's required deadline of Sunday morning, he had told me on a very short phone call that I was fired from the family business. He was afraid I'd go too far with hurting Kyla, and she'd call the police and make me do jail time. He didn't want anything tarnishing the business in any manner.

Mom called me right after the call ended as she cried her eyes out over the phone. She told me it was my Dad's decision to fire me. She didn't even have to call me to tell me that. Mom was a laid-back parent. My dad was a strict parent, and whatever he wanted, he got, or there were major consequences to pay.

My life had been falling apart, piece by piece since Kyla left. If Kyla had never left, life would still be great. My parents and I wouldn't have anything to argue about. They would still see Bria daily, which I knew they loved.

When it came to money, I had no worries. I had more than enough money to cover my expenses for several years. If Dad didn't allow me back into the company, I'd just use my work skills and capabilities to get a job elsewhere when I arrived back home. My focus was Kyla and Bria. My parents couldn't even stop that focus, no matter how hard they tried.

Kyla and Bria were my life. They were the reason I still had breath in my body. They were the reason I worked as hard as I had these past few years. Now, there they were. In another state. In the presence of another man. I swore if my daughter called him daddy, I would rip his spline out.

Kyla was mine.

Bria was mine.

It was time to take back what was mine.

The take-back would be done in such a tasteful manner. Kyla won't ever see it coming.

Chapter Thirty-One

Kyla

"You are breathtaking."

Taking Ryan's hand and stepping out of my car, I smoothed down the maroon-colored evening gown that held my body like a glove. My hair was in a high pineapple style, with a few loose strands that hung around my face. I wore a pair of dainty silver earrings. On my feet were a pair of silver, sparkling high heels.

"Thank you, handsome."

He kissed my forehead.

Ryan's eyes widened as he handed me a red

rose. "Are you wearing makeup?"

"Sabrina went crazy when I told her we were going to dinner tonight."

"Your beauty is on full display."

"You are so sweet."

"If I weren't so hungry, I'd take you back to my place and slip you out of this dress."

Smiling, I responded, "I want everyone to see me tonight. I didn't spend a torturous hour being Sabrina's doll for nothing."

Ryan laughed as I looked him over in his sea-green dress shirt and gray dress pants.

"You look like a million bucks."

"I feel like a million bucks with you on my arm," he confessed as he placed his hand on my lower back.

Together, we walked into the Steakhouse restaurant.

Walking up to the hostess stand, Ryan stated, "Reservations for two under Walker."

"Follow me to your table." The hostess led the way.

We followed the hostess through the low-lit, modern decorated restaurant until we arrived at an empty booth. Sitting across from each other, the hostess stated, "Your waiter Peter will be with you shortly."

Opening the menu, I looked it over as my stomach growled on cue. My stomach growled so loud Ryan looked up and laughed. "You sound like you might be hungrier than I am."

Smiling, I nodded. "I skipped lunch today."

Peter, a tall, scrawny man with black hair, walked over to the table with a basket of warmed bread. "My name is Peter. I will be your waiter for the evening. May I interest you in our special bottle of wine?"

"What type of wine?" Ryan asked as he looked at Peter.

"It's a dry, white wine."

"Yes, we will take it." Ryan smiled.

"I will be back shortly."

As soon as Peter walked away, Ryan and I dived into the bread basket at the same time, our hands colliding with each other. At the same time, we both pulled our hands away.

"Ladies first."

Pulling out a piece of bread, I ripped a piece off. I held it outstretched, inches from Ryan's mouth. He ate the bread and moaned in satisfaction.

"I thought you said ladies first," I joked before I took a bite of the bread.

"I couldn't say no to warm bread in my face."

Silence settled over us as we looked over the menu. "Do you have any recommendations?"

"The filet mignon is to die for."

Peter walked over to our table, and he carried a bottle of white wine. He popped the cork and filled our glasses halfway.

"Are you two ready to order?"

"Not yet. Can you give us a few more minutes?"

"Of course. Take your time."

"How is the wine?" I asked him after he took a sip.

"It's great, but you might not like it. It's not sweet."

Picking up my glass, I took a sip, and my mouth scrunched up. Ryan laughed as he dug his hand into the bread basket and took out a piece.

"It is bitter."

"Dry wine at its finest."

"I think I'll stick to the sweet ones from now on."

I went back to looking at the menu when I felt eyes burning into me. My heartbeat quickened. I turned in my seat and looked around the restaurant. Everyone in the restaurant talked with their dinner partners, not giving me any attention. Sighing a breath of relief, I turned around in my seat, and I looked at Ryan.

"Are you okay?" Ryan asked, concern written all over his face.

"Yes, I am." I looked back at the menu for a few moments before I looked up to see Ryan staring at me. "Why are you staring?"

Skepticism was prominent in my voice.

"I'm just admiring the beautiful woman sitting across from me."

I smiled at his compliment. "You always know the right words to make me feel special."

"You should feel special. You rock your strength and confidence for all to see."

I placed my hand over his and gave it a squeeze.

"The strength and confidence have come from your unconditional love and support," I admitted as Peter walked over to us.

"How is the wine?" He said as he approached our table.

Ryan and I locked eyes before we laughed. "I think it's great."

"I think the complete opposite." I brought my hand up to my chest.

"I'm sorry to hear that. Would you like to try another wine? We can go for a sweet one this time."

I shook my head. "I'll just take a glass of water."

He nodded. "Are you two ready to order dinner?"

"I will have a filet mignon, medium, with a side of grilled asparagus." I closed my menu.

"I will have a filet mignon, medium rare, with a side of creamed spinach."

"I'll go put your orders in. I'll be right back with your water." Peter scribbled the order onto his notepad, grabbed the menus, and walked away.

Within minutes, Peter delivered my water to the table, and I took a hearty sip as Ryan sipped his wine.

"You could've ordered another drink."

I shook my head. "The water is fine."

Ryan and I talked as we snacked on our bread. Twenty minutes later, our food was delivered to our table. The presentation of the food was flawless. I only hoped the quality of the meal matched its beauty. Cutting into my steak, I took a bite, and the steak was exquisite, cooked to perfection.

"This is the best steak I have had in a very long time," Ryan said after a few minutes.

"This is the best steak that I have ever had."

As I cut my asparagus into smaller pieces, I saw a flash of strawberry blonde hair out of the corner of my eye. Looking over, I noticed Sabrina standing several feet away next to a beautiful, exotic sculpture.

"Is that Sabrina over there?" I pointed in the direction which was located close to the kitchen.

Ryan looked up from his plate of food. "Yeah, I believe that is her."

"I wonder what she is doing here?"

"Maybe she came for the amazing steak," Ryan suggested.

Excusing myself from the table, I walked over and placed my hand on Sabrina's shoulder. She spun around, and her eyes lit up.

"Hello, Kyla." She smiled.

"What are you doing here?"

Her eyes flickered around the restaurant before she said, "I'm here picking up some food."

Raising an eyebrow, I placed my hand on my hip. Sabrina was not the best liar, and I could see straight through her. "Sabrina, what is going on?"

Sabrina huffed as she rolled her eyes. "Okay, fine. I am not here picking up food."

"What's going on?" I repeated.

Sabrina stared into my eyes before she

looked past me. "I'm here to capture the moment."

It took several moments for her words to process in my head. Turning around in confusion, I looked at Ryan, down on one knee. In his hand was a maroon box with a beautiful, white gold one-carat diamond ring that sparkled in the restaurant's dim lighting. All the occupied tables in the vicinity looked at us with joy on their faces.

I placed a hand over my pounding heart as I stepped back in amazement. Ryan smiled as he said, "These past few months that I have gotten to know you have been amazing. There has been something about your aura that attracted me to you from the first day that I met you. The first day that I laid eyes on you. Not another day can go by without me confessing that I want you to be my wife. Will you do me the honor of marrying me?"

"You fell in love with me when I couldn't find the courage to love myself. Of course, I'll marry you."

As cheers and congratulations were murmured in the restaurant, Ryan stood and took the ring out of its box. He slipped the ring onto my finger before he wrapped his arms around me and kissed me.

"You knew about this?" I asked Sabrina as she continued her mission to take pictures of us.

"Of course, I knew. I've known for a few weeks now."

My mouth dropped open in shock. "You two did a great job of hiding this surprise from me."

"That was the plan," Ryan stated.

"I would never ruin my best friend's first and only proposal."

Wrapping my arms around her, I kissed her on the cheek. "Thank you for helping make this moment so special."

"You don't have to thank me. I was honored to be included in this special moment."

Turning to Ryan, I said, "I love you so much, Mr. Walker."

"I love you too, future Mrs. Walker. My love for you is never-ending."

"You have no idea how much the feeling is mutual."

Chapter Thirty-Two

Brad

There was not much more that I could handle. Watching Kyla move onto her new life with no cares in the world was painful. Did she ever think of me? Did I ever cross her mind anymore? Or was I just a distant memory of her past life that she wished to forget?

Following Kyla to the restaurant was the worse thing I could've done. She looked stunning in her maroon evening dress. I had never seen her dress up so elegantly.

It wasn't pleasant to watch her boyfriend help

her out of her car and kiss her on the forehead. My heart ached as I watched him place his hand on her lower back and guide her to the restaurant door.

Sitting outside for a while, I was tempted to go inside and order dinner when I saw a familiar face walk into the restaurant. I stopped and thought better of my decision. This must've been one of Kyla's friends as I had seen her at her job and Bria's party. Fearful of blowing my cover, I decided dinner would have to wait one more hour.

Thirty minutes later, I watched as Kyla's friend walked out of the restaurant and got into her car. The woman backed out and drove away as Kyla and her boyfriend walked out of the restaurant's doors. They both carried a to-go container. A sparkling object on Kyla's finger caught my eye. Squinting, I leaned forward as much as possible in my car, and I looked at an engagement ring. An enormous engagement ring. He was no longer her boyfriend but now a fiancé.

Kyla was engaged, but she wasn't engaged to me as I had always dreamed would happen. She was engaged to another guy. Tightening my grip on the steering wheel, I held on until my knuckles turned ash white.

I watched as Kyla and her fiancé sat their to-go containers on top of Kyla's car. They wrapped their arms around each other for a long time before sharing a sensual kiss. He tucked a stray piece of hair behind her ear and told her something. Kyla laughed as she smiled before they grabbed their to-go containers from the car. He opened the driver's door for her, and she slid inside. He smiled and closed the door before he turned and walked to his car.

Kyla waited until he was settled inside his car before she pulled out and left.

I watched him as he started his car up. He reversed and left the parking lot. It took every ounce of my being not to follow him to his house and beat him to a pulp.

As I watched his car disappear out of sight, I came to a decision. I could not wait any longer. I needed to act now and take back what was mine.

Kyla was mine, and she would come back home with me. I wouldn't take no for an answer.

Chapter Thirty-Three

Kyla

Thanksgiving was three weeks ago, and it came relatively quick. Amelia and James invited us over for the holiday. Even though they had just met us, they treated us like we were a part of their family. I could not have asked for a better holiday. We passed delicious food around the table and laughed at memories as we created new ones. Sophia wasn't able to come into town as she ended up spending the holiday with her boyfriend's parents.

I curled up on the couch, sipping a glass of

red wine while reading a book. The book was an intense mystery, which had me on the edge of my seat. I was halfway through the book, and I was hooked. I looked forward to a long, peaceful night that allowed me to dive deep into a book and explore a different world than my own.

Ten minutes into reading my book, Bria walked out of her room.

"Mommy, I don't feel good."

I exhaled, set my glass of wine on the end table, and closed my book.

"What's wrong, Sweetie?"

Bria coughed into her hand. "I think I have a cold."

I took her hand and pulled her closer to me. Placing the back of my hand on her forehead, she felt warm but not warm enough for her to have a fever.

"You do feel a bit warm. Would you like some soup?" Bria nodded. "Let me put on some chicken noodle soup, and then I'll be in your room to give you some medicine."

As I walked into the kitchen to prepare the soup, Bria returned to her room. Once the soup simmered on the stove, I went into the medicine cabinet and grabbed the children's cough medicine. After Bria drank her medicine, I said, "Your soup will be ready in five minutes."

I filled a bowl and placed the soup into the freezer to cool it down.

"Bria, your soup is ready."

Bria walked out and sat at the table as I put

her soup in front of her. I walked over to my phone on the couch as she ate.

Picking the phone up, I texted Ryan.

Me: Plans to go to the lake might be canceled for tomorrow. Bria is not feeling well. Will update you in the morning.

Within moments, a message came through.

Ryan: Ok beautiful. Tell Bria I hope she feels better. I love you.

Me: I will tell her. I love you too.

"Ryan said he hopes you feel better soon."

She smiled as she spooned soup into her mouth. "I still want to go to the lake tomorrow."

I shook my head. "We are not going anywhere tomorrow if you are sick."

I walked over to her and ran my fingers through her hair before I kissed her forehead.

She pouted before she dropped her spoon into her bowl of soup.

"I'm all better now."

Chuckling, I walked over to the soup on the stove and spooned two ladles into a bowl.

"Nice try. Eat that soup so you can shower and go to bed. Sleep is the best remedy to feeling better."

Bria did as she was told, and we finished our soup at the same time.

After dinner, I loaded the dirty dishes into the dishwasher as Bria took a shower. Once Bria was all clean, I kissed her forehead and tucked her into bed.

"Goodnight, Sweetie."

"Goodnight, Mommy. I love you."

"I love you too. I will see you in the morning."

Shutting the light off in Bria's room, I closed the door and returned to the couch. I still had time to read some more of my book before I had to go to bed. Opening my book up, I grabbed my glass of wine and dived back into my character's world. This book had captured my attention so intensely I considered staying up for another two hours to finish reading it.

As 11:00 PM crept around, I finished the last page of my book. I was relaxed from the two glasses of wine I had in the past three hours, and I was ready to go to bed.

I grabbed my phone to send Ryan a goodnight text.

Me: Goodnight, handsome. I love you so much. I cannot wait to become Mrs. Walker.

Ryan and I had discussed getting married in a few months. Some would think it was rushed, but what Ryan and I desired was all that mattered. We had considered eloping and coming back to throw a wedding party, but from a very young age, I had always wanted to walk down the aisle, and I couldn't say no to that opportunity.

After cleaning the kitchen up, I went to take a hot shower. The water rushed over my body and my muscles loosened up. I was ready for a good night's rest.

After toweling off my body, I dressed in my favorite flower print pajamas and walked into my bedroom. Ryan had not responded to my message, so I was sure he had fallen asleep before me. I couldn't wait for the day we would fall asleep next to each other for the rest of our lives. Plugging my phone into the charger, I turned off the lights and snuggled under my covers. Sleep had wrapped its comforting arms around me until I heard the sound of a door closing. My eyes shot open in the darkness as I pushed myself to a sitting position. My heart jumped out of my chest. Someone was in the house with us.

Shoving the covers off me, I stood and approached the door to my bedroom. There was no other option but to do everything possible to protect Bria. Taking a deep breath, I pushed the door open and walked out. I stopped dead in my tracks as my eyes continued to adjust to the darkness. Standing several feet away in the doorway was a dark figure. All I could make out was the black hoodie, baggy black pants, and black boots.

"We meet again," came an all too familiar voice.

A voice I knew all too well. A voice I didn't ever want to hear another day in my life. A voice that haunted me for years.

My breath hitched in my chest as goosebumps raised on my arms. After almost a year of staying under the radar, Brad had found me. Brad had found us. Deep down in my heart, I knew it was only a matter of time before Brad located us, but I didn't think it would be this soon.

I didn't think it would be tonight. Where did I slip up in my planning?

"You have no words to say to your boyfriend?" His voice was cold and a bit shaky. His arms moved at his sides as he continued. "Or shall I say, ex-boyfriend? I don't recall us breaking up, but I have seen you with another man."

I took a deep breath. "I can explain..."

"No, Kyla." Brad was too calm. "You cannot explain anything to me."

He took a step forward, causing me to take a step back. I looked at the light switch that sat behind Brad. "It's been almost a year since you've seen me. I thought I would get more of a welcome than this."

The pounding of my heart reached my ears. Whatever I did from this point forward, I needed to tread on thin ice. Brad was too calm, and the smallest thing could set him off. From experience, I knew the type of wrath Brad could muster, and I did not want to be on the receiving end again.

"H-h-how have you been?" I stuttered as I scratched my hair, my anxiety threatening to appear.

Brad chuckled, sending chills down my spine. "How have I been? Do you really want to know Kyla?"

"Of course, I want to know."

"I feel as if you couldn't care less."

"Why do you feel that way?"

"Well, if you want the truth, I have been

horrible. My life has crumbled since you left and took Bria with you."

Ryan paused as he lifted his hand to remove the hoodie from his head. He turned and flicked on the living room light. For the first time in almost a year, I looked at Brad in the flesh. His brown hair had grown a few inches. His mustache and beard had grown a bit too long. His green eyes had a dark tint to them. Yet, he was still every bit of attractive as I had remembered. If only his actions matched his looks. To be on the safe side, I hid my left hand behind my back.

"Why did you leave?" He looked into my eyes, waiting for an answer.

Searching his eyes, I noticed they were void of emotion.

Nervousness filled my body as my mouth went dry. I opened my mouth to respond to his question, but it seemed as if my brain had forgotten how to formulate any words.

Brad chuckled at my lack of response as he took a few more steps into my house. He acted as if this was not his first time there. As if he was invited inside and he didn't break into my house without my consent. I backed up two more steps before my back hit the wall.

"This is a nice place that you have here," he continued as he looked around, ignoring that I neglected to respond to his previous question.

"Thanks," I drawled out, not sure how to respond.

He walked over to the dining room table and

fingered the red rose Ryan had just given to me. A devilish smile appeared as his eyes flickered over to me. He picked up the rose.

"Did your boyfriend give you this rose?"

Going against my better judgment, I blurted out, "Brad, what are you doing in my house?"

Brad looked up as he dropped the rose back into the vase, his emotionless gaze now dark with anger.

"I believe you know why I am here."

He responded in a tone that was too calm for my liking. There was no way he was this calm inside.

Shaking my head, I placed my hand on my hip.

"Brad, I understand you must be upset. I took Bria from you, and we left, but I had to do what was best for me. What was best for us."

Brad picked up the vase and threw it across the room. The glass shattered and echoed through the house. I screamed in terror as I jumped.

To my horror, Bria's bedroom door swung open moments later.

"Mommy, what's wrong?"

She rubbed the sleep from her eyes as she looked at me.

"Honey, please go back into your room."

Brad smiled at the sight of Bria as his eyes brightened.

"Hi, baby girl."

His mood had taken a complete u-turn.

Bria turned and looked at Brad. "Daddy?"

"Oh my goodness Bria. I haven't seen you in so long. Come give daddy a hug."

Brad squatted down and opened his arms wide.

Bria was about to run over to Brad when I grabbed her hand and stopped her. "Bria, please go back into your room. Mommy will be in there soon."

Brad stood back up as he yelled, "Why are you preventing me from seeing my daughter?"

His mood had taken another turn, and it was for the worse.

Bria turned and looked at me. "Go to your room now."

Bria ran into the room. If looks could kill, I would've been buried six feet under.

"Why are you preventing me from seeing my daughter?" he asked me with bass in his voice. He stood by the dining room table. He stood too close for my comfort.

"Brad, please just leave, and we can do this another time."

Brad gave off a horrific laugh. "Do you really think I am going to leave?"

"No, I don't think you will leave, but that would be the best thing you could do right now."

Brad pointed towards the front door.

"If I walk out of that door, I am sure you will pack up Bria and take off again. I will not allow that to happen again. I will not let you take her from me. I will not let you leave me again."

I took a deep breath. "I had to leave. I had no choice but to remove my child from such a toxic environment."

"You mean our child?" He clarified.

"Yes, our child. I had to remove our child from a toxic environment."

Brad shook his head as he took two more steps closer. "I wouldn't say it was toxic."

"Screaming at the top of your lungs at us is toxic. Watching her mother get slapped, punched, or kicked is toxic."

Brad yelled at the top of his lungs as he grabbed his head in his hands. "Just shut up."

"Just leave Brad. Bria does not need to go through this anymore."

After a few moments, Brad removed his hands from his head and looked up at me.

"You can take your hand from behind your back. I know that you are engaged."

I allowed my arm to relax at my side, my ring showing on full display. "Please go," I pleaded.

Brad shook his head as he reached into the pocket of his hoodie. He produced a handgun, and my heart dropped into the pit of my stomach. I was going to be sick.

"I can't let you go. Just pack up your things. You and Bria are coming back home with me."

I stood frozen as my eyes zeroed in on the gun in his hand. To my knowledge, Brad had never, ever owned a gun. Him having one in his hand made me feel fearful.

In a soft tone, I said, "Brad, please don't do

this. Bria and I have started a life here. We can't just up and leave."

Brad scoffed as he scratched his beard. "I have seen the life that you started. You can leave Kyla. It's not all that special. You did it when you left me back home. I was miserable for months on end. You can pack up your things and leave now."

"H-how did you find me?"

I had to know where my plan went awry.

"I tried to find you on my own, but you left me absolutely no crumbs to trail." Brad laughed before he continued talking. "So I had to spend a lot of money on a private investigator."

Brad moved the hand that the gun was in as he looked down at the ground. He looked up and his eyes were red-rimmed with tears threatening to fall.

"When he told me the extent that you went to not be found, I was devastated. You can't tell me that life with me was really that bad."

Silence settled in the room as I was too fearful to speak. I didn't want to be killed by Brad, the first man I had ever loved. The first man that I had trusted.

"I've been watching you for a while. So many times I just wanted to walk up to you and Bria and make my presence known, but I had to wait. I had to wait for the perfect time."

I kept silent, allowing Brad to get everything he wanted to say off his chest.

"The first time I saw you in town, I thought you looked so beautiful. Of course, you looked different with the bangs, but I knew my sweet Kyla. I wanted to wrap my arms around you and never let you go. I missed you a lot." He paused as a tear fell from his right eye. He took a deep breath. "But you tried to replace me with that guy. I don't appreciate it."

He lifted the gun and pointed it at me.

The blood drained from my face as I raised my hands up. Was this how my life was going to end? Was I going to die tonight? Before I was even given a chance to live?

"W-wait."

"Wait for what? I don't want to hurt you. I just want you to pack your stuff and come back home. This is all that I ask. I'll forgive you for everything you did here. We just need to go now. We can start over. I love you. I love Bria."

"Wait, Brad. Just wait. Can you just listen to me?"

He looked into my eyes, his emotions on full display.

"I'm all ears."

"I cannot leave with you. I will not put Bria back into that toxic environment. She does not deserve that type of lifestyle. Please do not do something that you will regret. If you love me, you will leave. If you love Bria, you will leave. Just please leave and don't come back."

"Kyla, I love you and Bria with all my heart. I have always told you that you would never leave me. I have made it plain and simple for years. No one will have you if I can't have you."

A loud piercing pop rang throughout the room. Searing pain radiated as I looked down at my stomach. My flower-printed pajamas were now blood-stained. I dropped to my knees and fell onto my face, experiencing weakness all over. My vision blurred as sleepiness settled over me. I heard loud, heavy footsteps grow softer before they disappeared. The door slammed shut. I was not going to die today. I could not die. I had Bria to live for. I was a fighter. I was a warrior. I escaped into black darkness.

Chapter Thirty-Four

Ryan

My phone ringing startled me out of my sleep. Reaching to grab my phone, I picked it up and answered.

"Hello," I mumbled into the phone.

"What's up," came a familiar male voice.

I scrunched my eyes as I pushed myself up. "Who is this?" I was disoriented.

"Did you delete my number or something? I know you didn't do your best friend like that."

I gasped. "Marky Mark. What the hell are you doing calling me at..." I pulled the phone away to look at the time and said, "midnight."

"Marky Mark is back in town, baby."

"For good?"

"For good. The Mrs. and I just settled into a town not too far from you."

"I can't believe you are back home. We must get together soon. Now, why in the hell are you calling me at midnight?" I pushed my covers off me.

Mark laughed into the phone. "Midnight used to be eight on a weekday for us."

"Yes, it used to be, but that was in our college days."

"Ryan, don't tell me you are now going to sleep at nine o'clock every night."

I laughed at Mark's statement as I walked downstairs. "Of course not. I go to sleep at nine-thirty now." I received a howl of a response from Mark as I walked into the kitchen.

"Same old Ryan, I missed so much."

"Same old Marky Mark I haven't heard from in quite a few months."

"Marky Mark has been too busy with the Mrs."

"How is Chels doing?" I grabbed a glass from the cupboard and filled it with water. Chelsea was Mark's wife. We had gone to the same college, but she was a year younger than us. They messed around for a few months before they became a couple. I had called her Chels for as long as I could remember. Finally, Mark was down on one knee four years later, asking her to become his wife. Watching my best friend get hitched as the best man was a beautiful sight.

"She's doing all right. So happy to be back home. She missed her family."

"Are you telling me Marky Mark, also known as Momma's boy, hasn't missed his family?" I took a sip of my water as I leaned on the counter.

"You do not know how much I missed them. But I had my fix today when I crashed dinner. It was epic, mashed potatoes and meatloaf night."

"I know you did not crash dinner. I can only imagine you made dinner amazing with your presence.

"Of course. Whenever I am in anyone's presence, they are having a great time. So, I must ask you a question."

"Ask away." Knowing Mark, anything could come out of his mouth.

"Are you seeing anyone?"

"Yes, I am. Do you remember the woman I told you about the last time we talked?"

The phone became silent as I took a few sips of my water. "The one you met at the coffee shop?"

"Yes. That is the one."

"How is the relationship going?"

I could not hold it inside anymore. "We are engaged."

"What? When? How? Where?" Mark blurted out.

"We became engaged last week. I took her to a nice dinner and proposed in front of the entire restaurant."

"Where in the hell was this Ryan years ago? You were always faithful to your studies and your work. You didn't bat an eye on all the pretty girls who threw their goodies at you."

"Something changed when I laid eyes on her."

"Are you telling me it was love at first sight?"

I took a deep breath as I thought for a moment. "All I know is that I wanted her to become a part of my life."

"This woman must be special to have changed you. I must meet her."

"Well, we were planning to go to the lake tomorrow with her daughter to hang out. You and Chels are more than welcome to join us."

"Chelsea and I might take you up on that offer. I have to meet the woman who has captured my best friend's heart."

"You'll meet her, and I promise you, you will know why I love her as soon as you talk to her."

As Mark responded, a noise sounded in my ear, alerting me of an incoming call. When I pulled the phone away from my phone, and I saw Aunt Lily's name pop up on my phone, curiosity came over me. "Mark, I'll call you in the morning. I have another call coming through, and I need to take it."

"I know that excuse. I bet your woman just arrived at your bedroom with nothing on but a pair of red pumps."

"Yeah, if only that was the case. I love you, Mark. I'll talk with you tomorrow."

"Love you too, buddy. Goodnight."

Switching the call over, I answered.

"Hey, Aunt Lily. What's going on?" Aunt Lily was such a family-oriented and sweet individual. Even though I was not related to her by blood, she wanted me to call her Aunt, and I had no issue with that.

I heard an emotion-filled, gut-wrenching scream travel through the phone, which caused my heart to pump hard in my chest and my stomach to sour.

"Aunt Lily. What's wrong?" I asked, on high alert.

"I just received a call. I am trying to book a flight there right now," Aunt Lily wailed into the phone.

"Received a call about what?"

"It's Kyla. I just received a call from the police. Kyla was shot."

As soon as those words entered my ear and were processed in my brain, the glass I held dropped out of my hand and shattered into a million pieces. My heart shattered as water and glass bounced off the floor and hit my legs and feet.

"What?" I yelled as I ran for my car keys and wallet.

"I am booking the next flight out of Washington. I should be there in a few hours."

"What happened?" My voice cracked as I choked out the words. Tears burned the back of my eyes as I gathered everything I needed to leave.

"All I know is that the police called me and told me they received a call from a neighbor. Kyla was found unresponsive with a gunshot wound."

Unresponsive? Tears streamed down my face as I ran to the front door. After locking the door, I ran to my car and jumped inside. "Is Bria okay?"

"Bria is in police care. She is safe. No harm done."

"Is Kyla going to be okay?" I asked as my car roared to life.

"I don't know Ryan. I just know I can't lose her. I just got her back a few months ago. I can't say goodbye to her again."

"I'm on my way to the hospital. I'll keep you updated until you arrive," I said into the phone before I hung up. As I zoomed out of my neighborhood, I prayed there were no cops on the road because a high-speed chase would ensue before I'd ever pull over and waste precious time. Calling the support system I needed, the phone rang three times before it was picked up.

I heard a muffled, "Hello."

"Momma, I need you." I wailed into the phone as the tears streamed down my face like a water faucet at full capacity.

There was ruffling on the phone before Mom said, "Ryan? What's the matter?"

"Aunt Lily just called. She said Kyla has been shot."

"What?" I heard her say, "James, wake up. We need to go now."

"What's wrong? Go where?" I heard Dad ask.

"Kyla has been shot," she said to dad. "Honey, what happened?"

"I don't know, but I can't take it if something happens to her. She is my everything. She is my world."

"I know, honey, I know. Let's just hope and pray she will be fine. We are on our way to the hospital. Please drive safe, and we will see you soon."

Hanging up the phone with my Momma, I focused my attention on the road as I squeezed the steering wheel tight. I had told Kyla months ago that I would protect her and Bria with my entire being. Somehow, someone had caused harm to her, and I was not there to protect her. What had happened? What monster could have done such a horrific thing? Kyla was such a pure-hearted woman. Why would someone want to cause her any harm?

I remembered when I stared into her beautiful brown eyes for the very first time. She had me so mesmerized, I could feel it deep within my bones. I knew then that I was smitten and had to see if I had a chance with her. When I looked at her hand and saw no ring, I knew I could convince her to go out with me, but I would take my time charming her before taking that leap of faith. Who would've known we would be engaged almost a year after meeting? I knew because she had captured my heart within days.

I reminisced on when I held her hands in mine for the first time. Something spooked her after dinner, and I told her I would love to help her get over whatever she was dealing with that caused her fright. Her hands were so soft and small, and they fit perfectly in my grasp.

I remembered the first time I wrapped my arms around her. She felt perfect tucked into my warm embrace. She smelled delightful, like a garden of fresh flowers. I knew at that moment she completed me. I had found the missing piece I had waited years for, and I didn't want to let her go.

I reminisced about when I kissed her for the first time. Her soft, irresistible, delicious lips met mine, and the moment of truth was revealed when I felt the fireworks set off within my soul. My soul had found its soulmate, and I knew he couldn't live without her.

I remembered the first time I told her I loved her. The look on Kyla's face was priceless. She was surprised, but I could see all over her face that she felt the same way I did. The twinkle in her eye gave it away.

I reminisced on the first time we made love. It was the day when we became one. I had claimed her as mine in one of the best ways possible, and I knew I never wanted to say goodbye to her.

Remembering all the first times further proved I couldn't lose the wonderful woman who helped me become the man I am now. She helped me realize there was more to life than focusing on work. Instead, she helped me focus on life itself and the beauty it entailed.

I prayed Kyla would be fine. I prayed the bullet did not cause any permanent damage that would cause me to lose her forever. That would cause Bria to lose her forever. Kyla was a fighter. Kyla was a warrior, and I knew she would not give up. She had fought for years, and I knew she would continue to fight.

After twenty minutes of speeding, I pulled into the emergency room drop-off area and killed the ignition.

A woman that stood outside under the awning addressed me. "Sir, you can't park there."

I ignored her comment as I walked past her. I had only one thing in mind; she would not stop me. The sliding doors opened, and I looked around. Six individuals sat in the waiting area. I walked up to the check-in counter. There was a woman with a bun that wore a pair of scrubs. She typed away on her computer. After a few moments, she looked at me.

"You can sign in right there." She pointed at the clipboard that contained a sign-in sheet.

"I don't need to sign in. I am here to check on my fiancée."

"What is your fiancée's name?"

"Kyla Williams."

She typed into the computer and clicked a few times. "There are some detectives that are here to see you." She picked the phone up and pressed a few numbers. "The fiancé has arrived." A few moments of silence passed. "Okay." She hung up the phone. "The detectives are coming to speak with you."

Two men dressed in suits walked through the double doors that led to the back area. One was tall and muscular with a head full of wavy black hair, and the other was short and stocky with a bald head. They approached me, and the short man spoke.

"Hello, my name is Detective Simpson." He stuck his hand out, and I shook his hand. "This is Detective Black." Detective Black shook my hand.

"Hello, detectives."

"We are working on the case of your fiancée, and we'd like to gather more information from you."

"I don't mind assisting in your case, but can you tell me how she is doing before we discuss anything else."

Detective Black and Detective Simpson looked at each other before they looked back at me. Before they could respond, I heard, "Ryan, we are here, honey."

Turning around, my mother and father ran into the emergency waiting room. My parents were in such a rush they didn't even bother to change out of their pajamas. Looking down, I noticed I only wore pajama pants and a T-shirt.

We had just rolled out of bed, and we looked like it.

"Thank you for coming, momma and dad." They stood on each side of me and wrapped their arms around me.

We turned and placed our attention on the detectives. "Come follow us so we can find somewhere private to sit down and talk," Detective Simpson said.

The detectives led us through the double doors and walked until we came across an unoccupied conference room. We walked inside and sat around the table as Detective Black shut the door behind us. Once Detective Black sat down, he opened a notepad and spoke.

"She was unresponsive when she was taken from the scene. They have her in emergency surgery right now."

"How long has she been in surgery?" Dad asked.

Detective Simpson looked at the expensive watch on his wrist. "About thirty minutes."

"What happened?" Momma asked.

"We aren't too sure. That is why we want to question your son."

My eyebrows raised. "Wait. Am I being questioned as if I am a suspect?"

The detectives looked at each of us before Detective Black responded. "It is a part of the investigation process. We suspect those closest to the victim first. In this case, you are the fiancé."

"I would never hurt her. I just proposed to her

last week." It was difficult to mutter the words as tears threatened to fall.

"We just need to find out where you were tonight and go off witness statements."

"I arrived home around 8:00 PM. I had dinner with my parents."

"We can vouch for that." Mom nodded in agreement.

Detective Black scribbled on his notepad. "What did you do once you arrived home?"

"I did some laundry while I watched some TV."

"Is there any way you can corroborate that you were home and never left the house?"

I thought for a moment as I went through the night's events. Pulling my phone out of my pocket, I noticed I had an incoming text. Opening the message up, I read the last message Kyla had sent me. I hadn't seen it earlier because I had fallen asleep. Reading the message for the first time since the shooting happened caused my tears to flow down my cheeks like a waterfall.

"What is it son?" Dad rubbed my back.

"A text I am just now seeing from Kyla." Turning the phone around for the detectives to see, they leaned in closer as they squinted their eyes. "Does this look like the text that would come from a woman right before she is shot by her fiancé?"

Detective Simpson read the text out loud. "Goodnight, handsome. I love you so much. I cannot wait to become Mrs. Walker."

After a few moments, Detective Black tapped his pen on the table.

"Let's get a statement."

He flipped a few pages in the notepad.

"I have here that Kyla's next-door neighbor called to report screaming and gunshots. The neighbor reported seeing a hooded figure run out of the house and flee on foot. From the height provided, we have determined it was a male running away from the scene."

"We know for a fact that it was not a robbery. Nothing was taken from the scene that had any value," Detective Simpson said.

"Whoever did this shooting had a personal connection to the victim. When there are cases where nothing is taken from the scene, but there was a crime committed, we are almost ninety-nine percent sure it was done by someone the victim knew," Detective Black informed us.

I gasped as I thought back to my conversation with Kyla the first time she came to my house. "I know who did it."

"Did what?" Mom asked.

"I know who shot Kyla."

"How do you know?" Detective Simpson asked me.

"Kyla came to South Carolina in an attempt to get away from her abusive ex. She had always told me he would find her sooner or later. He must have found her."

"Can you provide me with this man's name?"

"All I know is that his name is Brad, and he is

from Miami." Then my mind went in another direction. "Did you question Bria? She was in the house when the shooting happened, right?"

"Poor, Pumpkin," Mom commented as she poked her lip out.

"We wanted to take the route that would not involve having a child provide details when her mother was just shot in the room next door."

"That would be the perfect person to ask. Bria is smart, and I can assure you that she will tell you who was in that house before her mother was shot."

The detectives looked at each other.

"I'll call the unit with Bria so we can question her. Sit tight, folks. We will get to the bottom of this."

Detective Black and Detective Simpson stood and walked out of the conference room.

Dad waited until the door to the conference room closed. "Kyla will be okay, son."

"I hope so."

I wasn't feeling as optimistic.

I couldn't believe I hadn't thought of Brad sooner. No wonder Kyla was so fearful of him. He was a downright monster if he was behind all of this. What pained me the most was that I was not there to protect her as promised.

Chapter Thirty-Five

Kyla

I felt light as a feather. Everything was white and pure around me, with no color or impurities to see for miles. Was I floating on a cloud? Was this the afterlife that everyone wondered about a time or two in their life?

The random sound of a beep evaded my brain. Or was it my ears? The sound continued, drawing me away from the fluffy cloud I found comfort in.

"I think she's waking up," floated from somewhere close as the stench of antiseptic entered my nose.

"I'll go get the doctor."

A hand touched me, and my eyes fluttered open for a brief second. All I saw was a bright light before my eyes closed again.

"Look at me," said a familiar voice, pulling me away from the cloud I didn't want to leave.

Opening my eyes again, I looked at the face of the person I knew and loved. For some reason, the face was tear-streaked, and the eyes were red.

"Handsome, what's wrong?"

My throat was irritated. Another hand was placed on my arm, and I turned to see another familiar face saddened and wet with tears.

"Amelia," I gasped in a voice not recognizable.

Amelia grabbed a cup of water and held the straw a few inches in front of my mouth. Leaning forward, a pain emitted in my stomach which caused me to groan and wince.

"Honey, sit back. I'm sorry." She put the straw right to my lips. I took sip after sip, the water soothing my parched, irritated throat.

A doctor came into the room and he carried a clipboard. Aunt Lily followed close behind, clutching tight onto her purse.

"Hello, Kyla. My name is Dr. Tyson. How are you feeling?"

"My stomach hurts."

I looked around the room. I realized that I sat in a hospital, hooked up to several machines.

Memories of Brad in my house took residence in my mind. The moment Brad snapped and could no longer maintain his composure, I fell to the floor with a gunshot wound. Brad had caused physical harm to me before, but I never imagined it would go this extreme. My intuition over a year ago was correct. He wanted my body to be scraped up by a forensic crew. Thank goodness, I sat in a hospital bed surrounded by the people that loved me.

"That is going to be the case for a while. The great news is, you have already started the healing process."

"Where is Bria? Is she safe?" I asked.

"She is fine. She is with James. She hasn't been getting any rest, so she is at our house resting," Amelia stated.

"Where is Brad?"

Silence settled upon the room as I looked from Dr. Tyson, Aunt Lily, Ryan, and Amelia. Everyone had a look of pity in their eyes, and at that moment, it bothered me deep within my core.

"The good news is that we had success removing the bullet. It was mere inches from hitting any vital organs, so we are thankful for that. You are expected to make a full recovery." Dr. Tyson said as he smiled.

"Thank goodness," Aunt Lily exclaimed. She placed a hand over her heart and closed her eyes.

"I'll have a nurse come in and give you some more medicine for your pain."

"Thank you, Dr. Tyson," I said.

"You are welcome, Kyla." He walked out of the room.

"Honey, I am so glad you are fine." Aunt Lily's eyes welled with tears. "When I received that call, I thought I had lost you forever."

"Don't cry, Aunt Lily. I could never leave you."

My own emotions started to go haywire as I watched tears stream down Aunt Lily's cheeks. My actions were the reason for those tears. Brad's action was the reason for those tears.

"You better not. You are stuck with me for life." Aunt Lily kissed me on the cheek.

"I hope you'll never leave me," Ryan said.

I turned my attention to him. "I don't plan on leaving you. My love for you is never-ending."

Ryan smiled as his mouth wobbled. Tears streamed down his face as he grabbed my face and kissed me.

Wiping away his tears as I stared into his eyes, Amelia asked, "Isn't young love so beautiful?"

"Yes, it is," Aunt Lily agreed.

After the emotions in the room died down, a nurse walked into the room. After she introduced herself, I asked, "So, can anyone tell me where Brad is?" I cleared my irritated throat as Amelia brought the cup back up to my lips so I could sip more water.

"We don't know," Aunt Lily admitted.

"What do you mean?"

Disappointment settled over me as the nurse

put medicine into my IV.

"He left after shooting you," Ryan informed me.

He balled his hands into a fist.

"How long ago was the shooting?"

I placed my hand on Ryan's hand to stop his fit of rage.

"It was two days ago."

"Two days? As in forty-eight hours?" I screeched.

"You are safe, beautiful. I promise you. He is not going to come near you ever again. If he even tries... I will personally..."

"Honey, stop speaking out of anger," Amelia interrupted Ryan as I gave his hand a squeeze.

"There are two police officers outside that door standing guard." My eyes widened, and Aunt Lily placed a comforting hand on mine. "They are only there in case he decides to come back, but the detectives doubted he would do that."

A knock sounded on the door.

"Come in," Ryan called out.

The door opened, and two men in suits walked in. One was tall and muscular with a head full of wavy black hair, and the other was short and stocky with a bald head.

"Hello, Kyla. I am Detective Black," the taller of the two said as he waved at me before he motioned to the short man. "This is my partner Detective Simpson, and we are handling your case."

"It's nice to meet you two."

Detective Simpson looked at everyone in the room. "Is it okay if we speak to Kyla alone? It'll only be a few minutes."

"That's fine." Aunt Lily stood up. She gave me a reassuring smile before she walked out of the door.

"Come on, honey," Amelia stood and held her hand out to Ryan.

I released Ryan's hand as he leaned over and kissed my forehead. He took his mother's hand, stood up, and walked out the door.

I watched as they left the room. Once the door closed, the detectives sat down.

"First and foremost, I want to say I am happy to see that you survived the shooting," Detective Simpson said.

"Thank you."

"We want to make sure we receive a statement from you as you are the only eyewitness." Detective Black pulled out a notepad and pen and wrote down my account of that night. "Are you sure it was Brad Robertson who shot you?"

"I am 100% positive."

Detective Black continued to write on his notepad as Detective Simpson said, "Bria loves you with all of her heart."

"Why do you say that?"

"She told us it was her dad who was the shooter."

I smiled as I realized Bria did the right thing when she spoke with the Detectives.

"We have had cases similar to this one where there is a domestic dispute between two parents. The child has some recollection of what happened and won't give any information away as they are scared to get one of the parents in trouble. In this case, Bria had no problem telling us that her dad hurt her mom," Detective Black informed me.

"Kyla, good luck with your recovery." Detective Black gave me a reassuring smile as he stood up.

"We will be in touch once we locate Brad," Detective Simpson stated as they headed for the door.

"Thank you so much for all that you have done."

As the door was about to close, it was pulled open. Amelia walked into the room and sat next to me. She reached out and took my hand in hers. "Pumpkin, I am so glad you are okay. We were worried sick about you."

"I'm glad to be alive. I couldn't imagine leaving Bria in this world all alone."

"She loves you with all her heart. James and I had her for the first night, and she refused to sleep. She cried her eyes out and begged for you to come home. We didn't get much rest that night, so Lily took her the second night so we could get some rest."

"She is my everything."

"We know, Pumpkin."

"I don't know what I'd do with myself if I didn't

have her."

Amelia as she squeezed my hand. "Can I tell you something?"

I looked into her eyes and could see plenty hid behind them. "Of course."

"I would love to talk to you about Stephanie. She was my younger sister."

"I never knew you had a sister."

"That is because I don't speak of her too often. Stephanie passed away."

"I am so sorry to hear that." Amelia smiled sadly as she looked around the room. "How long ago did she pass away?"

"Thirty years ago. She was murdered."

I gasped as I brought my hand up to my mouth. "What happened?"

Amelia took a deep breath before she spoke. "Stephanie was in a relationship with Chandler, a guy she met in college. At the beginning of the relationship, he treated her like the princess she was." Amelia smiled at the memory before she continued. "He proposed to her within three months of them dating. She was in love with him, so she said yes. After they had married for a year, it seemed like a switch was flipped. She would disappear for days on end, which was not common as we talked daily. When she would reach out to me, she would act very strange. When it had been months since I had seen her with my own two eyes, I decided to show up at her house one day."

"Was she happy when you showed up at her

house?"

Amelia shook her head as her eyes became red-rimmed and filled with tears. "I received more of a shocked reaction. When she flung open the door, I saw her black eye, and I lost it."

My heart dropped in my stomach. Dealing with years of abuse was difficult, but it was even harder to hear about others who also endured it.

"When I asked her what happened, she told me she ran into a door."

"Did you believe her?"

Amelia shook her head as the tears fell from her eyes. "I begged her to leave Chandler. I begged her to come to stay with us. I told her we would keep her safe, but she told me he promised not to hit her again, but all he did was lie." Amelia's eyes flickered over to the door before she continued. "One day, about three years later, my life fell apart. I received a call from an unfamiliar number while I worked, and I usually don't answer during work hours. But something told me that I needed to take that call. As soon as the person on the other end introduced themselves to me as a detective in the Homicide Unit, I dropped the phone and screamed at the top of my lungs."

Salty tears fell from my eyes as I gave Amelia's hand a comforting squeeze. Pushing myself up to sit, I wrapped my arms around Amelia as we cried together in silence. Thankful for the pain medication, there was no pain.

I rubbed her back as she continued to cry.

Stephanie was killed by her abuser. Somehow, I survived my abuse. Thinking back to the first day I met Amelia and James, I now understood her comment at the end of dinner.

'Thank you for leaving when you had the chance. Not everyone is given that opportunity.'

"The cause of death was an injury to the back of the head," she admitted, once she could speak again.

"Let me guess. Chandler tried to deny causing any harm to her."

"Of course, he tried, but I informed the detectives of all the bruises and marks I had observed over the years. In her heart, she thought he would change, but he proved her wrong in the worse way."

Silence settled upon the room as we separated.

"Stephanie proved her own case, though. After an extensive search of the house, the detectives found hidden cameras. Unfortunately, she died from Chandler pushing her down the stairs."

My heart went out to Amelia. She still carried the burden of her sister passing away on her shoulders.

"Amelia." Amelia looked at me. I wiped the tears away from her eyes. "The pain of losing your sister is still a raw wound that has yet to heal after all these years."

"It is, but I am just so grateful to have met such an amazing woman tired of the abuse. That ran from the abuse. That survived her abuse."

"It was difficult for me to leave Brad. It was one of the hardest decisions I have ever had to make. Like Stephanie, I believed in the lies that were told to me. I stuck around several years before I decided to love myself enough to escape that situation."

"You are an inspiration."

Amelia and I wrapped our arms around each other and hugged again. In the past few months, I was blessed to have encountered two women I considered mother figures. I wouldn't change the love I received for anything in this world.

The door opened, and Ryan walked in carrying a cup of coffee.

"What's going on in here?"

Amelia and I separated as we looked at Ryan and said, bonding simultaneously.

"It's a beautiful sight."

The door opened again, and in ran Bria. "Mommy," she yelled at the top of her lungs.

"Bria," I yelled back as I opened my arms.

She jumped into my arms, and the movement caused pain in my stomach, but I could care less. I held onto her tight as I ran my fingers through her hair. Aunt Lily and James walked into the room with smiles.

"I'm so happy you are okay, Mommy."

"I'm glad I am okay as well. I'm glad you are okay."

Tears fell from my eyes. My emotions were all over the place, and I had zero control over them.

"Why did Daddy try to hurt you?"

The room fell silent as I had no response to Bria's question. There was no answer I could think to tell a child, just like there was no answer I could think to tell anyone else.

"I don't know, Sweetie, but Daddy will get the help he needs now."

Cradling Bria in my arms, my mind traveled to places I preferred not to go. Yet, I couldn't help but think what would've happened if the bullet had hit any vital organs. Bria would have been motherless with a father I hoped would spend the rest of his life behind bars.

I was thankful to be alive.

I was grateful to be alive.

I was a survivor.

Chapter Thirty-Six

Kyla

My Christmas was spent in the hospital. The best gift I was given was life, so there were no complaints. Amelia, James, Bria, and Ryan came to visit with me. Amelia and James took it upon themselves to buy Bria all her gifts. They refused to take any money from me for the presents. To say they spoiled her was an understatement. Aunt Lily had to return to Washington but promised to return as soon as she could make the trip.

Each passing day spent in the hospital was

difficult for me. Even though the doctor had told me the bullet had not hit any vital organs, he suggested I stay in the hospital while my wound healed. Unfortunately, my physical wound was not the only one that needed to heal. My mental wound was more damaged.

Every time I closed my eyes to rest them, I saw Brad in my house with the gun. I saw the desire in his eyes to hurt me, and it prevented me from getting any type of restful sleep. When the nurses saw the bags that formed under my eyes, they told the doctors I needed counseling. So, every day, I was scheduled for counseling. It was a process, but it started to positively impact me.

The day after I woke up, Sabrina had waltzed into my room as she carried a bouquet of red roses and a cappuccino.

"Hello, Kyla."

"Hey, Sabrina."

"It's so amazing to see you up and smiling. How do you feel?"

She sat the bouquet and cappuccino on a table before she walked over to me and wrapped her arms around me.

"I am sore, but I can't complain."

Sabrina grabbed her cappuccino and took a sip before she sat in the unoccupied chair to the left of my bed.

"I arrived right after you were admitted, but Amelia kicked me out. She told me I needed to go home to Emily and she would keep me updated."

"Amelia meant all love and no harm."

Sabrina nodded. "I just wanted to be here for you. I never wanted to leave your side. You mean the world to me. Our friendship means the world to me. You'd be right by my side if the shoe was on the other foot."

"Of course, I would've been. That is what best friends do." I looked over at the roses. "Those are so beautiful. Red roses are my favorite."

"I know. I bought them at the floristry right next door to our job."

"I give them a five-star rating."

Sabrina took another sip of her drink. She smiled before we made eye contact. Her smile disappeared before she spoke.

"I can't believe Brad found you. You were always so careful with how you handled yourself."

I nodded. "I know. It was a shock to me when I woke up to him in my house."

"Did he ever mention how he found you?"

"He told me he hired a private investigator."

Sabrina gasped. "He went to the extreme. How long has he been around town?"

I shrugged my shoulders. "Regarding how long he has been here, I am not sure. In my heart, I believe he's been here at least a month."

"How could you be so sure?"

"He mentioned the engagement."

Sabrina's mouth dropped open as she brought her manicured hand up to her mouth.

"Unbelievable."

"Thinking on it now, I believe he was the dark

shadow I saw outside of our job that one day."

"That is shameful. We chalked it up to your mind playing games on you, but deep down, you knew. You knew he would find you."

I nodded. "I'm just grateful to be sitting here, talking to you."

"Kyla, you are a fighter. I had faith you would pull through."

For the next two hours, Sabrina and I continued to talk. It was great to have her company for a while. Sitting in a hospital bed and unable to go outside was hard on me mentally, physically, and emotionally. When it was time for her to leave, she stood and wrapped her arms around me before she kissed my cheek.

Three days after Sabrina came to see me, Detective Simpson and Detective Black paid me a visit.

"How are you doing, Kyla?" Detective Black asked me as they sat down.

I smiled. "I am doing better each day."

"We are glad to hear that," Detective Simpson stated.

"We come bearing good news." Detective Black gave off a comforting smile.

"You caught him?"

"We caught him." Detective Simpson said.

He smiled, lifting a huge weight off my shoulders. For the last few days, I had been on edge. Even though the detectives assumed that Brad had left the area, a small voice told me he wouldn't go until he could get Bria. Bria had been staying with Ryan's parents, and she had police supervision on her 24/7, even when she was at school.

"That is wonderful to hear. Where did you find him?"

"We found him in a motel in North Carolina," Detective Black stated.

"Wow," I gasped.

Even though I knew Brad wouldn't go back to his house, I never thought he'd be found in North Carolina.

"When we surrounded the motel, he barricaded himself in his room, and it took seven hours for us to get him to surrender," Detective Simpson informed me as he rubbed his bald head.

"He has always been stubborn."

"You don't have to worry about him anymore, Kyla. We might need you to testify if he decides to plead his innocence when the time comes. Would that be something you'd be okay with doing?"

"I'll do anything in my power to protect my daughter."

Once the detectives left that day, I smiled and relaxed in bed. That was the first time I could take an uninterrupted two-hour nap without jerking awake from fear.

The biggest surprise of my stay arrived a day later. I was watching a talk show when a soft knock at the door alerted me. It was unusual as everyone visiting never knocked. They just entered and announced themselves.

"Come in."

The door opened a crack, and a pink dreamcatcher was inserted into the opening. The dreamcatcher shook at a slow pace. After a few moments, the door opened, and I looked at a face I had not seen in several years.

"Amy," I yelped as my mouth dropped open.

"Kyla," she exclaimed as her eyes widened.

"What are you doing here?"

Shock settled in as I grabbed my cup of water from the table and sipped.

"I was just in town. Decided to come to see my old best friend from long ago."

Amy set the dreamcatcher on the table, and I admired its intricate details. It was so beautiful I made a mental note to replace it with the one Brad bought me.

Taking a hard look at Amy, she looked almost the same as the last time I saw her. The only difference is that her red hair used to hang to the top of her butt was now cut in a cute shoulder-length bob.

"I doubt you were just in town," I stated as she wrapped her arms around me and squeezed me tight.

"Well, that sounded a lot better than the bitter truth."

"I'd love to hear the truth."

She sat in a chair and looked at me as she tucked a piece of hair behind her ear. "I searched for you. Upon that search, I heard that you were injured. I had no other choice but to come to visit you."

"Thank you for coming to visit me. It means the world to me. What, has it been a little over four years since we've last seen each other?"

"Five years, darling. You were pregnant the last time I laid my eyes on you."

"Now I have a five-year-old daughter." Where has the time gone?

"I heard her name is Bria."

I took another sip of water and replied, "How did you know?"

"Brad called me several months back. He told me you two had a daughter, and you took her away from him."

I gasped as my mouth dropped open. "He called you?"

"Yeah. He wanted to know if I knew where you had gone." She nonchalantly shrugged her shoulders.

"I'm so curious about what your response was."

She smirked as she threw her left leg over her right knee. "I told him I was glad you finally left him."

I laughed. "I know he didn't like that response in the least."

"Of course not, but I had to be honest with him. I owed it to myself. He hung up on me when he didn't hear what he wanted."

"You were always against my relationship with Brad."

Amy motioned with her hand to me in the hospital bed. "Now you see why. When he told me you had left him, I searched to find you as soon as I got off the phone. Can I ask you something?"

"I'll tell you anything. You know that, Amy."

"Why in the hell do you not have any social media active? You made it ten times harder to find you."

"I had to do what was best for us to stay safe. I knew he'd use social media to find me, so I had to let it go."

Amy smiled. "That is what amazing, strong mothers do."

"Thank you. What did you do with yourself after foster care?"

"I ended up going to college."

"You were always so smart." I rubbed Amy's hand. "I knew you'd end up going to college. But, you always told me you were undecided."

"I was undecided until I received a full-ride scholarship. After that, there was no way I would get buried in student loans."

"Understandable," I commented.

"I went to the University of Arkansas. That is where I met my husband, Alexander." Amy held her hand out to me, and I looked at the beautiful ring that looked colossal on her small finger.

"Amy, I'm so happy for you. Congratulations. How long have you two been married?"

"Two years." Amy's eyes zoomed in on the ring on my finger. "Oh my gosh, what did I miss?

Didn't you leave Brad like a year ago?"

I nodded in excitement. "I did, but Ryan came into my job one day and had me in his sights. Ever since that day, he has shown me he is the kindest gentleman I have ever met. Eight months later, I am engaged."

"I can't express how happy I am for you. That is a beautiful ring. Beautiful, just like you."

My heart warmed. I felt like our friendship had never taken a break, and it was a wonderful feeling.

"So, when do I get to meet the amazing Alexander?"

"Very soon. He had to stay back home with Julia."

I raised an eyebrow. "Who is Julia?"

"Our four-month-old daughter."

"You had a baby?"

Amy smiled. "Yes, I did. She is my angel."

I did a once over her small frame. "You do not look like you just gave birth."

"I can thank my absent parents for the wonderful genes they provided me," she stated before we laughed.

"Yes, you can."

"So when is the wedding? Or are you two going to elope?"

"We have not decided on a date for the wedding. I want it to happen within the next few months. We are going to have an intimate gathering with friends and family. If you can make it, it would mean the world to me."

"Of course, I will make it. I will clear my entire schedule to watch you walk down the aisle."

"Give me your number so I can text you the details when the time comes."

Amy and I exchanged information. After another two hours of catching up, we said our goodbyes and agreed to chat soon.

Watching Amy walk out of my hospital room brought tears to my eyes. She was my support system all those years through foster care. Brad split us up as he was aware Amy was not a fan of his. Even though it took me years to come to my senses, I am glad to be free of Brad and his abusive ways.

During my two-week stay, Ryan visited me several times throughout the day. I wasn't sure how he did that many visits with his schedule, but he always made time to come by, even if it was only for five minutes at a time.

When it was time for me to be released from the hospital, Ryan came to pick me up.

"Are you sure you want to return to your house?" he asked me as he pulled out of the hospital parking lot.

"I think I will be fine." I settled into the passenger side of his car.

"I don't think it's a good idea. You might as well pack up your things and come live with me."

I took a deep breath as I considered what Ryan said. Deciding not to respond, we quietly drove the rest of the way to my house.

Stepping out of Ryan's car, I glanced over at

my car. I made a mental note to start it up later to make sure the battery wasn't dead.

Approaching the front door, I unlocked it. Taking a deep breath, I walked three steps into the house. The atmosphere seemed different even though everything in the house looked in place and spotless. I looked over to where I had fallen after I had been shot, and my heart sank deep into my stomach. There was no way I would be able to walk over that spot and not think about what had happened. My healing would never start until I was far away from this place.

Spinning around, I bumped into Ryan's hard chest.

Startled, I stepped back a step. "I can't stay here."

Ryan placed his hand in the middle of my back. "I'll take you home and have a friend help me pack your things."

As Ryan led me back to his car, I turned and looked at him. Ryan had shown me the type of man I needed in my life. In a few short months, I would walk down the aisle to start my forever with him.

"Why are you smiling at me like that?" He pulled open the passenger door.

"I'm just blessed to have you in my life."

"The feeling is mutual, beautiful."

I never doubted that statement for a second.

Chapter Thirty-Seven

Kyla

The soft melody of the processional song flowed through the speakers. I held the bouquet tightly as I stared at the beautiful array of flowers I had picked out.

Today was the day. The day I said 'I do' to the man that taught me how to love again. The man that loved me when I didn't think I could be loved.

"You look so beautiful, Mommy," Bria said before she settled her hand in the flower basket she held.

Bria had her hair pinned up and wore a cream-colored flair dress.

"Thank you. So do you, Sweetie."

I took a deep breath, my nerves on edge.

Bria disappeared out of the back door right after she smiled at me.

I looked down at my white short-sleeved, a-lined, flared wedding dress that I wore. This dress was designed by my wonderful future sister-in-law, who couldn't attend the wedding today due to a fashion show set in stone a year prior. My hair was pulled up into a pineapple style. I couldn't help but agree with Bria.

Taking a deep breath, I looked over at Sabrina. She wore her hair in a low bun with a small amount of makeup. She was dolled up in a peach-colored floor-length dress.

Sabrina smiled before she leaned over and kissed my cheek. She walked out the door towards the backyard.

Over five months, Ryan and I had planned and put together our wedding. We couldn't have done it without the help of Amelia, Sabrina, and Aunt Lily. The shooting scared us so much that we wanted to get married as soon as possible to get our lives started. We invited close friends and family to our house for our wedding. The entire backyard had been transformed into a beautiful rustic atmosphere.

"It's showtime." Aunt Lily beamed.

Aunt Lily had her hair pulled back into a low formal bun. She wore a satin peach-colored long-sleeved jumpsuit that accentuated her curves.

Hooking her arm through mine, I took one more deep breath before I walked toward the backyard.

Stepping over the threshold, my eyes scanned the backyard as I stood in place. I was in rustic heaven. The backyard was decorated with tasteful rustic scenery. It was filled with friends and family that sat on wooden chairs.

"Please rise," the officiant said.

On cue, everyone rose to their feet as they turned and looked at me.

I looked at Ryan, who stood beside the officiant and his best man Mark. He wore a tuxedo with a white tie. His eyes met mine, and his gaze sent a shiver down my spine. He gave a nervous smile before I noticed his bottom lip quiver.

"Are you ready?" Aunt Lily whispered to me.

Nodding, Aunt Lily walked me down the aisle as the melody flowed through the speakers. I never desired to be the center of attention, so I planted my eyes on Ryan. As we walked closer, I saw tears of joy wetting his cheeks.

Once we arrived at the aisle's end, the officiant asked, "Who gives this woman to this man today?"

"I do." Aunt Lily kissed me on the cheek.

Reaching my hand out, I wiped Ryan's tears away. Taking a deep breath, I willed myself not to cry. I did not want to shed tears and smear the makeup artist worked on for over an hour. Ryan grabbed my hands. Looking deep into his eyes, the officiant began the ceremony.

As the ceremony went on, I would look into the crowd and receive joyful smiles from the people we loved the most.

"With the power invested in me, I now pronounce you husband and wife. You may now kiss your bride."

Ryan released my hands. He placed one hand behind my head and one hand on my back. My eyes fluttered closed right before his soft lips met mine. Just like the first time we kissed, it felt as if fireworks were set off inside me.

Cheers erupted around us as I interrupted our kiss with a smile.

Hand in hand, we walked down the aisle together. 'Congratulations' and 'You two look stunning together' were thrown our way as we headed over to where our pictures would be taken.

Over the next forty-five minutes, we took pictures of our wedding party and our immediate family. It was amazing to wrap my arms around my new extended family and smile into the camera. I wouldn't trade the day for anything else in this world.

"Are you ready to get this party started?" Ryan asked me before he kissed my forehead.

"I've looked forward to this moment for a lifetime. Of course."

Ryan and I walked over to the tented area set up for the reception. We stood a few feet from the entrance as the DJ cut the music. "Introducing for the first time Mr. and Mrs. Ryan Walker."

The entire tent erupted into cheers as Ryan, and I walked hand in hand into the beautiful, air-conditioned, decorated tent. We smiled and waved at our guests as we approached the dance floor. As the first dance song flowed through the speakers, Ryan placed his hand in the middle of my back as he grasped my free hand. We moved to the song's beat as we stared into each other's eyes. The entire world dissipated, and our love enveloped us whole. The cheers that rang out as the song ended brought me back to reality.

Dinner was announced after our first dance. Ryan and I talked with a few guests as we walked to our table for dinner. Two servers walked over to us and sat our plates in front of us. Dinner tonight consisted of filet mignon, a medley of vegetables, and a bed of wild rice.

After dinner, the dance floor opened for everyone to dance.

Ryan and I parted ways to mingle for the first time during the wedding.

"Darling, you look stunning. Congratulations," Amy exclaimed as I walked over to her on the dance floor.

"Thank you." Amy kissed me on the cheek.

I focused on the tall man beside Amy as I waited on the necessary introductions. He held an adorable, bouncy baby girl.

"Kyla, this is my husband, Alexander."

"Hello, Alexander." I reached my hand out,

and he shook my hand.

"Hello, Kyla. Congratulations on your marriage."

"Thank you."

Amy smiled. "This is Julia. She turns nine months tomorrow."

"Hello, Julia," I cooed as I reached my finger out to her. She stared at my finger for a few moments before she grabbed it and gave it a squeeze. "She is just the cutest."

"Tell me that when she is screaming at the top of her lungs at 3:00 A.M.," Alexander joked, receiving a hearty laugh from us.

"Thank you for coming. Please, enjoy the reception."

After parting ways with Amy, I made my way over to Sabrina and her family on the dance floor.

"You have to save me a dance," I called out as I walked up behind her.

Sabrina turned around with a huge smile before she threw her arms around me and hugged me tightly. "Of course, I will save you a dance. You are finally a Mrs." Sabrina sipped from her cocktail.

I shrugged my shoulders. "It only took five years and a child being brought into this world."

"More like eight months and a man being able to care for another man's child as his own."

"You look so pretty, Auntie Kyla." Emily touched my dress.

"Your words mean the world to me, Emily."

Emily beamed as she turned in a complete

circle. Spotting something or someone in the distance, Emily took off at a fast pace.

"Congratulations. Married life has its ups and downs, but it is worth it in the end," Julian admitted before he hugged me.

"The advice is much appreciated. Please, enjoy the reception."

Turning my attention to Sabrina, I said, "I will be back for my dance later."

Sabrina winked at me as someone tapped me on my shoulder. Turning around, I looked at Scott.

"Oh my gosh, Scott. Thank you for coming."

Wrapping my arms around Scott, I gave him a hearty squeeze.

"Of course, I came. I wouldn't miss your wedding if the world was falling apart. How have you been?"

Right after the shooting, the doctor advised me not to work for a few weeks to heal. A few weeks turned into a few months, and I did not return after an extensive conversation with Kelsey. I decided to leave the customer service atmosphere and take some time off to recover, more mentally than physically. Visits to the counselor became more frequent, and my PTSD had become easier to deal with, even if just by a little bit. I spent the last five months healing and planning every little detail of my wedding from start to finish. Both activities combined proved to be a full-time job for me.

"I've been okay. Missing you and my job like crazy. I miss seeing my regulars."

"Well, you just married one of them. I told you that someone was in love," Scott sang out.

I laughed. "You did tell me that. Months later, voila," I exclaimed as I showed him my ring.

Scott's eyes widened. "It'll take years for Vanessa to get a beautiful and humongous ring."

"Where is Vanessa?" Scott had RSVP'd with a plus one, so I was sure he would bring her along.

"She had to stay home and care for her grandmother. She came down with the flu."

I winced as I frowned. Vanessa had come into the coffee shop a few times while I worked, and we always had good conversations when I was not swamped with customers.

"I hope her grandmother feels better soon."

He nodded. "I will let her know. She told me to pass along her good wishes as well."

"Thank you."

Scott pointed at me as a guest brushed past him. "Make sure you come in for a drink sometime so we can chat like old times."

"You know I despise coffee."

Scott shrugged. "Come for a blueberry muffin then. Or our amazing hot chocolate that you love so much."

I nodded. "I'll take you up on that offer."

Scott leaned a bit to the left to look around my head. "I must go steal a dance with Sabrina. I'll dance with you later."

Scott scurried away right as an arm snaked around my lower back. A kiss was pressed to my right temple as I shut my eyes, enjoying the sweet bliss of the moment.

"You look beautiful tonight," Ryan whispered in my ear.

"You look handsome tonight," I replied back.

Ryan wrapped his arm around my lower back. "I can't believe we are married."

"I feel as if I waited my entire life for this moment."

Ryan smiled before he kissed me.

"Hello, Mr. and Mrs. Walker," boomed a deep voice.

Breaking apart from our kiss, I looked at Mark and Chelsea. Chelsea stood taller than me by a few inches. She had wavy blonde hair and crystal blue eyes. Mark was a tall man with brown curly hair and green eyes. Mark had a beer in one hand, and his arm wrapped tight around Chelsea's waist.

"Congratulations." Chelsea kissed me on the cheek before she hugged Ryan.

"Never thought the day would come when you would tie the knot." Mark gave Ryan a bear hug. "Especially to this woman. How did you snag someone so beautiful?" Mark hugged and kissed me on the cheek. My cheeks received a lot of attention tonight.

"She managed to put up with my flirtatious comments and drooling for weeks on end."

Mark raised his eyebrows. "I've never known

this guy to drool. Or to flirt. Keep it up, whatever you are doing."

Mark and Chelsea said another round of congratulations before they walked over to the bar in the corner.

"Your best friend is something else."

"Yes," Ryan agreed. "Marky Mark is a special type of unique."

Hands are thrown over my eyes, putting me in complete darkness. Once the hands were removed, I spun around, and Ryan's parents stood behind us.

"I get to call you my daughter-in-law now. Yay," Amelia squealed as she threw her arms around me and squeezed me tight.

"She has been waiting five long months to call you that." James playfully rolled his eyes before he took a sip of his beer.

"I have. I cannot lie."

"If it were up to Amelia, Ryan would've married you after the first time we met you."

"She is amazing. How could someone not want her as a daughter?"

Hearing the word daughter come out of Amelia's mouth caused my mind to wonder about my mother and my father, the people I would never meet. The father that would've walked me down the aisle if he had chosen to be in my life.

"You are right about that. Welcome to the family." James hugged me tightly before he kissed my forehead.

"I don't get any love? It's my wedding day,

too," Ryan pointed out.

"You've received enough of our love for the past thirty years. Kyla gets all the loving tonight," James responded before he grabbed Ryan into a hug.

Amelia hugged and kissed Ryan next. "I want some loving," floated over my shoulder as Aunt Lily wrapped her arm around my shoulders.

"Thank you so much for walking me down the aisle."

"You do not have to thank me, Sweetie. It was my pleasure." She took a sip of the wine she held.

"You do not know how much that meant to me."

"I promised you I would be in your life no matter what. I am keeping that promise."

Someone brushed against my dress. I got a glimpse of Bria and Emily as they ran past us.

"Bria," I yelled, but the music was too loud.

"I'll go slow them down," Aunt Lily assured me as she headed in the direction they went.

Throughout the rest of the night, I sipped on a glass of champagne as I danced the night away with friends and family. We had a bouquet toss in which a beautiful young lady won. We played the shoe game and died of laughter from the responses. The funniest question asked was, "who has the better shower-singing voice?" My shoes flew high into the sky at record speed. Ryan's singing voice was comparable to nails screeching on a chalkboard. My wedding day was more than I could have ever imagined for myself at a young age. I had always imagined a fairytale wedding. This wedding was far from the fairytale wedding I envisioned at a young age, but I wouldn't change anything. I couldn't wait to see what marriage life had in store for us.

Chapter Thirty-Eight

Kyla

My back encountered the silky, satin bed sheet that adorned the king-sized bed, and my arms splayed out beside me. Ryan stood over me, lust-darkened eyes stared down at me as he unbuttoned his pants.

We had been in Bora Bora for our honeymoon for five days. We left for our honeymoon two nights after our wedding, and we had been having a blast. This was the first time Ryan, and I had ever been outside the country, and it was a beautiful experience.

We had snorkeled with the school of fish in the clear, sparkling water. Received a massage five feet from the ocean, listening to the rhythmic sound of the waves crashing ashore as the knots in our bodies were rubbed out. Climbed to the top of both extinct volcanoes, receiving the most intense exercise I had ever done in my entire life. Last but not least, we parasailed over the ocean and enjoyed all the island's sights.

Biting on my bottom lip with my teeth seductively, Ryan grunted as he tugged his pants down and they dropped to the floor with his discarded shirt.

Pushing my legs open, Ryan settled between them and looked into my eyes.

"Mrs. Walker," Ryan whispered, tracing his index finger on my top and bottom lip.

"Yes, Mr. Walker?" I flicked my tongue out of my mouth to touch his finger, and he smiled.

"I'm so glad you are my wife."

"You've been telling me that every day since we said, I do."

"Officially, you've been Mrs. Walker for a week now." Ryan dipped his head and nibbled on my neck, causing a shiver to vibrate my body.

"I know. I still feel like I am dreaming. How did I ever get this lucky to marry you?"

Ryan looked into my eyes. "I wouldn't call it luck. You were too irresistible not to marry. I blame your unconditional love and support."

"Mr. Walker?"

"Yes, Mrs. Walker?"

"I'd love it if you made Mrs. Walker feel ecstasy right about now."

A seductive grin made it onto Ryan's face as he pushed himself up on his elbows. Ryan placed feather-soft kisses on my lips before he moved farther south. Ryan's kisses trailed from the sensitive spot on my neck and to my chest, which thrilled my body with what would take place next. Ryan gave my nipple a soft tug with his teeth, sending more involuntary shivers through my body. Repeating the same action with my other nipple, the excitement in my body was close to sending me to pure bliss.

Ryan plunged into me which caused me to gasp from pure, utter ecstasy. Reaching my hand around Ryan's back, I dug my nails into his back as I bit into his shoulder. Even though we had made love every day for the past week, it still felt as wonderful as the first night. I couldn't get enough of this feeling. I couldn't get enough of Ryan. I could picture myself doing this for the rest of my life.

Ryan's thrusts intensified as he captured my mouth with his. Swirling his tongue into my mouth, my eyes rolled to the back of my head as our tongues tangled together. Releasing a moan, my body lost all control as pleasure traveled from my head down to my toes. Ryan groaned, and his body stilled as he attempted to hold himself up. Ryan's eyes closed as he took a few deep breaths.

Ryan flopped onto the bed next to me once

he caught his breath, and we lay in silence for a few minutes.

Getting up off the bed, I went into the bathroom and wiped myself down. Ryan walked into the bathroom a short time later and said, "I swear it doesn't get better than that."

Smiling, I walked back into the room and wrapped a robe tight around my body before I tied it. Approaching the sliding doors, I walked out onto the balcony. The cloudless night was heaven on earth and all the stars shined bright in the sky. We were staying in an over-water bungalow, and the view was breathtaking.

The sliding door opened and closed. Seconds later, muscular arms wrapped around my waist as Ryan pressed his body against mine. A kiss was pressed to my right temple.

"If only we could just stay in this paradise forever."

"We could stay for a while, but we would go broke quickly," Ryan joked.

I playfully elbowed him as I looked out to the calm ocean. The ocean was so calm, a soft rhythmic movement could be seen.

"I lived my entire life near the ocean. The ocean has always been my escape, but I have never experienced this."

"I can promise you this won't be the only time you experience this type of calm."

"How are you so sure?" I asked him as I looked at him over my shoulder.

"I plan for us to do something like this at least

once a year."

Silence settled upon us as I leaned my back into Ryan's chest. "Can I be honest with you?"

"Of course, you can be honest with me."

Turning around in a complete circle, I looked into Ryan's eyes. The eyes that were lust-filled minutes ago were now filled with pure love. Pure love for me.

"You saved me. You saved my sanity. You saved my life. I will forever be grateful to you for that. Thank you for loving me for the imperfect person I am."

Ryan tucked a stray piece of hair behind my ear before he pinched my cheek. "I never want to hear you thank me again. I love you with all my heart. I promise to love you for the rest of my life."

"Until death does us part."

Ryan's lips met mine as my eyes fluttered closed. Truth be told, one kiss could have two souls bound together for eternity.

Chapter Thirty-Nine

Brad

I tapped my fingers on my uncomfortable bed and stared at the concrete wall. It had an impressive display of graffiti sprawled across the wall. The graffiti ranged from sloppy, amateur artwork to fantastic creations that took some time to complete.

Kyla had won the battle this time around. I looked over at the metal bars that imprisoned me in a room the size of a shoebox. Kyla had placed me in prison, and I could not do much about it right now. She was unaware that I had many plans up my sleeve, though. I'm sure she had probably gone back to her house to sleep with no cares in the world. I'm sure she felt great keeping Bria away from me. What she did not know was that the fight was not over. The fight was just beginning. The fight would not be over until she felt the wrath that I had brewing within me. She was far from being correct if she thought she had experienced the worst. Next time, I wouldn't be so nice. She would feel every ounce of pain and sorrow I had to dish out. I just had to come up with a plan to make my escape.

Next time, I would ensure the deed was complete before I walked away. I bet my life on that fact.

OTHER TITLES BY ANA DENISE

His Crazy Obsession Series

His Crazy Obsession

His Unstable Obsession

Dangers in Love Series

Dangers in Love

Lost in Love

Thank you for reading!

Please add a review on Amazon, Goodreads, or TikTok and let me know what you thought!

Reviews are extremely helpful for authors, thank you for taking the time to support me and my work. Don't forget to share your review on social media and with hashtag #HisCrazyObsession and encourage others to read the story too!

Ana Denise was born and raised on the Treasure Coast of Florida in 1999. She considers her family and friends to be most significant in her life. Growing up, she has always been fascinated with reading and writing short stories. Following her passion, she has decided to become a romance author after obtaining a Bachelor's Degree in Business Administration.